THE NOTHING JOB

The new Detective Chief Inspector
Henry Christie novel

Reluctantly agreeing to track down three dangerous criminals, DCI Henry Christie's philosophy is that anything that keeps him at the cutting edge of coppering can't be all bad. But then he's asked to close down an investigation into a fatal police shooting, and he uncovers a number of worrying connections. Henry charges headlong into a terrifying conspiracy and finds himself much closer to the cutting edge than even he would have wanted...

THE NOTHING JOB

Nick Oldham

Severn House Large Print
London & New York

This first large print edition published 2012
in Great Britain and the USA by
SEVERN HOUSE PUBLISHERS LTD of
9-15 High Street, Sutton, Surrey, SM1 1DF.
First world regular print edition published 2009 by
Severn House Publishers Ltd., London and New York.

British Library Cataloguing in Publication Data

Oldham, Nick, 1956-
    The nothing job. -- (A Henry Christie novel)
    1. Christie, Henry (Fictitious character)--Fiction.
    2. Police--England--Blackpool--Fiction. 3. Detective and
    mystery stories. 4. Large type books.
    I. Title II. Series
    823.9'2-dc23

    ISBN-13: 978-0-7278-9886-9

Severn House Publishers support The Forest Stewardship Council
[FSC], the leading international forest certification organisation. All
our titles that are printed on Greenpeace-approved FSC-certified paper
carry the FSC logo.

MIX
Paper from
responsible sources
FSC
www.fsc.org   FSC® C018575

Printed and bound in Great Britain by the
MPG Books Group, Bodmin, Cornwall.

To the memory of my father

ONE

She had been chased through the streets half-naked, screaming in terror, her clothing having been ripped from her puny olive-skinned body. Ultimately she had made the mistake of running into a dead-end alley at the back of the shopping centre where her attacker had cornered her. Then in a murderous frenzy the knife had been driven twenty-two times into her chest, neck and face, puncturing an eye, slicing the carotid artery and skewering the heart. She had bled quickly to death in a reeking alleyway in the newest city in north-west England, two thousand miles from her home.

As DCI Henry Christie stared down at the body, at 3.23 on a balmy early summer morning with the dawn light not too far away, he did not know her identity, nor exactly how many times she had been stabbed. In fact, all he knew was that there was the murdered body of a frail young woman in front of him, splayed brokenly and pathetically between two giant metal rubbish bins, that she had died a brutal, horrifying death – and it was his job to get a murder investigation underway.

An hour and a half earlier, unable to sleep

properly for yet another night, Henry Christie had been sitting in the living room of his recently renovated and redecorated house, which only months before had been virtually destroyed by a deranged arsonist bent on murder and retribution. His eyes were closed but his mind was focused on an image that was over twenty-five years old. It was as clear as a photograph ... in fact it was almost exactly the same as the photograph he was holding in his fingers. He opened his gritty eyes and looked at it and saw that there was one minor, critical difference between what his mind recalled and the actual photograph itself.

Henry sighed and sank back in the armchair, his fingertips holding the edge of the photograph which he knew had been taken with a Pentax K1000, the standard issue of Lancashire Constabulary's Scenes of Crime Department (as it was then called; now it was CSI) in the early 1980s. He knew this because he'd done a short secondment on SOCO as part of his initial in-force training at the start of his police career. At that time in his life he'd been going through a phase of being interested in photography, hence the memory recall. And he too had also owned a Pentax way back then and remembered the K1000 as being a solid, reliable, if unspectacular camera. Just right for the knocks and bangs of life on SOCO. It was certainly a good enough camera to record the scene of a murder in vivid detail.

Henry leaned forward, put the photograph down on the smoked-glass coffee table and picked up another from the stack. This one showed a different angle of the same murder scene.

Then, one by one, he went through the whole set, shuffling and arranging them into a logical order, which made sense to him.

Firstly there were the shots of the general approach to the scene: from the main road, in through the car-park entrance, then yard by yard (oh, how Henry missed that Imperial measure) up the path which led to the moors; then through another narrow winding path in the pine trees and the point where the body had been discovered.

There were the tantalizing glimpses of something lying between the trees as the SOCO got closer. Then the body became more distinct and identifiable.

A ten-year-old girl: abducted, raped, murdered.

Jenny Colville. The year 1982.

Henry Christie had been a PC in uniform then. He'd been a tenacious thief-taker working on Task Force on the days just before it was disbanded and the world of policing had moved on when Lord Scarman published his reports into the riots which had stunned Britain and shaken up the cosy 'old-world' culture of the cops who thought they could do anything and get away with it.

Henry, now a chief inspector, fast approaching the time when he could retire if he chose to do so, exhaled another long, deep sigh. His mind was firmly on that day when Jenny's body had

9

been found.

His mouth curved into a half-smile, realizing that was the day he'd met Kate Marsden for the first time, later to become his wife, then ex-wife and, full circle, his wife again. She had been out walking her golden retriever – a dog Henry professed to adore – on the moors above Haslingden in the east of Lancashire. She had stumbled across the girl's body. And that was how he'd met her – over a dead body. Henry, along with the local DI, had been one of the first officers on the scene and he'd been instantly mesmerized by Kate.

Unable to believe his good luck when the DI tasked him to take a witness statement from this gorgeous young woman, Henry didn't linger at the scene. But before leaving, he did see the dead girl *in situ* and like every other dead body he had ever seen, before or after – and there were many – it was a vision that was indelibly imprinted in his brain, like a brand in cowhide. It was filed away for easy reference and consultation when necessary.

But at that time, Henry did not give the dead girl and the physical evidence surrounding her too much thought. He was busy concentrating on Kate and, to coin a phrase, his head was a long way up his own arse, being in love and lust at the same time. A fearful combination designed to dull the senses of any man, but particularly one in his early twenties with hormones a-raging. It had taken him this long – a lifetime, a whole career almost – to realize what a naive idiot he'd been to take things for granted, go along with it

10

all, accept his orders and not to question what he innately knew to be false.

But that is how things were in the good old days – underlings blindly doing what they were told and if they didn't like it, tough, fuck off.

Plus there had been no time for Henry to sit back and chew things over. Everything moved at top speed in those days: work, play, work, all in a relentless, unbroken cycle.

Now, though, as he moved through his silent house into the conservatory, Henry did have time for uncomfortable reflection, brought about by a series of events that had made him do a double-take in 1982 and catch his breath. Because in his hands and in his brain he knew he possessed something which could have a massive effect on the organization that was called Lancashire Constabulary.

'Shit,' he said quietly and sat down on the cane sofa. He liked the conservatory, probably the only family member who did. However, tonight it was chilly and made him shiver.

He placed the SOCO photographs on the glass-topped coffee table and squared them into a neat pile. They were all 8 by 6s and still as sharp and as clear as on the day they'd been taken. He wrapped an elastic band around them, slid them back into the envelope, which he tied with string, then placed that into his briefcase. And locked it.

No wonder I was dumped from that investigation, he thought bitterly, especially after I'd been manipulated to do the dirty deed for the DI. If I'd stayed on it, I would've been a possible

11

threat. I might have realized what had happened. I might've blabbed.

Henry stretched his whole body. It was still painful as the cracked ribs and other cuts and bruises he'd received following his last foray into the world of operational policing were slow to heal, even months later. That little jaunt had been the one during which he had discovered the felony that was now troubling him. He needed to stand up and move around again because sitting induced stiffness and soreness. Moving kept the first of these at bay and reduced the latter.

He rose from the sofa, both he and it creaking, then walked back through the house, eyeing the drinks cabinet set in the new sideboard. A strong whiskey would have been a delight just at that moment, a pleasant accompaniment to the Cuprofen he'd swallowed ten minutes earlier. He paused and touched the handle of the cabinet, trying to resist the temptation. He weakened after a quick check of the wall clock. Surely it would be safe now, he thought. He opened the cabinet and inspected the row of bottles, none full. He picked a Jack Daniel's and a heavy whiskey glass, pouring just enough of the golden-brown liquid to cover the base. That's all I need, he thought. 40 per cent proof. Fast, powerful pain relief, plus the tablets, then I'll be able to ease my aches and pains, get the photos out of my mind and get some sleep.

'Surely no one's going to get murdered at this time of night,' he mumbled as he returned to the living room and sank on to the settee, placing the drink on the coffee table, untouched.

12

Was it worth the hassle, he thought. To rake up the past, to bring something to light that didn't matter any more?

Thing was, he knew that he himself had often been less than one hundred per cent straight down the line, honest and ethical when it came to putting villains behind bars. But there was one line he had never crossed to secure a conviction, even in the days of yore, when such things were rife.

He had never planted evidence.

Not like that detective inspector had done all those years before.

He picked up the glass and held it to his nose, inhaling and savouring the smoky aroma of the spirit. 'This is tempting fate,' he said. It was the early hours of Tuesday morning, the first of a seven-night run of being the on-call DCI for the county. Even though he knew he was merely, and gladly, helping out because other DCIs were either on leave, at court or off sick, Henry knew drinking was a no-no. If something happened that required his presence, even the faintest whiff of alcohol would see it being his last night ever. The people further up the chain of command who disliked him would see to that and he didn't want to give them any ammunition to use against him.

But drink had been sustaining him recently. Not a lot of it, but regular, small amounts. It had become a habit.

Please, he thought, no one get killed.

The glass moved to his bottom lip.

And the phone rang.

Sod's law.

Instinctively he checked the clock and mentally logged the time, then with relief put the glass down and reached for the phone.

'Henry Christie.'

He immediately recognized the voice at the other end as that of Chief Inspector Andy Laker.

'You must still be a desperate man,' Laker said gloating, 'putting your name down on every call-out rota on the off-chance you might get something.' Laker's voice was cynical, mocking.

Henry held back. Until recently Laker had been the chief constable's staff officer (or brown-nosed bag-carrier as the role was known colloquially) and during his tenure in that post he and Henry had rubbed each other up the wrong way. There was no love lost between the two men. Laker thought Henry was a long-in-the-tooth dinosaur and Henry thought Laker was a jumped-up twat. However, Laker had been sidelined by the chief and found himself in the role of the control-room chief inspector because, rumour had it, the chief 'couldn't stand the smarmy git'. Henry could easily have dropped into a verbal tussle with Laker but did not have the time or inclination.

'I'm assuming there's a job,' he said, 'or have you just called to insult me?'

'I'd like to say just to insult you,' Laker chuckled, 'but sadly there is a job. Can you cover it?'

'What is it?'

'Body of a female discovered by an armed-

14

response unit in Preston. Looks as if she's been stabbed.'

Henry felt a surge of adrenaline rush into his system.

TWO

'Two questions: what the hell are you doing on duty and out in division at this time of night and why even drive down the back street?'

Henry had directed his queries at the bulky but fit figure of PC Bill Robbins, a headquarters firearms trainer, but for that night only he was the armed-response patrol referred to by Andy Laker. He had been the one who had made the gruesome discovery.

Robbins blew out his cheeks in an exaggerated, pissed-off way. 'Effin' silly idea from the dream factory,' he moaned, talking about the initiative from headquarters, a place often referred to as the dream factory by cops out at the sharp end. 'Working shifts out in division, as well as training ... I'm back in the firing range teaching an initial firearms course at ten this morning, knackered.'

Now Henry remembered. Last time he'd bumped into Bill, he'd been doing the same but in another division.

'Might as well apply for a transfer out of training to a division. At least I'd only be doing one job. All I need is a brush up my arse,' he continued.

Henry patted him on the shoulder. The two

16

men went back a long way, having worked together briefly as uniformed constables in the early eighties. 'Never mind, mate.'

'As for the other question – I was bored and nosy.'

'Not a good combination.'

'So I was just moochin', seein' how far I could get the car up various alleyways ... as you do. Found her purely by chance.'

Henry looked closely into Bill's eyes. 'And are you OK? It's a pretty horrible thing to find.'

'Oh, aye. Seen worse.'

Henry had asked the question because last time he and Robbins had been flung together it had ended up with two of their colleagues being brutally murdered and Henry and the firearms officer coming face-to-face with a deranged suicide-bomber. He knew Robbins was made of stern stuff, though – but as a boss, it was something he had to ask.

'Don't really affect me,' Robbins added. 'How about you, pal?'

'Bearing up,' Henry said.

Robbins nodded sagely.

The two officers were standing in Friargate, one of Preston's main shopping streets. They were at the junction with Anchor Court, which was the name of the alley in which the dead girl had been discovered. A police crime-scene tape had been drawn across the entrance, and down the alley emergency lighting had been brought in and switched on to enable a proper investigation of the death scene.

The man now bending over the body stood

upright and began to peel off his latex gloves as he walked back towards Henry, who was standing on the public side of the crime-scene tape. The man was back-lit by the mobile lighting, making him a silhouette and accentuating the fact that his big ears stuck out at right angles from the side of his head like handles of a football trophy. He was a thin man and the baggy white paper suit he wore for forensic purposes billowed loosely on his frame.

'I'll get my statement done, if that's OK,' Robbins said to Henry.

Henry turned to the firearms officer. 'Yeah, Bill, that'd be good.'

Robbins headed to his car and Henry rotated back to the figure in the alley, who had just reached the tape. Henry folded his arms. 'What's the verdict, Prof?'

The man was Dr Baines, the Home Office pathologist, someone Henry had known for many years and had discussed many a brutal murder and post-mortem with over a pint or two. Henry hadn't seen much of him of late as the murders he had recently investigated had been covered by a much prettier female pathologist who'd stood in for Baines whilst he'd been attending various conferences and seminars on dental forensics, which was his specialism.

'Well,' Baines declared, snapping off the second glove, 'you probably know as much as I do at this moment in time.'

'Professor,' Henry said, 'you are paid an absolute mint for your incisive knowledge and vast experience and it's not really good enough to say

18

I know as much as you do; you are supposed to know more than me.' The words were spoken in jest.

Baines eyed him like a naughty child. 'As I was saying,' he blinked, 'all my observations will be superficial until, (*a*), I'm allowed to move the body – which can only happen once your CSIs and forensic bods have done their bit – and, (*b*), I get the poor lass on to a mortuary slab.' He pulled his tongue out at the detective. 'However, multiple stab wounds, many deep, probably one to the heart or neck could be the one that killed her. So, female, sixteen to eighteen years old...'

'That the best you can do?'

'Standing in a fucking alleyway – yes!' he said haughtily and ducked under the tape. 'Except to add that she looks to be from Eastern Europe, maybe of Balkan origin ... once I get to inspect her teeth properly, I might even be able to pinpoint a town.' Henry raised his eyebrows, impressed. He knew Baines was compiling a dental database for forensic use. The professor went on, 'And she's a drug addict ... I can see track lines on her inner right arm, which is flung over her head ... I'd even hazard a guess that she's a sex worker, probably in this country illegally ... but that's for you to find out.'

'Time of death?'

'Recent – two hours ago,' Baines speculated.

Henry's mind ticked over. He glanced up and down Friargate, then fished his personal radio out of his pocket. He was about to call the Preston comms room when the radio blared out

19

his name. 'DCI Christie receiving?'

'Receiving.'

'Can you make to the CCTV room, boss? Urgently?'

'On my way.' Henry turned to Baines. 'I'll maybe see you over a dead body,' he said quickly before spinning on his heels and hurrying away.

His jaw rotated angrily and a huge surge of annoyance pulsed through him. His breathing became shallow as he attempted to suppress his emotions and remain calm and rational. Even so, he could not prevent a burst of air breaking out from his lungs as he regarded the young woman in the wheelchair with contempt. Her eyes could not meet his and she looked sharply away from Henry's steel-sharp, accusatory glare.

'I'm sorry I missed it,' she mewed meekly.

'I'm sorry you missed it, too.' Henry's ironic tone stung and she blushed up. 'You missed someone being chased through the streets? A victim pursued by her attacker?' His voice rose incredulously.

'Boss...?' Henry's eyed flickered to the night-duty detective constable, who gestured with the flat of his hands for Henry to calm it.

Nostrils flaring, head shaking, Henry said, 'We've lost a lot of valuable time because of this and trails can go cold very quickly on murder enquiries ... so, what've we got?'

They were in the CCTV room situated in the high-rise monstrosity of a building that was once Preston's main police station, just off the city centre. Now the operational side of the job, cells included, had been moved to a modern operating centre further away from the centre. This building on Lawson Street, a child of the sixties, remained police property and still housed the admin function for the division as well as the comms and CCTV rooms. A cell complex, now unused and mothballed, could still be found in the basement, but it was off-limits to all now.

The CCTV suite was jointly funded by the local council and other agencies and staffed by non-police personnel. Because of the nature of the work it could provide employment for disabled people, such as this wheelchair-bound lady who, Henry had discovered, had been on an extended toilet break, leaving the room unstaffed at a crucial time. Just how crucial had been unearthed by a quick review of the tapes.

She gave Henry a worried look, then manoeuvred her electric wheelchair to the bank of CCTV monitors trained via a small army of cameras on various key points in the city.

'This camera is situated on Friargate at its junction with Ring Way.' She pointed to one of the screens which relayed a scene which Henry recognized. Ring Way is the dual carriageway curving around the perimeter of the city; Friargate crossed Ring Way at a set of traffic lights, effectively dividing the shopping street in half. One part of it remained mainly pedestrianized and the other northerly section was still a traffic thoroughfare. The girl's body had been discovered in an alley at the top of the pedestrianized section which also backed on to the main shopping arcade, St George's. The wheelchair-bound lady pressed a couple of buttons and the screen jumped.

Then Henry's insides tightened as he saw a young woman fleeing for her life.

And behind her was a man. But he was not running, just loping with a purpose like wild dogs do in Africa when hunting down prey. He was only metres behind the girl.

Henry's breathing stopped momentarily – then the two figures were gone off screen because the camera did not follow them, merely captured them moving across the width of its lens. The recording lasted maybe three seconds – from the girl appearing on the left edge of the screen, then the man behind her, then they were both out of shot and because the CCTV operator was having a well-earned piss, that was it.

Henry growled inwardly.

The time on the screen read 01.56.

'Is that it?' Henry asked, voice brittle.

'Not quite,' the lady said. She pressed a few more buttons and the screen went dead, then flickered back to life, showing the time, 02.08, the exact same scene. 'This is him coming back.'

Henry watched transfixed.

The man who had chased the girl trotted un-hurriedly back into shot, keeping his head low. Then he was gone.

Henry exhaled long and hard. 'Anything on any of the other cameras?'

She shook her head.

'I take it there are other cameras up Friargate?'

She nodded.

'So remind me, how come there's only you here tonight?'

'My colleague went sick at short notice.'

Henry could not prevent a 'tut' from escaping.

'I needed the loo,' she said defensively. 'Otherwise I don't leave the room. I eat and drink in here, but sometimes I need to pee. How did I know someone would be murdered?'

'Sod's law,' Henry said. He looked away disdainfully, then back at the monitors. 'Run that first one back, will you?' he instructed, reflecting how glad he was he hadn't taken that mouthful of sour-mash whiskey because you just never can tell when someone's going to get whacked.

'OK, they've come down the north part of Friargate – we assume – from the direction of Moor Lane, crossed over Ring Way then continued up Friargate, the traffic-free bit, in the direction of Cheapside and the victim has been cornered and murdered in Anchor Place. The offender has then returned in the direction he came from.'

Henry's eyes roved across the four uniformed cops crammed into the CCTV room, the most he could pull together at short notice. His mind was working quickly. It was 4.15 a.m., over an hour and a half since the body was discovered, over two hours since the crime was committed and twenty minutes since he'd viewed the CCTV footage. He was desperate to do as much as he could with the time and resources available to him, so that when he handed the investigation over, as he knew he would have to, he would

23

have ensured that the package would be much more than a well-cared-for crime scene and nothing else. It was a matter of professional pride for him to do as much as possible in the little time available.

'From what we can see, the guy is in his mid-twenties, wearing a brown zip-up jacket, maybe a motorcycle jacket or flying jacket, and blue jeans. These will be bloodstained. He has dark-brown, maybe black hair, he's well-built, around the six-foot mark and he's a white man.' Henry glanced at the paused image on the TV screen. It would be enhanced at some stage, but he didn't hold out much hope of it turning out much better than it already was. The make-believe technology on TV cop dramas that portrayed super-sharp enhancement simply did not exist. In real life it was just a series of fuzzy images, as anyone who has watched *Crimewatch* will know. 'Does he ring any bells with anyone?' he asked hopefully. They all shook their heads and muttered negatively. 'Right, OK, two pairs. It's a bit of a mooching job, this,' he said rubbing his hands. 'One pair start at the crime scene and work your way down Friargate towards and then across Ring Way; the other pair start at Moor Lane and work your way slowly up towards Ring Way in the opposite direction. Look in bins, peer down grids, in flowerbeds et cetera, to see if we can locate a murder weapon, a knife or blade of some sort, obviously. Don't disturb too much, though, because there'll be a search team on this later this morning – but for now I want a cursory search of the immediate area.'

24

The four PCs exchanged glances and hesitated until Henry said, 'Go,' and gestured with his hands as though he was pushing them out.

Henry looked at the night-duty DC. 'I'm going for a stroll, too.'

The DC nodded.

'You check the footage for fifteen minutes before and after what we've already seen. Might turn up possible witnesses.'

'OK.'

Henry gave the CCTV operator a curt nod and when his back was turned, she shoved her tongue down between her bottom set of teeth and bottom lip and pulled a monkey face at him. He, in turn, not seeing this, left the room rolling his eyes at her inefficiency.

Back on the streets it had turned predawn chilly, even though the night had been warm. A kind of light mist had formed and hung wispily like a ghost. Henry walked back up Friargate where he'd left his car, pulled a three-quarter-length zip-up jacket from the boot and slid it on. Then he went back to the point where the CCTV camera was affixed to a lamp post above the Ring Way/ Friargate junction. He looked up at the camera that angled back down at him guiltily.

Hands thrust deep in his pockets, Henry stood on the exact spot that victim and pursuer had crossed at four minutes to two, then twelve minutes later had been re-crossed by the pursuer, now murderer – alone, having committed his brutal deed.

His eyes searched the pavements for a trail of

blood. No such luck.

Twelve minutes, he thought.

Henry ran the footage through his mind again, brief though it was. The girl had been fleeing, desperate for her life. As she'd run across the screen with her ripped clothing and shoeless feet, her head had whipped round to look at the man behind her. And even though the image was fuzzy, unclear, it was plain to see it had been a look of terror.

And then the man came into shot, unhurried, with that sure gait, knowing he would catch and destroy her. No knife in hand, though, not even on the return journey.

So he followed her, killed her, then came back.

And she had no shoes on her feet ... and she was a drug addict according to the observation from the pathologist.

Henry's eyes moved around, over to the Grey Friar pub on the opposite side of the road, one of the Wetherspoon chain, and the smaller pub on the opposite corner, the Old Black Bull. They were positioned like sentinels to that section of Friargate, one of Preston's oldest thoroughfares, which, if Henry was honest, had seen much better days. Now, despite the best intentions of the city council, parts of it were quite run-down and almost derelict. It was a mixture of Indian restaurants, iffy pubs and a smattering of half-decent shops ... and, Henry thought again, *the girl had nothing on her feet*. Just how far could someone run barefoot, he speculated. Not far, not even when running for your life. He crossed the deserted road at the traffic lights, stood outside the Grey Friar, his brow creased as he mulled it through.

Raising his eyes skywards, he squinted at the approaching dawn for a few moments, watching the sky change hue. A few cars came down Ring Way. In the distance he heard the glass-rattle of an electric milk cart. The city was easing itself reluctantly out of bed. He walked a few more metres north along Friargate to the minor junction with Union Street on his right, feeling unsettled.

Nothing on her feet. To Henry that meant two things: she'd either been chased from a nearby premises, or she'd jumped from a car. It was the former hypothesis that captured his imagination there and then so with that in mind, he began to stroll. Hands clasped behind his back, the regulation two miles an hour – cop pace.

He worked his way up Union Street, then across Great Shaw Street until he dropped back on to Friargate where he bumped into the pair of constables making their way from Moor Lane to Ring Way.

There was a short conversation – nothing to report – before parting. Henry crossed the road on to Edward Street, not really knowing what he might be looking for, and basically finding absolutely nothing, nor anyone, as he worked his way back to the traffic lights, his starting point, slightly annoyed at himself.

He rubbed his eyes. They squelched obscenely. He knew that later in the morning this section of town would be torn asunder by the murder enquiry and house-to-house teams. He was

27

already frustrated it would not be him deploying officers on their tasks, which is why he felt driven to find something out here and now, something tangible for the murder team to get their teeth into.

'Once more,' he told himself.

This time he walked three-quarters the length of the north side of Friargate, then looped right into Great Shaw Street and back again.

'*DCI Christie?*' his PR called.

He stopped outside the Preston Playhouse Theatre and fished the PR out of his pocket. It was the comms room contacting him. 'Message from the CSI – can you attend the crime scene removement of the body?'

'Roger ... I'll make my way back up. ETA two minutes.' As he spoke he rotated on his heels and found himself looking down a narrow, high-walled alley. At first glance it appeared to be a dead end. He had peered down it on his first walk-through, but hadn't seen anything which drew his attention, other than a battered-looking Fiat Panda at the far end of it. Henry slid his radio back into his jacket and walked down the centre of the alley towards the car, feeling broken glass crunch like cockroaches under his feet. It was becoming easier to see as dawn broke.

Suddenly he froze, mid-stride, patting down his pockets for his mini-Maglite torch, which he found in his outer jacket pocket. He twisted the lens cap to turn it on and flashed the tiny but intense beam on the object that had caught his eye. It was on the ground by the front nearside

28

wheel of the car.

Initially he had thought it to be just litter, a discarded chip paper or burger wrapper, scrunched up then thrown down.

He swallowed drily with excitement as his eyes focused on a woman's slip-on shoe, white, rather like a ballet shoe. He squatted, hearing and feeling his knees crack, to inspect the find. Definitely a shoe.

Standing back up stiffly he glanced further down the alley to see if he could spot its partner.

The alley narrowed considerably into nothing wider than a ginnel and then came out on Friargate between two shops. Just to Henry's right, beyond the car, a tight junction in the alley turned ninety degrees and ran parallel behind the shopping street. Henry's whole being tensed as he heard the sound of footsteps in this section of the alley, then a door gently closing and the sound of a latch dropping. His second surge of adrenaline of the night gushed into him, purging his mouth of saliva.

The footsteps came closer.

Henry stepped back and pushed himself against the wall, waiting for whoever this was to emerge. His breathing was put on hold. He covered the torch beam with the palm of his hand.

As he waited, he spotted a motorbike propped up in the shadows against the wall on the opposite side of the alley, the first time he'd seen it. It was a trials bike of some description.

Suddenly a man appeared from the alley within feet of him, fitting a full-face motorcycle helmet over his head and walking over to the bike. He hadn't noticed Henry – and he was wearing the same sort of jacket as the killer in the CCTV footage.

Henry took one step so he was standing behind the man. He'd already fished out his warrant card which was in his fingers, ready to be displayed.

'Excuse me,' he coughed.

The words seemed to send a charge of electricity into the man. Henry saw him jump, then spin quickly and aggressively. Henry extended his arm and flashed the warrant card, flashing the torch beam to it so the man could see the ID and make no mistake.

'I'm a police officer,' Henry said, waving the ID. He quickly took stock of the man. He could not see his face in the helmet, but could see he was strongly built, maybe a little shorter than himself.

The man lifted the visor of his helmet. 'Don't know,' he shrugged, the voice deep, guttural.

'Don't know what?' Henry said, taking a further stride towards him, that feeling inside him which said, *'Don't let this guy go.'*

'I'd just like a word, please.'

'For what? Why?'

'Remove your helmet, please.'

'For what?'

'Helmet – off.' Henry mimicked its removal. 'Let me see your face.'

The man shrugged again as if he did not understand Henry's words. 'No, no.' He wagged a finger as though he had no time for this

30

nonsense.

'Yes, yes,' Henry said, stepping even closer, but getting a bad vibe. Was this the murderer? His gut said yes. 'I need to talk. I'm a policeman,' he insisted, still displaying his warrant card clearly.

The man edged away, getting closer to the motorbike.

'No – must go.'

'No,' Henry said firmly. 'You stop now.' Inside he was regretting not being correctly tooled up. He didn't have his handcuffs or his extendable baton on him.

The man turned his back on Henry and made to the bike. Henry reached out intending to grab his arm and spin him round. No one had ever successfully ignored Henry in almost thirty years of coppering and this guy was not going to be the exception. But somehow, sensing this was about to happen, the man pivoted without warning. It didn't take Henry by surprise. His cop instinct was already sounding clanging bells, but the man did move very quickly, faster than Henry had anticipated, and as he span, he flung out his left hand and caught Henry a glancing blow across the chin. Henry reared away, staggering back a step or two, not really losing his balance, just dropping into a defensive stance like a wrestler.

The suspect – as the man now was – had taken up a similar position, like a mirror image of Henry, but with one major difference: there was now a knife in his right hand, long, slim-bladed. In Henry's right hand was a tiny torch.

31

The men paused in a stand-off.

Henry gulped, finding his mouth still barren. 'I'm a cop,' he reiterated so there was no misunderstanding. He held out the warrant card again. 'Don't be silly. Drop the knife.'

'No,' the man uttered, his voice slightly muffled by the crash helmet.

'You drop it,' Henry said warningly. He slowly placed the warrant card in his jacket pocket, extracting his PR, his eyes transfixed on the man and knife. He raised the PR to his face and pressed the transmit button and managed to say, 'DCI Christie to Preston...' They were the only words he got out before the man lunged at him.

Henry saw it coming, prepared for it.

He sidestepped and crashed the PR down on to the man's wrist, hard and violently, intending to hurt him with the solid radio.

The knife clattered to the cobbles, but the man curved into Henry, driving him back against the wall. Henry's arms flailed upwards like a broken windmill and everything was released. The PR crashed down and his torch skittered away towards the main channel in the centre of the alley.

The man came on. He grabbed Henry's right arm and with a display of great strength hurled him bodily against the Fiat Panda.

Henry lashed out desperately with his foot, feeling his right toecap connect somewhere on the man's right shin – but the man still powered in, his crash-helmeted head rearing back about to head-butt Henry in the face.

Even in that brief flash of time, Henry was

able to visualize the damage such a blow could do to his handsome features. He squirmed away and his right hand shot underneath the jawline of the helmet, grabbing for the windpipe. He squeezed his fingernails either side of the Adam's apple, then using all the force he could muster heaved the man backwards – a man who was now fighting like a demented being. Henry's muscles screamed with the effort, his face contorted, his neck sinews like steel twine. The man broke free and reeled away, but gave Henry only a moment of relief because he was back on the cop again, laying into him with a series of well-placed body blows. Henry was powerless to resist them and was not a skilled enough fighter to avoid them.

He sagged down as the man punched and kicked, raining blow after blow on him. He toppled over, groaning, and found himself belly-down on the cold ground, his face twisted and able to see underneath the Fiat Panda. And even despite the violent onslaught he registered another slip-on shoe. Then his vision swam as though he'd dived into a swimming pool – but the sight of the second shoe and the certainty that he'd accidentally come across a murderer had a massive surging effect on him. He managed to roll away and back up to his knees – only to be kicked in the side of the head and sent splaying across the car again.

He gasped, his senses ebbing and flowing, expecting more, to be pounded into oblivion – but the man picked up the knife, ran to the motorbike, leaped on it and fired it up instantly.

He revved the engine and slew away up the cobblestoned alley, doing a sharp right at the end and disappearing.

'Fuck!' Henry spat in rage, forcing all the feelings of pain aside and shaking his head to clear his thinking. He yanked himself to his feet by using the wing mirror of the Panda and rescued his PR, which he began to scream into whilst being completely embarrassed and annoyed at himself. He calmed his voice and relayed the situation, then in pure anger kicked out at the Fiat Panda. As he did he noticed a glint of something hanging in the steering column. The keys were in the ignition.

He wrenched the driver's door handle, found it open and dropped in behind the wheel. Slamming the clutch down and jabbing the accelerator, he twisted the key with all his might, subconsciously hoping that his display of strength would transfer through the ignition system to the starter motor and start the car. It seemed to work, as the engine fired up first time.

He almost cheered, but muttered, 'Long time since I commandeered a car.'

Not that he had any real right to do what he did, but there was no way he was going to allow a murder suspect to get out of his clutches so easily, especially not one who'd assaulted him.

He scrunched the car into first gear, shaving away some of those nasty cogs, and gunned the little car up the alley, causing the small engine to howl. He braked hard at the junction before turning in the direction the motorcyclist had taken – and at the same time hearing and feeling some-

34

thing heavy roll in the boot of the car with a dull thud.

Braking at the junction with Friargate, Henry was amazed to see the motorcyclist race across his headlights, having just avoided contact with the ARV car driven by Bill Robbins which was now, according to the shouted airwave traffic, enmeshed in some roadside railings.

Waiting a moment to hear that Bill was OK – he was – Henry rammed the accelerator down and went in pursuit of the bike.

Arrogantly, the rider reared the machine up on to its back wheel and executed a superb wheelie along the centre line of the street, then dropped the bike back down. With his left hand he cut a dismissive 'You'll never get me' gesture and twisted down the grip.

The Panda – bless it – accelerated gamely as Henry, with one hand on the wheel and the other operating his PR, and still trying to clear his brain, relayed his position and mode of transport.

'And what exactly has this person done?' the comms operator asked Henry. 'Other than assault you?'

'I think that's enough to start with, don't you? Let's just get him stopped,' Henry snapped in his best DCI tones. He wedged his PR between his thighs, but even as he gave chase he realized there was little chance of success here as most of the available cops in Preston were trudging around the city centre on foot and Bill Robbins' ARV was now connected to railings.

Catching this man would now be down to

35

Henry Christie – armed with an ancient Fiat Panda.

'Do you have a registered number?' the comms operator asked.

'Only partial,' Henry admitted after picking up his PR again. He gave the control room the first two letters, all he'd seen through his swimming vision. 'Which,' he added, 'if I'm correct means the bike's registered in Liverpool.'

'I'll see what I can do,' the operator said. Meanwhile Henry had reached the junction of Friargate and Moor Lane, where there was a huge double roundabout. He saw the bike tearing down Fylde Road in the general direction of Preston docks.

He imparted this piece of information over the air and screwed the Panda as hard as he dared in the same direction, acutely aware that the distance between hunter and hunted was ever-increasing. And he knew there were no cop cars in the area. So though he had no way of telling in what direction the bike had gone, he still carried on hopefully, never one to call off a chase just because he couldn't see his quarry.

He was also acutely aware that the little engine was now emitting a horrible overheating smell and he hoped it wouldn't blow.

Then he thought, Fuck it.

He was chasing a murderer.

He found second gear and made the engine scream for mercy, feeling the whole thing almost lift off the ground as the front wheels smacked up and across the first of a series of traffic-calming ramps (Why not sleeping policemen any

36

more, Henry thought) in the 20mph zone surrounding the university campus. As the car
crashed down on to worn shock absorbers, it
rattled worryingly, and once again, something
hefty bounced in the boot.

He fully expected the car to fall apart at any
moment.

It didn't.

He was so pleased about this, he hit the next
ramp at fifty.

'DCI receiving?'

'Go 'head.'

'A BMW F800GS motorcycle was stolen
earlier this evening from Merseyside,' the
comms operator came on to inform him. 'Could
this be the one?'

'Could be,' Henry said, not knowing the first
thing about motorbikes, other than they were
dangerous things. 'Let's work on that assumption and get it circulated. It could be linked to
the incident in Friargate, so it needs stopping
and the rider arresting. Approach with caution ...
he is armed with a knife ... How about calling
out the helicopter?'

'Already done.'

'Plus, if it has been stolen from Merseyside,
there's every chance it could be going back
there, so get a checkpoint set up on the A59 at
Tarleton, please.'

'Will do.'

The checkpoint would ensure that any vehicle
travelling on the five-nine towards Liverpool
would be seen. There were other routes, obviously, but there was no way they could all be

covered.

Re-wedging the radio between his thighs as the Panda lifted off the last speed ramp, Henry sped down the incline that was Fylde Road under the stone-built railway arch which held up the west-coast line, then under the next railway bridge and left on to Strand Road. He was still working on the assumption that the bike was returning to Merseyside, but he knew he didn't have a cat in hell's chance of catching it in a ropy Fiat Panda. He began to calm down a little, putting his theft of this vehicle down to his anger at having been bettered in a scrap.

Frustrated, he banged the wheel, cursed and jammed the brakes on at the next set of lights, once again feeling something shift in the back. He wondered if he should bother going right out of the city, or should he return the Panda to where he'd found it and leave the chasing to others. He had a crime scene to get back to and manage as well as the discovery of a pair of shoes, which was probably connected to it, to investigate.

At the lights, which stayed on red forever, his adrenaline evaporated and his body started hurting from the hammering he'd just had. He glanced around the inside of the car for the first time. In terms of spec it was spare and very lacking; in terms of being a complete mess, it was excessive. The passenger footwell was littered with fast-food cartons, newspapers and plastic bottles. The back seat was strewn with discarded female clothing.

Henry had a thought.

He was still at the lights. He pulled through them, parked at the side of the road and applied the handbrake, and got out. He called the registration number in for a PNC check, again noticing that the letters denoted that the vehicle's origin was Liverpool. He frowned.

'No trace, no current keeper,' the comms operator came back to him.

Henry acknowledged that. He glanced up at the sky and saw the police helicopter curve across the River Ribble and head out towards Liverpool. 'Good luck,' he said to himself. 'Let's hope he's not the one that got away.'

He walked around to the back of the Panda and twisted the handle on the hatchback, pulling it open.

And there, folded into the cramped space between the back seat and the hatchback, was the naked body of another young woman. Her face was scrunched up at an acute angle, looking at him through wide-open, but dead eyes.

THREE

Henry Christie sat on the kerb, his heels in the gutter, his bare knees drawn up, short pants exposing his gangly tanned legs. Securely positioned in the 'v' formed at his groin he had wedged the bottom half of an empty tobacco tin, the lid removed and placed on the kerb next to him. In his right hand he held a four-day-old chick, warm, fluffy, yellow, very much alive, recently stolen from its mother. It was held firmly but gently in his small palm and Henry looked at it, smiled and wondered innocently if it would fit in the tobacco tin. The tin was just about the right size, as was the bird, and he guessed that if he pushed it in and pressed down with his thumbs, as though it was modelling clay, it would fit very nicely, thank you very much. The chicken's legs flapped and it made a strained sort of noise. Henry smiled, certain the chick would fit well, then he'd be able to put the lid on and take it round to show to his mates.

He placed the bird sideways in the tin and began to use his thumbs, feeling its tiny wings and delicate bone structure give as he kneaded it into place...

Henry shot bolt upright, perspiration cascading off him.

He groaned and took deep breaths, turning to Kate as she reached out for him.

'Oh God, sorry love,' he said, flopping back into the bed, the back of his right hand on his brow.

'Was it the chicken dream?' she muttered sleepily.

'Yeah ... other people dream about running naked through shopping centres; I dream about filling a tobacco tin with a baby bird,' he whined. 'Give me naked any time.' He wiped his eyes, yawned, exhaled.

'Difference is,' Kate mumbled, turning over and hauling the duvet back over her head, 'you haven't done naked...' And then she was asleep again.

'No, but I've done chicken,' he said.

He twisted his head and checked the time: almost 6 a.m.

Was there any point, he wondered, even trying to get back to sleep? He decided not, gently eased the cover off and pulled on his pyjama shorts, then dressing gown, before inserting his feet in his slippers and sneaking quietly out of the bedroom. He walked past the two empty bedrooms that belonged to his daughters, Jenny and Leanne, feeling a fatherly twinge of guilt. They had almost flown the coop now, he thought wryly, keeping up the chicken analogy, and as a dad he had missed most of their growth. He swallowed back something big and emotional in his throat then wondered which of the rooms he would use for his planned model railway and Scalextric combined. Humming at this prospect he made his way down to the kitchen.

Then, coffee in hand, he retreated to the chilly conservatory to watch the day arrive.

It was Tuesday morning, the week after he had been called out for the murder on Friargate, which had turned into a double murder. The girl in the back of the Panda had been stabbed to death by the same knife as the girl in the alley, tests had shown.

Henry had done as much as he could on the night, but had been obliged to hand it all over to a 'real' senior investigating officer to deal with, as much as it stuck in his craw. The remainder of his week-long stretch on cover had been fire-brigading call-outs from all over the county, most of which he had resolved. By the end of the stint he was exhausted and was grateful when Monday morning came around. Just because he was on call did not mean he could forget his day job and despite a call-out each night he had still been required to be in his office at headquarters in the mornings at least to show his face. As the week had progressed, he'd become more and more dog-tired than he'd been in a long time and had slept in most of Saturday and Sunday, much to Kate's annoyance.

His week on the rota had finished at 6 a.m. on Monday. He had rolled into his office later to shift the paperwork which continually appeared on his desk and then he had an ED – early dart – at 3 p.m. so he could make up for the weekend and spend the evening with Kate and have his first touch of alcohol in a week.

He'd expected to sleep well for a change, but

as usual he'd tossed and turned and had a recurrence of the chicken dream when he eventually got to sleep, which is what had thrown him back to wakefulness.

The chicken dream was actually a retelling of a real-life incident, something that had happened to him at the age of five but had resurfaced from his subconscious only in the last few days. At that age, he and his family were living in a rural, but fairly tatty village in Lancashire in a tumbledown house that came with a few acres of land. His father, God rest his soul, decided to keep hens to make ends meet. The only problem was that there was no one in the family who could bring themselves to execute a chicken for food and that foxes and rats had no such qualms and continually caused mayhem in the run.

But for a young Henry James Christie, the hens were a delight, particularly the newly hatched chicks, which is why he liberated one for himself and pushed it into a tobacco tin, finding that it fitted really well if squeezed in hard enough.

Fortunately his mother spotted what he was doing and saved the life of the poor chick just before Henry clamped the lid down.

The bird lived, but it would always have a limp, and Henry – his bum smacked soundly at the time – had never really lived it down for the rest of his life. It became one of those embarrassing family anecdotes trotted out on birthdays and Christmases and was something he was never allowed to forget until recent years when the family became more fragmented.

The memory had been brought to the surface by the dead girl in the back of the Panda. The way she had been folded into the meagre space available made a direct subconscious mind-link for him to the chicken incident, only surfacing when he fell asleep. Obviously the chicken incident had left him deeply psychologically scarred. He just hadn't realized it.

Henry laughed at the comparison – girl v. chicken – and looked out across his back garden to the fields beyond.

It really wasn't in the same league, except that in his dream the head of the chicken had been replaced by the face of the dead girl and in the dream he was stuffing a huge hen with a human head into the back of a Fiat Panda.

He always suspected himself of being slightly bonkers and perhaps this was proof of that pudding.

'Too friggin' old for this,' he muttered. Finishing his coffee he made his way back upstairs and got into the shower, which he turned on hot and hard. He had intended to take the day off but had changed his mind ... there was something he needed to do to help save his own sanity.

'Henry, we're talking about something that happened over twenty-five years ago.' The chief constable peered over his half-rimmed glasses and across the expanse of his highly polished desk at the chief inspector who had managed to blag a last-minute appointment with the man who now led Lancashire Constabulary. His name was Robert Fanshaw-Bayley and all those

44

years ago he had been a rough-diamond DI who would think nothing of stooping to the lowest level – including the planting of evidence – to get a conviction. FB, as he was known by friends and enemies alike, sighed in a very pissed-off way. 'What is it with you, Henry, that makes you rake up muck and get everybody's backs up?'

'You took those girl's panties from the murder scene and planted them in the suspect's car,' Henry whined. 'And I was dumb enough to be a part of it.'

'Look, Henry.' The chief pointed a fat, sausage-like finger at his subordinate. 'You can't even begin to prove that.'

'I saw the scene and I distinctly recall her knickers were down around her left ankle.'

'But yet the crime-scene photo does not show that,' FB said firmly.

'Because you snaffled them before the SOCO got there. I remember seeing them.'

'Memory is such a fuzzy thing,' FB said blandly.

'Then you secreted them in the suspect's car, which had already been searched and nothing was found. And then you got me to re-search it and *voila*! Girl's knickers under the driver's seat and naive, dickhead me just went, "Uuh, fancy that, we must've missed them first time".' Henry put on a dumb voice for that last bit.

'Exactly what happened. The first search wasn't thorough enough and then the second one was. You did a great job, Henry, and a man got convicted of a murder he *did* commit.'

'That was the only evidence against him,'

45

Henry protested, his ring-piece twitching madly.

'And what you thought you saw at the scene you didn't really see and there's no way you can prove what you thought you saw. The SOCO photos don't lie – not in those days, anyway. The pre-digital era.'

Henry baulked inwardly as he realized that FB knew he had found the crime-scene photos, something which had taken a lot of doing. Word must have got back to the chief somehow.

'Look, the guy's son has just been to court for harassing you and Kate and almost killing her into the bargain just because he thought – *thought* – that evidence had been planted which incriminated his dear old dad, who has now croaked in prison anyway. His claims were fully investigated during his trial and found to be groundless, as you fucking well know!' Another sausage finger jabbed in Henry's direction. 'If you thought I planted the evidence, why didn't you speak up in court?'

Henry looked away, shamefaced. 'Because I didn't, but I should've done,' his voice rose defiantly.

'And because there's no evidence of it, that's why.'

'There's my evidence, my recollection.'

FB snuffled a grunt of contempt and checked the wall clock.

There was a beat of spiky silence between the two officers, then Henry's brow furrowed as he thought of something.

'What?' FB said suspiciously, sensing Henry's sudden stiffening.

'Nothing,' he said quickly, looking at the boss of Lancashire Constabulary. He and Henry had a long history that had begun at the scene of Jenny Colville's murder in 1982. Since then they had maintained a screwed-up relationship based very firmly in FB's favour, who would use Henry's undoubted skills, often ruthlessly, to achieve results, then toss Henry aside when it suited. Henry knew he had some things to thank FB for, but on the whole the senior officer was more in Henry's debt than vice versa.

'The devil,' FB said, removing his glasses and cleaning them on a tissue, 'makes work for idle hands, or something like that,' he declared. 'Trouble with you, Henry, is that you've too much bloody time on your hands, too much time sat around on your arse, thinking and getting twisted up about things.' He shook his head sadly, replaced his glasses and adjusted his wristwatch, which Henry noted was a chunky Rolex. 'How long before you retire?'

'Nine months.'

'Do you intend to go?'

He shrugged. 'Dunno.'

'Mm ... you know that guy *was* guilty of murdering that girl.'

Henry did know. Because of the circumstances of why the offender's son was harassing Henry, and other incidents, it had been necessary to re-examine the murder case, and a DNA test had been carried out which conclusively linked the man to the murder. Henry knew the man was guilty for sure, yet it didn't excuse the planting of evidence. Somehow it attacked his sense of justice.

'If those panties hadn't been found in his car, he would not have been convicted of her murder based on the rest of the evidence at that time, because DNA wasn't around then. If that had happened, he would have killed again – and again...'

'You can't be sure of that,' Henry said weakly, though he knew it to be true.

Once again the men regarded each other stonily. 'Yes I can, because I think he killed before and we could not prove it.'

Henry's mouth clamped shut.

'Henry,' FB said patiently, 'if you want to pursue this, go ahead, I can't stop you. But you'll never prove it, not in a month of Sundays. You'll stir shit, people's names will get blackened and there'll be no end benefit from it. No one will emerge smelling of 4711 ... and your already shaky reputation will crumble even further. Think about it.'

FB sat back and twiddled his thumbs ruminatively on his belly. 'How about getting off your constantly spreading lardy arse and getting involved in some real police work for a change?'

Henry barely suppressed a laugh. In the last two years he'd been involved in the disruption of a major terrorist atrocity in the north-west when two excellent officers had been brutally murdered by a man intent on assassinating the American State Secretary and also been involved in a major undercover operation ... but he kind of knew what FB was getting at. He'd become involved in these jobs more through

48

luck than anything and he was pretty desperate to break out of the office and get back to the sharp end of policing on a regular basis, rather than just in guest appearances.

However, he was suspicious of FB – as ever. 'What would that be?'

When FB winced slightly, Henry's low expectations sank even further.

Nothing jobs, he thought sourly.

FB reached across his desk for a buff file, which he opened. It was thin, with a few sheets of paper in it. 'Time, resources,' he said painfully, 'have meant we haven't been in a position to chase these up.' His voice was almost apologetic, confirming Henry's guess. He tried to keep a look of exasperation off his face but his flickering eyelids were a dead giveaway.

'Hey – you don't have to do this. I just thought you might like to get out and about again. I can't get your job back on FMIT, nor can I wangle a place for you on SOCA or any divisional CID, so you can take this, or leave it. I'll fix up someone to stand in for you at Special Projects, so you don't need to worry about that, just concentrate on this.' He tapped the file. 'I've siphoned off some travel and expenses money from another budget because I thought we needed to show the public we're doing something about this problem and these are pretty high-profile cases. But I can always find someone else.'

FB closed the file.

Henry held out a hand and FB passed it across.

'See accounts about the money. It's under Operation Wanted. Have fun.'

49

Henry nodded shortly and rose to his feet without opening the file.

'Not want to see what's in there?'

'I'll keep it as a surprise.'

'Good hunting,' FB said. 'And Henry?'

Henry paused at the door. 'Let it go?'

FB gave him a nod and a wink.

Henry did a mental coin toss. The penny fell heads-up, deciding him to avoid his office upstairs in one corner of the Special Projects larger office. Instead he trotted down to the dining room on the ground floor, which was alive with breakfast traffic. He took his place at the back of the queue and served himself with a toasted sausage sandwich and a large black coffee from the machine. He carried them to a table in the corner.

He arranged his sandwich, drink and file carefully in front of him, noticing for the first time that the word 'WANTED' was emblazoned across the front of the file in red letters. Henry still did not open it.

His sandwich tasted guiltily wonderful, the machine-brewed coffee less so, being bitter and sludgy.

It was only as the soporific effects of the food and drink wafted over him did he open the file and browse through the meagre contents.

He tutted and said under his breath, 'So I've become a bounty-hunter now, have I?'

FOUR

With the thin file under his arm, Henry made his way to the Intelligence Unit situated in the front corner of the ground floor of the headquarters building. He placed his thumb on the fingerprint ID entry system, tapped in a security code and entered a busy, pleasant office. He paused just inside the door, his eyes roving: the DI in the far glass-fronted office was chatting earnestly to the DS behind the closed door; everyone else was busy at their workstations, faces transfixed on computer screens or reading paper files. Spotting DC Jerry Tope sitting at a desk with his back to him, Henry grinned. He would do. Tope was a quiet, diligent officer who had been of great assistance to Henry on a complex murder enquiry a while back. It had been Tope's crucial analysis of intelligence and facts that had helped steamroller that investigation to a successful conclusion. And Henry quite liked the guy, which was a plus point.

Henry approached and stood behind him, allowing his presence to seep into Tope's psyche, making him turn round and raise his eyebrows.

'Saw your reflection in the computer screen,' Tope said, looking up. 'Can I help you, Henry?'

'May I?' Henry indicated the chair positioned

at the gable end of Tope's desk.

'Help yourself.'

Henry spun and slotted his backside on to the plastic chair, clutching the file to his chest. Tope eyed it and him with scepticism. 'You OK, Jerry?'

'Tip-top. You?'

'Ditto.'

Tope's eyes fell to the file again.

'You busy?' Henry asked.

'Under an avalanche.' He smiled tiredly. 'Just been doing some Intel work on that double murder, but they don't want me anymore, so I'm catching up on everything else.'

'Good.' Henry placed the file on the desk, opened it and turned it so Tope could see its contents. The DC picked up the three sheets and scanned them briefly, picking out the names.

'Ring any bells?' Henry asked.

'All three,' he confirmed. He went through the sheets, one at a time. 'Anthony Downie, Jane Kinsella and last but not least, Paulo Scartarelli.' He looked at Henry.

'And their connection is?'

'No actual connections as far as I know, other than all three are fugitives from justice,' he said grandly, with a short smile. He placed the sheets back into the file one at a time. 'Murder, murder and more murder ... not nice people ... So, *is* there a connection I don't know about, Henry?'

'Yep – all three fugitives are now my business. Acting on a direct edict from the chief constable no less, I've been selected from many, many volunteers and pressed men to bring these so-called fugitives to face justice in order that the courts can immediately release them again,' Henry said proudly.

Jerry Tope's nickname was 'Bung' – short for 'Bungalow' – because it was claimcd that he had 'nowt up top'. How he had accrued the moniker was a mystery because it was the direct opposite of the truth. Tope was a deeply intelligent man who had found his niche, appropriately, in the world of police intelligence where he was an analyst and no one's fool. Which was why, when he looked at Henry, squinting again, Henry wasn't in the least surprised to see that his little white lie had been seen through instantly.

'Shit end of the stick comes to mind,' Tope said.

Henry gave the impression that he was going to counter this assertion for a moment before relenting and saying, 'Not far off the mark there, Jerry.'

'As I recall, the chief got his arse soundly thrashed at the last Police Authority meeting. Apparently, one of the members got a bee in his bonnet about villains at large, these three in particular – and asked the chief what the hell he's been doing about catching such people. I believe there's actually six hundred wanted people on our books. These three miscreants are the cream of the crop.'

Henry suddenly liked Jerry Tope even more. He kept his ear to the ground and anyone who used the word miscreant went straight into Henry's top ten. He'd be saying shenanigans next.

'You're telling me things I don't know, Jerry. I'm not a political animal and the Police Authority doesn't interest me in the least.'

'I just read the newspapers. It's what I do.'

'Mm, I don't,' Henry admitted.

'I hope you've got some sort of budget,' Tope said.

It was a cautious 'Why?' from Henry.

'Well, let's see...' Tope picked up the first sheet. 'Not too much of a problem with Downie, he's supposed to be local-ish; Jane Kinsella could be in Australia and Paulo Scartarelli is supposed to be in Cyprus, linked up with some Maltese gangs operating out there, so they say. Living like an old-style Mafioso in the mountains, or something ... so there could be a bit of travelling involved.'

'FB said he'd siphoned some money from some budget or other specifically for this.'

'Want me to find out?'

Henry's eyebrows came together. 'And how would you do that?'

Tope twinkled his fingers like a master pianist over his computer keyboard and despite Henry's stomach doing a somersault, he said, 'Fetch, boy,' then leaned back in the creaky chair to watch a computer maestro at work. His fingertips danced across the keys as Henry recalled what a bit of a whiz Tope was in the Ethernet. He had the ability to hack into databases all over the world.

However, Henry's attention was distracted from this virtuoso performance by the entry into the office of a newly promoted DCI by the name

54

of Jack Carradine. It was this man who had replaced Henry on what had been the SIO team, but was now FMIT, the Force Major Incident Team. Carradine was one of Dave Anger's buddies, or arse-lickers, as Henry preferred to call them. Anger was the detective chief superintendent in charge of FMIT, having been brought in a few years earlier on a free transfer from Merseyside Police. Henry was under no illusion: Anger was slowly surrounding himself with his cronies. Carradine was a Scouser and went way back with Anger, so it must be true. Stereotypically, Henry wondered if the two men wore shell suits when off duty.

Carradine blanked Henry out as he strutted across to the DI's office, but Henry rose to his feet and collared him.

'Jack – how's it going?'

'Henry. Didn't see you lurking there.'

'Whatever,' Henry said indifferently. 'Just wondering how the job at Preston is going.' Carradine was the SIO who took up the reins of the double murder Henry had initially covered.

'You mean the one where you took a dead passenger out for an early morning drive and nearly completely fucked up any possibility of getting any useful evidence from that crime scene? That one, you mean?'

Henry's bottom lip twisted.

'You know, Henry, you are a fucking laughing stock, pal.' He gave him a patronizing tap on the shoulder and eased past, end of conversation.

Henry stood immobile for a moment, getting a grip on himself, his fingers folding and unfold-

55

ing into tightly clenched fists, his breath shortening as ire rose. All eyes in the office were on him, some sniggerers – he thought – some waiting for an outburst which would entertain them all in their drab little day.

Slowly he sat, controlling his breathing, blinking away the red mist.

Jerry Tope eyed him worriedly. 'You OK, boss?'

'Not really,' Henry said tightly.

'The man's a knob, if that's any consolation.'

'A knob with my job.' He inhaled deeply and blinked to shake himself out of his jagged state, then looked at Tope, self-control having returned. 'Nearly lost it there,' he admitted.

'He'll get his comeuppance.'

Henry smiled. 'Comeuppance – another good word, Jerry. I like a man with a bit of vocabulary ... So, found anything?' Tope had been tapping away at his computer keys.

'Thing is, once you know your way around the force intranet, if you've got half a computer-literate brain in your noggin, you can just about spy on anyone in the organization – email, files, departments, whatever.'

'But can't you be traced?' Henry asked, not completely sure he wanted to be a party to Tope's hacking.

The DC gave him a withering glance.

'I'll take that as a no.'

'Here we go.' Tope pushed the monitor around so Henry could see without craning his neck. It showed a lot of figures and balances. 'This is one of the chief's special accounts ... I mean, there's money sloshing around the constabulary all over the place ... this is Operation Wanted and there's twenty-five grand in it from somewhere ... This'll be the money siphoned from somewhere else.'

'Twenty-five grand?' Henry hissed. 'Where's it come from?'

Tope tapped a few more keys. 'Backtracking here,' he explained. 'Four grand from some Home Office funding for street crime...' More keys tapped. 'Eight from the central training budget – everybody nicks cash from training...' Tap, tap, tap. 'Three from corporate development.'

'OK, heard enough. Unbelievable.' Henry raised his hands in surrender.

'All kosher, though.'

'Not saying it isn't, Jerry ... just shows that money can be found from anywhere when necessary. Twenty-five grand, though. Seems a lot. Maybe a trip to Cyprus isn't completely out of the question,' he mused. 'Never been. They say it's pretty nice.'

'I've been. I could show you around,' Tope volunteered hopefully, batting his eyes at Henry.

'I'm afraid it's a job for a man of rank,' Henry said sonorously. 'Anyway, these miscreants.' He patted the file. 'Can you dig out everything we have about them all?'

There was a roar of muted laughter from the DI's office, then his door opened and DCI Carradine stepped out, the DI in tow. Henry wound around in the chair, a dark shadow crossing his face as he watched Carradine shake the DI's

57

hand effusively and then walk back across the office. As he passed Henry he gave him another pat on the shoulder, but didn't look at him, and carried on walking towards the door. It was all Henry could do not to jump up after him and fell him with a kung-fu-style kick in the back.

As ever, he remained a model of professional restraint, simply scrunching up a piece of A4 paper his left hand had been resting on, turning it into a tight ball.

The DI stopped by Henry's shoulder and exchanged a knowing glance with him.

'That man is a total wanker,' he stated, folding his arms, then grinned at Henry and said, 'Has Jerry been of help to you?'

Henry shrugged non-committally. 'Suppose so.'

'Fancy a brew, then – kettle's on in the office,' the DI offered.

'Don't mind if I do.'

An hour later, brews being a leisurely affair in the Intelligence Unit, Henry stopped off at the accounts department on the journey back to his top-floor office. There he spoke to a woman of his age who he'd known for many years and had once, indeed, had a one-night stand with about twenty-odd years before when he'd bumped into her on a CID night out in Preston.

'Henry Christie,' she said warmly, almost purring.

'Madeline Payne,' he responded, recalling the night of debauchery that had ended up in her grotty flat in the town centre. Memory gave him a little golden glow.

'Madeline Rooney, actually,' she said, holding up her left hand and wiggling the third finger.

'Oh, nice.'

'Third time around ... last time around.'

'Congratulations ... anyone I know?'

'A DC over in commerce – John.'

Henry nodded. He knew John Rooney. 'Yeah, good man,' he said and hoped that their little liaison would never rear its head again like the one he'd had with the woman who became Dave Anger's wife. Almost thirty years on, that little indiscretion still cost him dearly.

'I still remember, you know,' Madeline said demurely, looking at him in a sultry, dirty manner. She pursed her lips, which were not as full and soft as they had been in the flush of youth. Having said that, Henry happily admitted that he too was drying up with age.

His heart missed a thump and he thought tensely, Too much bloody history in this organization, too many skeletons in my cupboard, mostly based around my dick. He smiled fondly and said, 'Me, too.'

'Mm, anyway, water under the bridge. What can I do for you?'

Relieved, he said, 'Operation Wanted. How much have I got to spend?'

'Follow me.' She beckoned him, as she had once done all those years before and he followed (as he had done). Only this time she took him to her desk, noting that whilst the lips might have lost their fullness, the hips had expanded, but in a very shapely way. She manoeuvred herself into

59

her chair and bade him pull up another one next to her. She gave her mouse a shake and the screen came to life.

'Operation Wanted,' she confirmed, tapping a few keys to bring up a file full of figures. She placed a pair of specs on her nose to look at the monitor. From where Henry was sitting, he could not really make any sense of what he saw.

She whistled appreciatively.

'You've got a nice round figure to play with,' she said, giving him a suggestive sideways glance. She shuffled her shoulders and her large breasts moved provocatively.

Henry gave an inward, sad sigh. 'How much?' he asked, deciding to ignore the blatant double meaning. Madeline had been, and obviously still was, a girl with a reputation.

'Four grand.'

'Four grand,' Henry spluttered in disbelief.

Eventually back in his office, Henry leaned in his chair and wondered what had happened to the outstanding twenty-one thousand pounds that he knew, unofficially, was in the budget for Operation Wanted. Madeline had been insistent that four thousand was the only money available and though Henry suggested with subtlety that she look again, he didn't feel he had the right to come out and say he knew there were twenty-five big ones in the budget.

He scratched his head and decided it was probably nothing to sweat about. The four grand was probably just his sub-allocation from the larger budget, or however accounts worked. He was no expert and now knocked himself for not attending the two-day course called 'Finance for Non-Financial Managers' about two years before. Like most cops he had an aversion to handling money as well as an aversion to attending training events. He would never have missed a session on serial killers, though, but he'd thought that two days of figures and more figures was an appalling prospect and he'd made his excuses.

He rocked forward and reached for the three envelopes that had appeared on his desk from Jerry Tope, efficient as ever. He splayed them out and read the names on each: Downie, Kinsella, Scartarelli.

Eeney, meeney ... he thought, but decided to make the choice on a financial basis crossed with a weighting on whether there was any chance of success.

Kinsella, according to Tope, was supposed to have fled to Australia. That meant if Henry physically went there, his vastly reduced budget would get wiped out straight away. Scartarelli might be in Cyprus, which was a possibility, but the definite quick win would be Anthony Downie. There was a good chance he wasn't too far away and just needed flushing out. So, decision made, Henry's finger and thumb slid inside the envelope and pulled out the now thicker file.

He smiled as he read the front sheet, which was a copy of *The Informer*, the constabulary's crime intelligence bulletin, and wished he'd chosen a trip to the Antipodes instead.

The headline screamed, *Wanted for Murder,*

61

Rape and Indecent Assault.

Under the headline in thicker, fatter, bolder lettering were the words: 'DOWNIE IS VIOLENT AND DANGEROUS TOWARDS POLICE OFFICERS'.

Under that it read, 'Known to frequent the Blackpool, Leyland, Rochdale and Central Manchester areas.'

Then there was a colour photo of the man staring back at the lens with an expression of loathing and arrogance.

'Nice choice,' Henry said, sitting back and starting to read the file on the first of three people he was expected to go out and arrest.

Anthony Downie sat in the back of a police car. The car was a Vauxhall Astra owned by Greater Manchester Police and he was being driven to Rochdale police station with two uniformed constables in the front, passing an occasional comment to each other. Both were pretty pleased by the fact that Downie was in the back. So pleased that they'd just got a little bit complacent.

Downie huddled down in the seat. He was a big man, six-eight, broad-shouldered and just on the verge of being very fit. He was strong and agile and already cursing his stupidity in getting caught. He should have suspected this would happen. He'd stayed too long in one place and had paid the price.

He had been in Rochdale for three months, living under the stolen identity of a man he'd killed and buried under the patio of the previous house he'd rented, in Nottingham. No one had

62

noticed the man was missing yet. Downie knew this would happen because the man, a nonentity, had been carefully chosen for just that reason. It had been easy to live off the capital he had stashed in several bank accounts, all of which were accessible via plastic. Before he had killed the man – a very satisfactory strangulation following a wild bout of male-on-male intercourse – Downie had tortured him for four days and made him reveal all his PIN numbers. After the midnight backyard burial, Downie had moved up to Rochdale, withdrawing three hundred pounds per day from each of three accounts, renting a room in a modest terrace and hiring a nondescript car. Nine hundred pounds a day was about right and he had worked out that the accounts would last him about ten weeks at that rate.

His downfall came from a family in the same street. A hard-working family whose eldest son was gay. Downie had befriended him whilst pretending to be a supply teacher, as was his modus operandi, and started to steal from him and the family. The young man found some of his mother's property in Downie's rented room and challenged him. Downie made the mistake of apologizing and returning the property, only for the lad to blab to his mother what had happened. She in turn told her husband, a suspicious fellow, who began to follow Downie and discovered that he never went near any school. Instead he drifted each day into the Canal Street area in Manchester, where he targeted gay men in bars and cafes.

Not happy, the father called the police, who

spoke to the son.

At that moment, the police believed they were dealing with a man called Tony Robinson and simply went round to the rented room for a chat.

Downie's defensive and suspicious demeanour set off a few alarm bells in the officers' heads and with a nod and a wink between them they arrested him in a very nice manner, still unaware they were dealing with a ruthless murderer.

They 'conned' him into the car, saying there was a complaint of theft from the family and they 'needed to go through the motions'.

'Yeah, I can see that,' Downie said and willingly got into the police car. The officers dropped their guard and with such a compliant prisoner, they neglected to put handcuffs on him, by no means an unknown occurrence.

On the journey to the station the officer in the front passenger seat turned and said, 'What's your name again, mate?'

'Ant...' Downie stopped in mid-name and corrected himself. 'Tony Robinson,' he said quickly, stupidly caught out.

A look of comprehension came over the officer's face, but before he could react, Downie launched himself at him, powering a terrible punch into the side of the cop's head, breaking his jaw instantly, then hitting him again.

The car swerved as the two men fought in the cramped space, mounted a pavement and glanced off a bollard before bouncing around and stalling with a gear-crunching lurch. Downie, knowing the back doors were child-locked, crushed his big frame through the gap between the front seats, his fists flying and connecting, and he went for the passenger-door handle and scrambled out over the injured cop.

They had come to a halt on a quiet side road, a location which went a long way to inform Downie of his next move.

As he emerged from the police car he started to run – but only took three strides before stopping abruptly, turning and making his way back to the police car.

He dragged the officer he'd assaulted out of the car and dumped him on the ground before stomping on his head a couple of times, bringing his whole weight to bear and feeling the skull crack sickeningly under his shoe.

The officer behind the wheel was trying to free himself from his seat belt, scream for assistance over the radio, get out his baton and CS spray and get the prisoner Robinson, or whoever the hell he was.

Downie saved him the trouble of going too far.

He walked casually around the front of the car and opened the door for the officer.

'Get back or I'll spray you with CS,' he was warned. Downie laughed uproariously as the CS canister was pointed at his face and he was sprayed with a face full of the very nasty, usually effective, irritant...

'Unfortunately it doesn't work on everyone,' Henry Christie said as he read to the end of the depressing report in Downie's file. Downie had laughed in the cop's face, punched him hard and repeatedly until he was senseless, then dragged him out of the car and thrown him to the ground.

He had then stolen the police car, calmly driven back to his rented room, collected an armful of his belongings, then disappeared.

Henry breathed out. He shook his head at the stupidity of cops. Putting a six-foot-eight prisoner into the back of an Astra, being taken in by the willingness to cooperate and then being surprised when it went boob-up.

Shit happened.

If young cops were stupid enough to post videos of themselves breaking traffic laws on YouTube, then they were daft enough to think it wouldn't happen to them.

One was left with a fractured skull and broken jaw, the other a broken cheekbone and hand.

They subsequently found out the true ID of the man they had arrested and some pretty diligent follow-up detective work discovered a whole string of offences connected to gay communities and ID thefts perpetrated by the big man Downie, as well as the previously unknown murder in Nottingham.

Six foot eight did make him a big, formidable bloke. But as Henry read on in the file, the Intel on him revealed he was known to change his appearance frequently by wearing a variety of wigs and he hunched down to try to give the effect of being smaller than he actually was.

The assaults on the police officers were the last time Downie had been seen by a cop. He was known to have committed further offences in Scotland and northern England and had let it be known to some of his victims that he 'just loved' the gay scene in Blackpool even though there

66

was no evidence to suggest he was gay himself. The Lancashire connection came about because he had committed further offences in the county and had seriously assaulted twelve-year-old boys in Leyland and Blackpool.

Henry rearranged the file neatly and looked at Downie's photograph.

'So how the hell am I going to catch you, big fella?' Henry asked the image.

It was going to be through routine, Henry knew that. Delving into the file, checking out where he'd been, who he'd spoken to, what he'd said and let slip, and from that, working out where he was now. In other words, plain old-fashioned detective work. Talking to people, putting two and two together.

Henry's musings were interrupted by a figure at the office door.

He regarded the man suspiciously.

'You still here, Henry?'

Henry's eyes went into slitty mode. 'What's that supposed to mean?'

'I heard you'd been seconded to some elite crime-fighting team.'

Chortling back a guffaw, Henry uttered, 'What?'

The man – it was Chief Inspector Andy Laker – shrugged and said, 'Whatever.'

'What can I do for you, Andy? The comms room is way over there somewhere, isn't it?'

'I'm stepping into the breach.'

'What breach would that be?'

'The one opened by your move.'

Then it dawned on Henry. 'You're the one

who's replacing me here?' He pointed down at his seat and his hands flapped at the office.

'The penny drops.'

'You really have upset someone – the chief's bag carrier, to comms and then to this!'

'The chief chose me personally.' He sounded offended.

'And I thought you had a career in front of you,' Henry said amused. 'How wrong I was.'

'I'm taking over something that hasn't been working well.' Laker turned and regarded the larger Special Projects Office disdainfully, then turned back to Henry. 'They wanted a mover and shaker in here, apparently.'

'And who would that be?' Henry asked mischievously.

Laker bristled. He reddened up from the neck and his shoulders rolled.

Henry collected the three files in front of him, logged out of the computer, picked up the framed photograph of Kate and the girls and stood up. He walked slowly across to Laker, who shrank away from him.

'That was your induction,' Henry said. 'That's the in-tray, pending and out-tray ... I'm sure you'll be able to work out the rest for yourself, being so smart.'

'Uh – what?'

Brushing ignorantly past the smaller man, Henry closed his ears to the babbling and, now office-and-desk-less, he clutched the files and his meagre personal possessions and walked upright and erect out of the Special Projects Office without a backwards glance.

FIVE

There was something about the whole Downie saga that made Henry believe it would be a relatively easy task to track him down. A quick win, one out of three, a tick in the box. The hard bit would be physically getting hold of the big bastard and getting him into a police cell. Not an encounter Henry relished, but something he would have to deal with. He was only just getting over the pounding he'd had on the back streets of Preston.

He had looked at the file repeatedly and wondered how best to approach it and eventually decided he would kick the enquiry off in Rochdale, the last place Downie had come into contact with the cops, by visiting the family he had befriended and then stolen from. He had thought of speaking to a couple of Downie's more recent victims from two attacks in Blackpool and one in Leyland. From all accounts, though, these people were still traumatized.

Unusually for Henry he made an appointment. He preferred to drop in on folk unexpectedly and catch them on the back foot, but because of the rising fuel costs and the possibility of a wasted journey, he made the call instead.

* * *

He cleared his throat and looked at the family, mother, father, gay son.

They were in the living room of their terraced house in Rochdale, close to its border with Whitworth, which was in Lancashire.

'You found the bastard yet?' the father demanded. He was a gruff, no-nonsense working-class man struggling with the concept of having a gay son. He continually shot dagger-like glances at his lad, who sat there with his hands wedged between his thighs, uncomfortable and shamefaced.

'That's why I'm here,' Henry said. 'I've been given the job of finding him.'

'Hm,' the father breathed, unimpressed.

'How can we help?' the mother asked. She was dressed in a dour skirt and apron and could have been a character from an early episode of *Coronation Street*. All that was missing was a hairnet, curlers, blue rinse and bottle of stout. 'We didn't have much to do with the man ... at least, me and Norman didn't.' She glanced at her husband, then at her son. 'Eric did...' Her voice trailed off uncertainly, disappointment evident.

Eric, the son, mid-twenties, slim build, round face and long eyelashes, gave Henry a wan look and a shrug.

'He was a thievin', devious, perverted bastard,' the father blurted. 'A conman and a killer. It's lucky you're still alive, by all accounts,' he said to Eric. 'You could've ended up under a fuckin' patio.'

'Norm!' the wife cut in. 'No need to swear.'

Norman's mouth clamped shut with impa-

70

tience and became a tight line of disapproval. But then he muttered, 'Shit-shovellers.'

Henry observed the exchange, feeling the tension in the room.

'Perhaps if I could have a word with Eric – alone?' he ventured.

Eric breathed a sigh of relief.

'You're welcome to him,' Dad said and barged out of the room.

'Do you want me to stay, darling?' Eric's mum asked him.

'Ma, I'm twenty-three. I know I'm gay and I know I got conned, but I can deal with this.'

She nodded, smiling sadly at Henry and rose to leave.

'Thank Christ for that,' Eric breathed when they were alone. 'They make everything ten times harder than it has to be. OK, I'm a big disappointment to them, can't help it. Dad wanted me to be a mechanic like him. Not into cars.' He raised his eyebrows. 'Embroidery, yes.'

Henry chuckled. 'OK, Eric. I've read your statement and I don't really feel I need to go over the actual offences Downie committed against you...'

'I knew him as Robinson.'

'I'm aware of that.'

'So what do you want from me?'

'A chat about the man himself, anything he might have said to you, any indication where I might start looking to find him. That sort of thing.'

'Well,' Pussy Beaver said. From his face he

71

pushed back his superbly trimmed, bobbed silver hair, dusted with a sprinkling of glitter. 'Let's have a proper look.' He held out his finely manicured hand and tapped his thumb and forefinger together indicating he wanted to peer more closely at the photograph Henry Christie was showing him. Beaver was smoking a cigarette which had been inserted into a long, fat penis-shaped holder.

Henry handed him the photograph of Anthony Downie and gave Beaver a quick once-over. As ever, he found that he looked stunning. From the low-cut silk blouse, tightly wrapped around and displaying one of the finest pairs of breasts Henry had ever seen wobble, to the equally tight, short skirt with a split, from which a pair of long, tapering legs extended of which Cyd Charisse would have been envious. The effect was slightly marred by the unmistakable male bulge at the groin, which Beaver made no effort to conceal. Pussy Beaver may have had the breasts, but was just as proud of his tackle and never wanted to lose it.

He and Henry were in the admin office behind the box office at the Pink Ladies' Club, which Beaver – real name John Howard – ran efficiently and well above the law. Howard described himself as Head Pussy and by running this establishment on the Promenade at Blackpool, one of the country's leading nightspots, he had become a multimillionaire.

The two had known each other for several years and had first met in the dark days when the club was petrol-bombed by some local youths who despised what people like Howard stood for. Henry investigated the offence and arrested and convicted two nineteen-year-olds who, to this day, were still in prison for their crime. The last time Henry had had any dealings with Beaver was when a bomb had exploded at the club, but since then things had been fairly quiet.

'Mm,' Beaver said as he carefully looked at the photo.

'Apparently he's drawn to this place,' Henry said, basing the statement on the interview with Eric. 'Always comes in here when he's in town.' Henry knew that Pussy always held court in the bars of the Pink Ladies' in between his stage act and kept a sharp eye on the comings and goings of the clientele.

Beaver nodded, took a long drag of the cigarette, making Henry wince.

'Big man,' Beaver said, 'very big man.'

Henry had purposely not given Downie's height, so as not to lead the witness.

'Spot on,' Henry confirmed.

'Six-seven, six-eight, I'd hazard.' Beaver exhaled the smoke upwards through lips coated in a perfect cherry gloss. He looked at Henry. 'About right?'

'Yup.' Despite himself, Henry had difficulty keeping his eyeline level with Beaver's, constantly allowing them to drop and ogle the breastwork. Beaver had once let him feel them and they had felt good. Henry guessed that Beaver had had another boob job since then and he found himself curious.

'Hair's been dyed, though. He's blond now –

73

and has a goatee.'

'He's been in the club, then?'

'Yes. He kind of tries to hide his height with a stoop.' He handed the photograph back. 'What's he done?'

Henry rolled his jaw. 'Many, many bad things ... Particularly against gay men and transvestites.'

'But he's not gay himself?'

'Who knows what he is, other than a violent and dangerous individual.'

'Has he killed?'

'Oh yes – after a four-day period of torturing.'

'He was in here last night.'

A feeling of great satisfaction came over Henry as he thought, They always come home to roost.

The club, as ever, was packed to the gunwales, as it was six nights each week, pulling in an excess of £40,000 per night. Henry took up a position in one of the quieter bars in the complex, just off the foyer, and watched life go by. There was a heaving mixture of girls' nights out and stag parties, as well as the club staff and performing artists providing wicked colour and gaiety as they pranced and paraded amongst the clientele before the first show of the night got underway in the main auditorium, known as the 'Willy's Womb'.

He leaned on the bar, mineral water in hand, mesmerized by the scene of surging colour and laughter. Everyone was here for a good time and there had never been any serious public-order problems that Henry was aware of.

Adorned in spangles, sequins and feathers, now attired also in a pink latex leotard, shimmering stockings and high heels, Pussy Beaver stepped up to Henry.

Henry gave him/her the once-over.

'You look terrific, I have to admit.' Henry's eyes were automatically drawn to the boobs. 'Have you?' Henry could not resist asking, nodding at Beaver's chest.

'I thought you'd noticed, you dirty bastard,' Pussy squeaked with delight, her male vocal tones having disappeared as they always did in public. 'Yes, had a great uplift done last year, as well as a tummy tuck and face lift.' She raised her chin and ran her glittering fingernails across the tight skin. 'And an ass job.' She wriggled her shapely buttocks. 'And just because I can't bear to let the damn thing go' – her voice dropped into a hoarse whisper – 'I had my cock enlarged. I still love it, really ... something to play with in the bath.'

'Too much detail.' Henry held up his right hand in the police number one stop signal.

Pussy jiggled her boobs. 'Wanna give them a squeeze, Henry? Just for old times' sake.'

'I am very tempted,' he said wistfully, 'but let's take a rain check on that one, shall we?'

'Suit yourself – bitch,' she pouted, but not for real.

Henry blinked at her and shook his head, unable to fathom her out at all. It was far too complicated for Henry's one hundred per cent heterosexual brain. He actually thought of him-

75

self rather like a greyhound: he'd once been told that the only thing a greyhound ever thought about was chasing rabbits. All Henry could ever think of was chasing members of the opposite sex and inseminating them, although since his remarriage his eyes and mind were kept solely on Kate.

'Think he'll come?' Henry said.

'Been here two nights running,' Pussy said. 'Flashing the cash.'

'Somebody else's cash, I'll wager.'

'No doubt.'

'I'll keep looking, and you too?'

Pussy nodded, wafted her face with a Chinese fan which he flicked open with a crack, making Henry jump. 'Show's on in ten minutes ... I've got you a place in the royal box, luvvie.'

'I'm honoured.' Henry bowed graciously.

'Aren't you just.' She pursed Henry a kiss and flounced off towards the stage. Henry decided to risk one beer, which he took into the main theatre and found his way up to the royal box giving him an excellent slightly raised view of the venue. It was a Victorian theatre that had gone to rack and ruin in the 1950s and been saved by Pussy Beaver in the early eighties and had never seen better days. Henry was alone in the fur-lined royal box, making him glad and uncomfortable at the same time. Glad because you never could be sure who or what you might be sitting next to, uncomfortable because he stood out like a sore thumb. But whatever, he settled down to watch the show and keep an eye out for Downie.

The entertainment was basically an old-fashioned variety act, professionally done with lots of innuendo and dancing girls who were really men in disguise. Pussy did a solo spot for about twenty minutes, rousing the already rowdy audience into a mini-frenzy with a medley of Abba and Bassey songs. The first-half finale was a musical playlet with about as much plot as a porn movie, but some funny lines and good rock music. Henry enjoyed it all, but thought he shouldn't.

There was no sign of Downie.

He raised himself from his comfortable seat and drifted back to the bars to mingle. There was a thirty-minute interval, during which he found a tight spot at a bar and kept nicks from there. He still could not spot Downie.

The second half of the show began about 11 p.m. It was due to last for an hour and was a salacious romp through the ages – backwards – starting in the present day and regressing to Roman times; it was a shirt-neck-pulling extravaganza and he wondered if he had the stamina to see it through to the bitter beginning. He decided to give it half an hour and if Downie hadn't shown by then, he'd call it quits and head home to his heterosexual household and curl up next to a warm female bum.

Just as the cast appeared as knights in shining leotards, Henry spotted Downie at a table in the far corner. The hair was thick and curly, obviously a wig, and he sported a thick moustache and goatee. But it was his size that gave him away as he stood up to walk across to the bar. He

77

could not disguise his excessive height. Six-eight doesn't give much room for manoeuvre.

Henry watched him carefully.

He was sitting with two other men Henry did not recognize.

At the bar Downie ordered a round of drinks which looked like expensive cocktails. He carried them back on a tray.

Now he'd got him in his sights, Henry pondered the next move.

He could call in the troops to effect an arrest. He was loath to do this because it might cause mayhem in the club, especially if Downie kicked off, which he was very likely to do. Secondly there was the question of where Downie had come across his present money supply. The cash flow from the murdered man in Nottingham had been plugged. Downie wasn't drawing any state benefits, so how was he financing himself? If Henry arrested him now he might never reveal his present living accommodation and what could be a good source of evidence. But if he allowed Downie to walk out of the club with a view to tailing him, that could all go wrong especially if Downie was surveillance-conscious.

'Spotted him?' Pussy Beaver had sidled up to Henry in the royal box.

'Yes, thanks. Who is he with?'

'Two gay guys. What are you going to do? I don't want any trouble in here, luvvie.'

'There won't be. I'm just wondering what to do for the best. One way or the other, I don't want to miss him. He's too dangerous to be free.

I could do with knowing where he's holed up.'

'Looks like you're gonna have to make a quick decision.'

The wanted man had just sunk the last mouthful of his cocktail and was getting to his feet. It was clear from the body language, nods, handshakes, that he was on the move.

'Bugger,' Henry hissed. 'Why isn't he watching the show?'

On stage the cast was performing a Monty Pythonesque knees- up and the audience were roaring their approval at the sight of a dozen high-kicking men in knights' outfits and spandex. Downie walked across the auditorium, glancing at the show as he threaded his way through the tables towards the exit. Henry rose to follow, his right hand dropping into the jacket pocket into which he had stuffed his personal radio, which was switched off. Downie walked across Henry's bows, less than ten feet away, and Henry had to resist the urge to vault over and grab him. He held back, allowing Downie to reach the exit, then trotted out behind him, wondering whether Downie had clocked him and made him for a cop.

As Henry entered the foyer, Downie was leaving through the front doors, turning left on to the promenade and heading south. Pausing agitatedly for a few moments, Henry then emerged and saw Downie turning left on to New Bonny Street without a backwards glance. Not that Henry made the assumption that Downie hadn't spotted him. It would have been easy for Henry to do a quick sprint and close the gap, stop at the corner,

79

peer round and come face to face with Downie who might be waiting there to pounce. Instead, Henry dashed across the road and walked quickly down the seaward side of the prom and reached the junction just in time to see Downie turn into Bonny Street near the police station.

Henry jumped the railings and trotted across the prom and into the same street, finding himself fifty metres behind the man.

Bonny Street ran parallel with the promenade; the buildings on Henry's right, the backs of amusement arcades and Sea Life Centre, had their main entrances on the prom itself. On the left was a huge car park and the multi-storey eyesore that was Blackpool nick.

The road was deserted and dark, allowing Henry to follow from shadow to shadow. At one point Henry walked underneath the huge plastic shark affixed to the wall at the back of the Sea Life Centre. It was a nasty-looking model he had christened 'Dave' after Dave Anger. It had Anger's look about it: a beady-eyed viciousness.

Ahead, Downie walked past the newly constructed ground-floor public entrance to the police station, now locked for the night, then past the pub opposite, the Pump and Truncheon, a hostelry frequented by off-duty cops.

Downie crossed the narrow road and stopped suddenly.

Henry froze, then sidestepped smartly into a recessed doorway, hoping the dark shadow would hide him.

Downie turned slowly.

He stood there for a few seconds, carefully

scanning the street behind him. Henry held his breath. Then Downie started moving again with more purpose. At the junction with Chapel Street he crossed the road quickly and entered the maze of terraced side streets opposite which contained a tight mix of B&Bs, guest houses, private houses, pubs and shops bordered by Chapel Street and Yorkshire Street. Henry knew he would have to close in on Downie if he didn't want to lose him in there.

He sprinted across into Dale Street, keeping his footfalls as quiet as possible, thinking Downie had gone out of sight, but just saw him turn into York Street. Henry bared his teeth. He was starting to sweat now, despite the chill of the night. Crouching low, he jogged up to the junction and saw Downie do a right into Singleton Street – and Henry knew for sure if he lost touch now, Downie would be gone for good. If the man increased his pace he had a variety of choices of direction to take and could disappear without a trace in a matter of seconds.

Henry took a chance. He legged it up to the next corner and just spotted Downie bearing left into Back Shannon Street. Henry ran.

With his back to a wall, he peered around the corner and saw Downie was now stopped outside a terraced house, inserting a key in the door and with a quick check each way, stepping inside the property.

Henry had found his lair.

There were two uniformed constables hidden in the back alley behind the address. Henry had picked them purposely, two of the biggest, meanest-looking guys on duty that night. They had to be in case Downie managed to break out at the rear. He would be like an angry lion and they had to be ready to flatten him without compromise.

That left him and a female PC to do the front door.

Having said that, she was a pretty-sturdy-looking girl and she certainly knew how to swing the door opener, the two-handed tube of solid metal used by the police to smash down locked doors. She had given Henry a quick demo for his benefit and nearly caved his ribs in.

'You two guys in position?' Henry asked the two PCs at the back via the PR.

'Affirmative.'

'You ready?' he asked the female officer.

'And willing,' she said, brandishing the lump of metal with relish.

'Let's do it, then.' Henry patted himself down. This time he had made sure he had his handcuffs and extendable baton with him. And he wore a lightweight stab vest.

They walked side by side down Back Shannon Street and stopped at the front of the house. It was in darkness. Henry inspected the front door, a fairly flimsy piece of joinery needing replacement. It would not withstand the door opener and its operator for long.

But before resorting to that, he gave it a gentle push and tried the handle to confirm it was in fact locked. It was.

Henry touched his stab vest for reassurance,

82

then cleared his throat.

He gave the PC a nod and at the same time radioed the two at the back to tell them to get ready, the door was about to go in.

With a grunt like a tennis player, the PC drove the flat-end of the opener against the Yale lock.

The door didn't even try to resist. It flew open on first impact, clattering back. The PC stepped aside and Henry strode over the threshold shouting, 'Police officers.'

The hallway was in darkness. On the right was a closed door leading to the lounge and straight ahead was the kitchen door, the stairs being slightly offset to the left.

For a very brief flash, Henry relived a memory of not too long ago when he had entered a similar hall and had to fight for his life against a man armed with a knife before discovering two murdered cops in the front room.

He shook away the memory, shouted 'Police officers' once more, louder, flicked on the light and went to the living room door, which he flung open. He held back from entering as this room too was in total darkness. The light switch was next to the doorjamb. Henry reached in, flicked it on.

The room was empty – as was the kitchen.

Henry told the female PC to stay at the front door while he went to the back door, opened it and beckoned the two cops in from the alley. He gave them the once-over and chose the slightly smaller one to accompany him upstairs.

Leading from the front with his trusty Maglite torch on, Henry went up cautiously, the steps creaky. He stepped on to the landing and tried the lights. They did not work. Looking up, he saw the bulb was missing. There were three doors off the landing, all open, and no lights on in any of the rooms. A quick check of what were two bedrooms and a bathroom found them un-inhabited.

'He definitely came in here ... let's see if there's a loft and a cellar.'

The entrance to the loft was in the ceiling above the landing and it took only a glance to see that it hadn't been opened for a long time. The gaps between the frame and the flap had been thickly painted over, probably years before.

'Cellar?' Henry said and went back down to the hallway. The cellar door was in the kitchen. Henry opened it slowly and peered down the tight and steep concrete steps ending at another door on the left at their foot. It was closed and obviously led into the cellar under the house. Even from the top step, Henry could see chinks of light around the edge of this ill-fitting door.

He exchanged a glance with all three officers, then a nod. After a quick readjustment of his stab vest, and pinning his warrant card to his chest so it was clearly visible, he took out his baton and flicked it out with a crack like a whip.

'He's got to be down here,' he hissed.

He dipped his head, wondering just how big folk used to be when these houses were built. Must have been midgets, he guessed and began to sidle down the steps and on to the tiny landing at their foot. The cellar door was secured by a latch, which he unhooked, then pushed the door open on hinges that groaned.

'Police officers,' he said again loudly.

The cellar was low-ceilinged – probably for the midgets of yesteryear – dank and poorly lit, but he could see across to the wall opposite, where a naked man was manacled and chained. The smell that hit his nostrils was atrocious: a miasma of vomit, urine and shit – and the man across the cellar was covered in all these. He was on his knees, sideways on to Henry, with handcuffed wrists in front of him as though he was praying. A chain hooked through the cuffs was secured to the wall by a metal ring. He turned to Henry, eyes wide, pleading and terrified. A strip of parcel tape was wrapped around his face. Henry heard him try to shout something from behind the tape, a muffled scream, and the man's head started to bob furiously.

Downie's latest prisoner and no doubt his current, unwilling, paymaster.

Henry's first instinct was to go across to the man – but he checked himself and stayed put at the door, a hand holding back the three officers who were behind him, unable to see what he could, eager to move forwards.

Where was Downie?

'Anthony Downie? This is the police. I'm DCI Christie. Please show yourself now.'

Henry's voice echoed around the painted brick cellar walls, but he got no response.

The manacled man continued to nod his head frantically and gesture as best he could with his hands.

He was telling Henry where Downie was

hiding.

'Downie – I know you're in there. You are wanted for murder, so please show yourself.'

Henry's words were greeted by no response again.

He glanced at the constable on the step behind him. 'He's in here, I'm sure,' he whispered, 'and knowing him, the first cop through that door gets it.' He paused. 'That'll be me, I guess. If I go down – don't hesitate with him, do what you have to.' Henry turned his attention back to the dingy cellar. 'Downie, I'll count to three and if you haven't given yourself up by then, we'll be coming in mob-handed to get you. One ... two...' He paused again, just to build up the tension because he wanted Downie to believe he'd be charging through that door on three, when in fact he wouldn't. He was hoping the cheap con would flush him out. 'Three,' Henry bawled – but didn't move.

And it did draw Downie out from the shadows like a huge vampire emerging from hell – but armed with a machete raised menacingly.

'Hell's teeth,' Henry uttered.

The problem for Downie, as it was for Henry, was space, or the lack of it. He was an extra-tall man and the ceiling was low and he could not stand upright, nor slash the machete down the perpendicular from ninety degrees. He had to swing it almost horizontal to the floor and so instead of being able to chop Henry in half from the head down, he had to slice him sideways.

Henry was trapped on the bottom step, unable

to move either way, literally one of the tightest situations he'd ever been in.

Downie's speed increased as he rushed towards Henry, screaming, the machete raised at forty-five degrees in his right hand. If he got it right, timed it right, aimed it right, he would slash the blade across Henry's chest from his shoulder to his hip. He might well have been wearing a stab vest for protection, but at that moment he felt very vulnerable.

In response, Henry had to time his reaction perfectly, whatever the reaction might be. No decision was made in his head. For a millisecond he was transfixed like an idiot, watching a man he didn't know, hadn't even had any sort of interaction with, intending to slice him up like a tuna.

Henry saw his opportunity as Downie whisked back the weapon. He launched himself low and hard, his right shoulder connecting with a crunch into Downie's lower intestine and driving him back across the cellar.

Henry was not as fit as he could have been, but the technique of a rugby tackle had not completely deserted him even though it was fifteen years since he'd pulled on a jersey in anger. He bowled Downie over on to the concrete floor as his three uniformed colleagues careered in behind him, no hesitations, as instructed. Within a few flurried moments he was pinned to the ground, then disarmed, flipped over on to his front and his wrists cuffed behind him. Henry kneeled triumphantly on his back, the policewoman lay across his legs and the two PCs held his arms down.

Henry breathed heavily and nodded his appreciation at the three officers. 'Thanks guys – and gal.'

He settled his breathing and thought, One down, two to go.

SIX

Four days later Henry was still feeling as smug as a cat that had got the cream – and two pigeons for dessert.

'I'm a great sheller of peas,' he said with a self-satisfied smirk and continued to mix metaphors, similes and idioms whilst less than modestly boasting about the arrest and subsequent processing of Anthony Downie. 'And it was just like shelling peas. Give a dog a bone, you know how it is. I'm like a bloody terrier,' he went on, and on. He licked the tip of his index finger and made an imaginary tick in the air. 'When you've got it, flaunt it. I am the man.'

It was true that capturing Downie had given him a real buzz. He'd received a few pats on the back from various people – not including FB or Dave Anger – but he knew that no one was allowed to live on their laurels in Lancashire Constabulary and he would soon have to come up trumps again – because that was how the cookie crumbled.

Just to confirm how short the victorious shelf-life was, Kate propped herself up on one elbow, gave him the look he imagined she reserved for nincompoops and said, 'You're actually beginning to bore me now, Henry. Anybody'd think you were the world's greatest detective ... all you did was find a wanted man. It wasn't hard. It wasn't like cracking a major case, was it?'

'Jesus, since you got that gold band on your finger you've changed into a real harridan. Now you think you can say anything to me, and diss me, and I'll let it ride. Well, let me tell you something' – he flipped round and in a flash had pinned her to the bed and clambered on top of her – 'I won't bloody well stand for it, wench.'

The expression in her eyes morphed from disdain to lust. Her head bobbed up and she clamped her teeth around Henry's bottom lip, making him squeal like a baby, before thrusting her tongue into his mouth and letting him position himself between her legs.

Since the remarriage, their sex life had taken off stratospherically and early-morning intercourse had found its way back on to the curriculum. Which is why at 7.30 that morning he and Kate were wrapped around each other going at it as though the four-minute nuclear warning had sounded.

As Kate heaved him off and climbed nimbly on top of him, pounding down remorselessly whilst he amused himself trying to prevent her breasts from wobbling, the phone went.

'Bugger it,' he said, meaning don't answer it.

'No probs.' Kate gasped as she upped the rate and Henry responded accordingly.

It continued to ring.

'They'll call back if it's important.'

'You betcha,' she bounced, more breathless with each thrust.

The phone stopped. The couple made further adjustments to their position as Kate twisted to her knees and Henry assumed the position from behind, both of them groaning out loud as he thrust away. Kate threw back her head. Henry grabbed her buttocks and emitted a lion-like growl.

The phone started again.

'We have an ansaphone,' Henry said.

'You betcha,' Kate said, chewing on her bottom lip.

'Let 'em use it,' he grunted. The phone stopped again.

In stereo each of them uttered moans of ecstasy.

And then there was a sharp knock on the bedroom door, freezing both of them mid-thrust. Kate craned her neck around and they looked at each other, horrified.

'Look,' came the irritated voice from the other side of the door, 'I know what you're doing and I find even the thought of it abhorrent.' It was Leanne, Kate and Henry's younger daughter. 'And there's someone on the phone for you, Dad.'

Wide-eyed, Kate hissed, 'I didn't know she was home.'

'I never heard her come in,' Henry gasped, withdrawing. He and Kate had hit the sack about 11.30 and had crashed out instantly, sleeping like drugged logs after a triple nightcap. Leanne must have crept in in the early hours, silently and unexpectedly. Her parents thought she was staying at a friend's house for the night.

91

'Damn.' Kate crabbed sideways and Henry scrambled off the bed, muttering something very parental about kids using the house as a bloody hotel. He took two strides across to the door, stood behind it to hide his nakedness and opened it a crack.

A foot-tapping Leanne stood there, one of the cordless phone extensions dangling loosely in her hand. She was in her Goth nightie, with ruffled hair and sleepy eyes, looking achingly beautiful to Henry, although the nose stud always jarred him a little.

She thrust the phone at him. 'For you,' she said crossly. Her face scrunched into an expression of disgust. 'You two!' she almost spat. 'Anybody would think you never had it off before. You gross me out.'

Henry's hand snaked out and took the phone. 'I'm surprised we even get the chance with you and your sister in and out all the time, using the place...'

'Like a hotel? I know – unh,' Leanne finished for him, spun away and stalked back to her room.

Henry closed the door and put the phone to his ear. 'Henry Christie,' he said, glancing over at Kate, who was smirking at him.

'Henry, I've obviously interrupted something,' came a knowing voice.

'No you haven't, go on.' He walked back to the bed and placed his naked rear on the edge of it, reaching out to squeeze Kate's arm.

'Jerry Tope here, by the way.'

'Mornin', Jerry, what can I do for you?'

92

'Just got some information for you, hot off the press. Paulo Scartarelli? One of the remaining two on your wanted list?'

'Yep?'

'Interpol have been liaising between us and the cops in Cyprus – remember I said he was supposed to be holed up there? Well, they've contacted us to say the police there have located Scartarelli, and what do we want to do about it?'

'Arrest him?' Henry said hopefully.

'They went on to say that if that *is* the chosen option, they need all the original paperwork and want someone from here to go across with it, assist in the arrest and processing, and if that's done they assure us that the bureaucracy and delay will be minimal.'

'How minimal is minimal?'

'Two days, maybe three.'

Henry pondered this, scratching his groin thoughtfully. 'You at your desk, Jerry?' Tope said he was. 'Just check how much is left in the Operation Wanted budget, will you?'

'I'm not really supposed to access that account,' Tope said doubtfully. 'If I get caught...'

'You've got my permission.'

'OK, then.' Tope got to work and Henry slumped languidly back on the bed. Kate's hand rubbed his chest hairs gently, making him feel like purring. 'Fourteen thousand, nine hundred and eighty pounds.'

'That's ten grand less than it was. I've only put in a claim for twenty quid out-of-pocket. Strange,' Henry said, then pulled a face of indifference. Probably wasn't anything to do with

93

him. The chief, according to the accounts department, had given him four grand and that was it. 'Right ... when do they need a response?'

'By end of play today, bearing in mind they're two hours ahead of us.'

'I'll be in at nine, local time.'

'Cyprus is really nice at this time of year,' Tope said. 'It'll be a two-man job, won't it?'

'Nice try, Jerry,' Henry laughed as he ended the call and hauled Kate back across the bed to complete some unfinished business. But with silent efficiency this time.

In his teens Henry had avidly read all the James Bond novels and been captivated by the fictional jet-set life of the iconic secret agent. One of the books he'd been particularly fond of had started with Bond sitting in comfort on board a plane about to land in New York, contemplating the luxurious life he led. From that moment on, Henry decided that he too wanted to be a spy, living on caviar and fast women. It wasn't to be; at the age of eighteen he had actually been for a job interview with the Diplomatic Corps and been laughed out of the office.

As he sat cramped up in the seriously confined space of an easyJet aeroplane seat, he reflected what might have been if he'd pursued a degree in modern languages and international politics (not that he could speak any of the former and knew nothing about the latter), and become one of Bond's colleagues.

As it was he was crushed between an overweight woman at the window and the sturdy form of Bill Robbins in the aisle seat. In front of him was a selfish bastard who had insisted on having his seat reclined for the whole four-and-a-half-hour flight from Manchester to Pafos. He was seriously wondering if he'd get DVT from being unable to move his legs for the journey. If only he'd gone to university instead of joining the cops at nineteen with two crappy A-levels. I'd've been travelling first class, he whined inwardly as the plane started its descent into Cyprus.

There had been an ungodly scramble for seats because none were actually allocated at check-in and Henry, accustomed to knowing exactly where he'd be sitting when he flew, had found himself in panic mode when the flight was called at the departure gate.

He and Bill managed to fight their way to a pair of seats and as Henry wedged himself into the available space he knew then there was no comparison between being a cop on a budget and a secret-service agent on an expense account.

Following the telephone conversation with Jerry Tope, after which Henry had completed his mission with Kate, he made his way to police headquarters and gone to find Tope who was chatting to DC John Rooney, husband of the flirtatious Madeline in accounts, the one with whom Henry'd had a one-nighter in the dim, distant past. When Tope spotted Henry entering the Intelligence Unit office, he brought the conversation with the DC to an end. Rooney shouldered his way out past Henry, giving him a curt nod and tight smile. They knew each other, but not well.

Tope was all smiles, his face expectant like a pet dog which knew it was in for a treat.

'Two-man job?' he asked hopefully, raising his eyebrows.

'Only if you roll over and play dead,' Henry countered.

'Eh?'

'Nothing. But you're probably right, Jerry. But, no disrespect, from what little I know of Scartarelli, it's likely I'll need someone with me who's got a little more in the brawn department. Which is a backhanded compliment, actually.'

Tope's face went south. 'I never get out of the bloody office.'

'Sorry, mate, next time maybe.' Henry gave his shoulder a manly tap.

'Ho-hum, no probs,' Tope said accepting his lot. 'Here's the file and contacts.' He gave Henry a thick folder. 'And you're right, he's a dangerous git. He'll need watching.'

Henry nodded. 'Thanks for that. I'll pop up to accounts and clear the money ... going to need plane tickets and lots of euros.'

Tope scowled.

Madeline was busy talking to her husband, who'd made his way up to see her after talking to Jerry Tope. They gave Henry a suspicious look at first, then Madeline waved at him and smiled, but made no move to speak to him. Henry had to speak to another lady in accounts instead and arranged to buy seven hundred euros, withdraw two hundred sterling and get an order number for a flight out to Cyprus. He was also given use of a constabulary credit card, just in case of emergencies.

He then found an empty meeting room on the ground floor where he sat and read Scartarelli's file and began making phone calls and sending emails.

It was on the following day he knew for sure he would be going and the day after that before he and Bill Robbins actually fought their way for a seat on the easyJet flight to Pafos.

The plane banked sharply, cutting across the magnificent Troodos Mountains then heading towards the south-west coast on its descent. Henry blew out his cheeks appreciatively as, banking again, he glimpsed the crystal-clear waters of the Mediterranean dotted with tiny whitecaps and boats across the bulk of the sleeping fat woman beside him.

He adjusted his seat belt, stored his food tray as per instructions, and held his nose between finger and thumb, blowing hard to level out the pressure between his ears.

'You OK, boss?' Bill Robbins had noticed Henry's discomfort.

'Yeah – always gets me on the way down. Very painful.' He blew again and his ears popped, suddenly making his hearing keener than Superman's. 'That's better.'

Henry had chosen Bill Robbins, the PC who was the disgruntled firearms officer, to come along for the ride. This was not because they were old mates, which they were, or because they'd worked together years back, which they had. It was because that by accident Henry had found himself working with Bill when he'd stumbled across the plot to assassinate the American State Secretary on her visit to Blackburn. Bill's laconic cynicism and his calmness under the most extreme duress had impressed Henry. Bill was the sort of guy you pushed in front of you in a crisis. He had an old, level head on his shoulders and because he'd been steeped in firearms lore for the past fifteen years, he could handle himself physically and mentally.

As the plane made its final trim adjustments prior to landing, Henry allowed his mind to do a quick skim through his knowledge of Paulo Scartarelli, the second person on his wanted list.

Henry found it amazing that he was no longer surprised to be arresting a foreign criminal who had been operating on British soil – Lancashire soil at that. Although he knew it wasn't a new phenomenon, it was far more common than it had ever been because of the immigration mess the country was in.

Not much was known about Scartarelli. He'd been operating on the periphery of some brothels that had been set up in the north of England and had been circulated as wanted for the savage attack on an Albanian prostitute who had subsequently died. But not before she named Scartarelli as her killer. By the time she'd blabbed his name – when she realized she would die – he was long gone and though the initial murder enquiry generated many leads, it wound up after nine months when Scartarelli failed to raise his head above the parapet. Many rumours as to his whereabouts abounded. All related to connections with people-trafficking and various European gangs, but nothing concrete came to light – until Cyprus.

Henry was eager to hear the full story as to how he'd been found.

He braced himself as the plane touched down on the short runway and the brakes and reverse thrust were applied and finally his ears came back to normal. A short while later the plane taxied up to the terminal building and everybody de-planed, was transferred across the tarmac by bendy bus to customs and baggage reclaim.

Henry Christie and Bill Robbins had set foot in Cyprus. British cops abroad.

SEVEN

Agonizingly, Henry's bag came last down the conveyor belt, whilst Bill's was one of the first to appear through the rubber flaps. The firearms officer waited patiently for Henry whilst the DCI became increasingly annoyed, suspecting that it might not even have made the flight.

'How can this be?' Henry moaned. 'Our bags went in together.'

'It'll come,' Bill assured him.

And it did, eventually, all by itself.

Henry tore it off the belt and angrily set off towards the doors which opened out into the comparatively tiny arrivals hall, Bill in tow.

By the time they appeared, all the other passengers from the flight had gone and the hall was quiet.

Henry stood and looked around. Bill tapped him on the shoulder and pointed to a person holding up an A4-sized piece of white card on which had been scribbled 'CHRISTIE & ROBBINS'. Bill set off, Henry a beat behind him.

Bill stretched out a hand in greeting and the woman holding the sign broke into a wide, welcoming smile as she shook Bill's hand.

'You must be Detective Christie,' she said to Bill, whose bottom lip dropped stupidly open as he took in the sight of the woman sent to meet and greet them. 'You're just as I imagined.'

'I'm ... er,' he blubbered.

'It's so lovely to meet you,' she said and looked at Henry as she prised her hand from Bill's grasp and proffered it to Henry. 'You must be Constable Robbins,' she said, shaking his hand firmly. 'I'm Detective Sergeant Papakostas ... Georgia Papakostas.'

Henry's mouth also drooped, almost flopping on to the tiled floor, his anger over his late luggage immediately evaporating, to be replaced by a sort of awe at the sight of one of the most stunning women he'd ever met. Her jet-black hair was pulled back tightly from her face and tied in a neat ponytail. She had honey-coloured skin, deep-brown eyes, an imperfect complexion with two tiny pockmarks on her left cheek that only added to the overall effect of a true Mediterranean beauty. There was no make up other than a touch of lip gloss which simply served to accentuate the full mouth and pure white teeth of her hot, real smile.

For a few moments Henry could not form any words. He and Bill just simply stood before this woman drooling like imbeciles from a Tom and Jerry cartoon.

'Pleased to meet you, Sergeant,' he managed to say.

Her thick black, but perfectly trimmed eyebrows knitted together in puzzlement. 'I have got it the right way round, haven't I?' she said in a lightly Greek-accented voice. 'You are Bill, yes?' she said to Henry.

'Oh no, I'm DCI Christie ... this is PC Robbins.' Henry moved forward a couple of steps, positioning himself slightly ahead of Bill because there were times when it was only right and proper for a DCI to lead from the front.

Georgia giggled. 'I've been looking at the names on the paperwork, imagining what you both would look like.' She gave an apologetic tilt of the head. 'Got it wrong.'

Henry caught the merest scent of light perfume from her, reminding him of strawberries.

'All you need to know is that I'm the brains and he' – he thumbed disrespectfully at Bill – 'is the muscle.' And immediately regretted what he'd said because he knew it made him look stupid.

'Thanks, boss,' Bill said under his breath.

To try and compensate, Henry gave Georgia his cute tilted-head half-smile he kept for use on such occasions, coupled with a few blinks of his eyes.

She smiled and emitted a pleasant chuckle. 'Anyway, I'm very pleased to meet you both. As you probably know I'm the officer in this case and may I formally welcome you to Cyprus, halfway to the Orient, as they say.' She bowed her head gracefully and gave a very minor curtsey.

She was wearing a black trouser suit with sensible black shoes, good practical clothing for a female detective. As she bowed, her unbuttoned jacket flapped open slightly, revealing her red blouse fastened just above her breasts. Obviously these caught Henry's eye, as they did

Bill's, but what really caught Henry's breath and what made him realize that this might not be just a jolly to a sunny holiday island was the sight of the pistol strapped to her right hip.

Stepping out of the terminal building, Henry was struck in the face by the incredible heat of the day and the myriad of intoxicating aromas associated with the island, particularly that of the sea, which was literally just across the road.

The two Lancashire officers followed DS Papakostas down the ramp, past a few lounging and moustachioed taxi drivers touting idly for work, all of who watched the female detective's progress with dirty eyes and thoughts. She led Henry and Bill across the car park to a Nissan Terrano, a big four-wheel drive beast, into the back of which they heaved their cases and then themselves.

'You can have use of this,' she explained, 'but I'll drop you off at your hotel first.'

'Sounds good,' said Henry, barging Bill out of the way to get into the front passenger seat alongside Georgia, who climbed in behind the wheel. The two men exchanged scowls, but Bill relented and got into the back seat with great reluctance. It was only as Henry settled himself in and pulled on his seat belt did he realize that the vehicle's steering wheel was on the right. He said, 'You drive on the left,' with surprise.

'Oh yes,' she said.

Bill tutted and Henry shot him a quick look which said, 'Watch it.'

'You haven't been to the island before?'

Henry shook his head. 'I have,' Bill piped up.

Georgia smiled. 'Lots of British influence here, still,' she explained, manoeuvring the Terrano out of its parking space. 'We only recently changed to the euro,' she added.

'From what?'

'Pounds ... Cypriot pounds, that is.' She drove on to the road, the shimmering Med on their right, and gunned the big, but lazy, diesel engine which responded sluggishly. There then followed one of those slightly stifled introductory conversations covering such inanities as flight comfort, in-flight meals and other bits of trivia to break the ice. This included the fact that her father was Cypriot and her mother English, hence her almost excellent use of the language.

That done, Henry asked about the plan for the remainder of the day ahead.

Georgia checked her wristwatch. 'If it's OK with you guys, I'll take you to your hotel and get you settled in. Then, maybe, we meet up and plan for tomorrow, which is when we'll move for Scartarelli. It will have been a long day for you today, so you just need to chill for the remainder of the day and maybe we get a meal later?'

'Sounds OK to me,' Henry said.

'And me,' Bill seconded from the rear. 'I'm dying for a large Keo.'

Henry turned and grimaced at him.

'The local brew – very nice.' Bill smiled and licked his lips.

'I'll go with that, Henry agreed, turning forwards huffily, then looking sideways at DS

104

Papakostas's profile. 'How far to the hotel?'

'Maybe half-hour. It's in a place called Coral Bay.'

'In that case could you give me a bit of background as to how Scartarelli came into your sights?'

She gave a short laugh. 'Good phrase, because that's what he did – come into my sights.' She patted the gun nestling against her right hip.

She had a good informant, one she had been keeping to herself, something Henry could relate to. He had been a smuggler for many years and was in his early sixties, though he looked fifteen years younger despite his weather-beaten face and grey moustache. Georgia had encountered the man known as Haram when she had been a keen rookie cop patrolling the streets of Nicosia, the island's capital, in the early days of her service. She had, in fact, worked her way up to Haram. He had been the one every cop in the southern half of Cyprus had wanted to catch red-handed. Her trail had begun with the spot-check and subsequent arrest of a minor drug-dealer under the battered ruin of Pafos Gate. A deal had been struck leading her to the next dealer up the chain and so on, until she reached the final link: Haram. He was known to smuggle Turkish heroin down through the north and then cheap cigarettes and booze in the opposite direction. Although he had been arrested on a multitude of occasions, no prosecutions ever ensued.

But Georgia – ambitious to be a detective – bided her time. Constantly digging and building a jigsaw of Haram until she had four informants, all with jail penalties hanging over them, passing on information to save their own arses.

All the patience came to fruition almost a year after the encounter with the first dealer under the gate in Nicosia. Haram was bringing a carload of drugs across the border from the Turkish north of the island by a circuitous route around the western tip from where he would be supplying the tourists and the British forces bases in the south.

If her intelligence was correct – and jail sentences would happen if it weren't – Haram would eventually be travelling south down the coastal E704 towards Polis, a town popular with backpackers. Once on that road, there would be no escape for him.

That had been ten years ago and Haram, terrified by the thought of losing his liberty, had reached an 'understanding' with Georgia who, after successfully transferring to CID, used his intimate knowledge of the Cypriot underworld to further her career.

She had met Haram most recently and clandestinely on the waterfront at Kato Pafos, where they sat at a quayside restaurant called the Pelican, sipping mineral water. It was called the Pelican because a real live one wandered around the tables, seeking scraps from the diners.

'I want to give you something,' he said in his quiet, gravelly voice.

'That's always good to hear.' She was always cool with him, always in control, never wanting to give him the impression he was anything more than a piece of useful shit.

He held up his hands. 'You want it, or not?'

'Haram,' she began patiently, her brown eyes taking on a glint of steel. 'Give.'

She knew that he still operated very much in the centre of the Cypriot underworld, often protected from the law by her, and that he had grown wealthy on the proceeds of crime because she had allowed him to do so. He could now so easily just be stepping out of a prison cell if the two of them hadn't reached that understanding – something none of her bosses knew about, incidentally.

'A man has appeared on the scene,' he said gruffly. 'An interloper.'

Georgia gave him a crooked smile. 'And he's treading on your toes?' she ventured.

Haram looked quickly away. Georgia knew she had struck a nerve, read his mind. 'Go on,' she urged.

'He's Italian, mixing with the Maltese guys in Nicosia. Low profile, but starting to throw his weight around with us. He has good connections...'

'And he's treading on your toes?' Georgia said again, knowing that many of Haram's snippets of information were given simply just to get the competition off his back. Such was the nature of informants. They were always in it for a reason, and Haram's was to keep operating unmolested – and not to go to prison.

Haram nodded. The pelican approached their table, its big beak clattering hungrily.

'What's he doing?'

'People, drugs, prostitutes ... trying to set up a new line. Hookers, mainly, but also a lot of drugs ... using Albanian girls.'

Try as she might, Georgia could not keep a sliver of interest out of her eyes.

'I want him caught, neutralized,' Haram stated.

'So you can continue to do the same?' she said cynically.

He raised his eyebrows. They were grey and overgrown. 'And there's something else – a bit of glory for not much work on your part,' he teased. 'I have checked out this man carefully. Here, on the island, he goes by the name of Corelli, but I have discovered he is really called Scartarelli.' Haram passed the detective a scrunched-up piece of paper. 'His details. Check him out on your computers. You will find something interesting that will get him out of both our hairs.'

Her hand covered the paper. She looked sideways at the expectant pelican. 'And how will that happen?'

'I will give him to you on a plate.'

It was just the sort of job a detective likes occasionally. A decent arrest, not much paperwork and some kudos to boot.

When Georgia checked out the name, the computer she was using became all bells and whistles. Corelli, also known more correctly as Paulo Scartarelli, was wanted by the English cops for murder. What better fun could there be? To execute a simple arrest and get a big-time player off her patch with hardly any paperwork.

108

There was a tense few days waiting for Haram to come through, but he did via a call to Georgia's mobile phone.

'Tonight ... he will be driving three Albanian prostitutes, illegals, from Pafos to Limassol using the B6 ... Audi A4.' He recited the registered number. 'Leaving Pafos seven-thirty.'

'How good is this, Haram?'

'The best. Take him, get rid of him, flush him down the shitter.'

She thumbed the end-call button and felt a pleasant tremor of anticipation shimmer through her.

Henry listened as the story unfolded, but something about the situation did not quite add up. 'I take it it didn't go to plan?'

She looked squarely at him for a moment. 'You could say that.' Her voice sounded bitter, upset. Her attention returned to driving as she negotiated her way through Pafos, a dusty town that struck Henry as sun-baked and not very picturesque.

Despite her fine arrest record, which outshone most other detectives on the island, she could only muster the use of one double-crewed car – and herself – to pull the vehicle a murderer might be in. She argued that two would be better, but the police in Cyprus had the same resource issues as every other police force the world over – i.e. never enough. One would have to do.

At seven on the evening on which Georgia had got her information she sat in the rear of a

109

liveried Fiat Bravo on the B6, facing the direction of Limassol, waiting for an Audi A4 to pass them, a male and female cop in the front seats.

Which it did one hour later, four people on board.

The Bravo slotted in behind and followed for a couple of miles, passing Secret Valley and reaching Aphrodite's birthplace, where they decided to tug the Audi. Using blue lights, a tweak of the siren and flashing headlights, they indicated for it to pull off on to a scrubby parking area overlooking the two spectacular rocks in the sea below them, set against white cliffs. It was from out of the foaming water here that Aphrodite herself was alleged to have emerged from the ocean. The Audi pulled in as instructed and the three cops were quickly out of the Bravo, covering both sides of the Audi. It was all going very smoothly.

Georgia tapped the driver's window. The man behind the wheel looked up through hooded, dangerous eyes and just so he made no mistake about who was who, she flashed her badge at him and indicated that he get out of the car – now! He climbed out slowly, like a cat, doing as instructed, placing his hands on the roof and spreading his feet. The two other cops were doing the same with the female passengers. They were young, pasty-faced girls, immediately reminding Georgia of pimp-fodder.

She searched the man, asking him questions, then expertly cuffed him. He made only guttural, non-committal responses.

Georgia looked up as the woman cop searched

110

the last of the females. She saw what happened next in slow motion, knowing she would be able to replay the scenario in her mind forever.

The female suspect acquiesced to the search, but as the officer spun her round to slap on the cuffs instead of doing it from behind, a knife appeared in the girl's right hand from somewhere, probably having been secreted up her sleeve. It had a short blade, no more than three inches, with one serrated edge. Georgia screamed a warning, started to hurl herself across the gap as the prisoner jerked up her hand and thrust the blade up to the hilt below the officer's ribcage.

'There was no need for it,' Georgia said sadly to Henry. She reduced the acceleration of the Terrano as the road inclined up to the Coral Bay junction. 'She was just a silly, frightened kid from Albania, she panicked and a cop got seriously injured.'

'She didn't die, then?' Henry asked.

'No, but she's still poorly and could die.'

'I'm slightly confused though. How come we're moving on Scartarelli if he's already in custody?' But he knew he had answered his own question then. 'The guy wasn't Scartarelli, was he?'

'Just some pathetic low-life enforcer and gofer. He wasn't anyone, really, just a driver.'

'What did your informant have to say about that?'

'It was two days before I managed to speak to him again.'

From the back of the Terrano, Bill interjected, 'Was it a set-up, then?'

They met back at the Pelican in Pafos, Papakostas and Haram, a desperate tense encounter. Haram had lost much of his laid-back cool, his eyes darting all around, and they were sitting inside the restaurant so he could have his back to the wall and watch both entry and exit. His hand shook as he raised his strong coffee to his mouth and he kicked out petulantly as the tame pelican waddled by.

'He knows ... he knows it was me,' he said jerkily.

'How?'

'I'm the only one who could have told you. He played me and I fell for it. No fool like an old one,' he said caustically.

'No argument with that, Haram,' Georgia said. 'Add to that one of my officers is fighting for her life. Unnecessary. For what?' she spat. 'Three whores from a lawless country? Someone treading on your toes? And your useless information. Have you any idea how much I am suffering personally and professionally from this, this, cock-up?'

'I think my life may be in danger,' Haram said bluntly as though he hadn't heard a word said.

She stared angrily at him, unable to speak, but then she said, 'All you wanted me to do was take him off the streets for you, isn't it? Just to suit you, nothing else.'

He looked away, sucked on the last of his cigarette and stubbed it out. He fumbled in his trouser pocket and extracted a crumpled piece of paper, the second one he'd passed her in days. 'It's up to you,' he said. 'He stays there from time to time. That's all I can do.'

He stood up wearily, his joints showing his age. He gave a curt nod and left the restaurant.

Georgia's fingers took the paper, then she finished her bitter espresso in one swallow and went to the toilet at the back of the restaurant.

As she washed her hands after peeing, she clearly heard four cracks in quick succession and knew it was not a car backfiring.

Haram had twisted out of the Pelican and walked along the quayside towards the car parks and shops of Kato Pafos. It was early season and there were not many tourists yet, so the front was rather quiet. He reached the wide-open promenade area and stopped by the low sea wall, looking into the clear water where he could see big fish swimming lazily. He flicked a cigarette out of the crumpled packet and drew it out between his lips, clicked the disposable lighter and dipped his head between his cupped hands to light up.

He never saw who killed him. Whoever it was walked quickly up behind him, placed the 9mm pistol against the base of his skull and pulled the trigger four times. The force of the impact rocketed Haram over the wall and into the water.

Weapon drawn, Georgia raced out of the restaurant and ran towards the small knot of shocked onlookers gaping over the sea wall. And she knew Haram was dead even before she slowed down. He had foretold his own demise only moments earlier and now he was in the water, face down, floating, his head blown apart and the fish, over their initial panic when he hit the water, now in a bubbling frenzy of feeding on the blood and brain.

She went silent as she reached this part of the story, then pulled the Terrano into a space by the roadside.

'Here we are,' she announced. 'It's a hotel, but split into apartments. Hope that's OK.'

'I'm sure it will be fine,' Henry said.

'Cosy,' Bill said casting his eye over the apartment. 'Which side are you sleeping on?'

It was a one-bedroom apartment, meaning a kitchen area, bathroom, lounge and one separate bedroom, a very common type of holiday accommodation for the unwashed masses.

Henry grimaced. The sofa obviously converted into a bed, but he wasn't sure if this was appropriate lodgings for two grown cops on an official job. The two would never have shared a normal hotel bedroom together and there was enough money in the kitty to have separate rooms, or at least a two-bedroom apartment, either of which would give a greater degree of privacy required by two men well into their middle age. It wasn't as though they were twenty-somethings on a piss-up holiday. They were blokes who had their own ways and foibles and needed somewhere private in which to do them.

Henry wished he had personally sorted out the hotel instead of leaving it to the judgement of the locals.

'I'll go down to reception,' Henry said, 'see if I can sort something out.'

'I'm not after bumming you, y'know,' Bill reassured him. 'But then again, after a few Keos I'm anybody's.' He blew Henry a kiss.

Appalled by the thought and related image, the recently married Henry hurried down to see if anything could be done.

The accommodation issue was easily sorted. They were transferred into a two-bedroom apartment overlooking the pool (even though the bathroom was still shared), which was a much better arrangement. They had quickly changed out of their travelling gear, showered (separately) and re-dressed in clothing more appropriate to a warmer climate. Henry was in a baggy T-shirt and three-quarter-length trousers and trainers; Bill was in a vividly coloured short-sleeved shirt with lots of names of cocktails splattered all over it, three-quarter pants and open-toed sandals.

'Hey – we might only have one night of debauchery,' he defended himself against Henry's chides. 'I'm into the holiday groove.'

'We won't have *any* nights of debauchery,' Henry said sternly like some kind of police supervisor. 'We're here on a job, OK?'

'You won't be saying that after a pint of Keo.'

The duo strolled down the main street in Coral Bay, past restaurants, mini-supermarkets and tat shops. The place was reasonably busy and had a nice, easy feel to it. The evening was warm, a bit clammy, and Henry was already dripping.

'She said meet here, didn't she?' Bill pointed to an open-air restaurant across the street to which they duly made their way. Bill treated Henry to a Keo, which came in an iced pint glass. It tasted better than any beer he had ever had before, immediately dissipating the dryness of the journey which, when everything was taken into consideration, had taken a full half-day. He could feel the beer spreading its icy tentacles out across his chest. 'Good, eh?' Bill said. His own pint was already gone.

'Bliss,' Henry gasped, his eyes half-lidded in ecstasy.

DS Papakostas walked into the bar accompanied by a surly man with a thick black moustache who looked like a stereotypical Greek straight from *Shirley Valentine*. However, Henry did not pay him much heed. His eyes were firmly fixed on Georgia, who, though dressed casually for the evening, looked more stunning than ever. Her hair was pinned up in a much more feminine way than earlier and now, with make-up expertly applied, she was the Greek beauty to the Greek beast that walked beside her, scraping his knuckles on the ground.

Henry stood up and shook hands with her.

'Hello, Henry ... Bill.' She nodded and smiled at the PC, who had a glazed expression on his face. 'May I introduce my inspector?' She stood aside and indicated the man with a gesture. 'Inspector Tekke.' He proffered his hand and

Georgia continued, 'This is Henry and this is Bill.'

Tekke regarded the British officers through dark, ringed eyes. He reminded Henry of a lemur with a 'tache, but even so, everything about him screamed, 'Cop!' Henry felt immediately at ease in his presence.

'Welcome to Cyprus,' Tekke said, flashing a set of unnaturally white teeth.

'Thank you.'

'I hope your visit here will be worthwhile.'

'I'm sure it will ... please, sit. Can I get you a drink?'

'Just a water for me,' Georgia said.

'And for you?'

'Call me Andrei, or Andrew if you like,' Tekke said easily. 'And water will be fine for me, also.'

Henry turned to Bill and raised his eyebrows.

'Er, I'll have another Keo, if that's OK?' Bill said, misunderstanding Henry's non-verbal signal that meant, 'You get 'em.' Henry looked at him as if he was stupid. 'Oh, you want me to get them?' he said.

'That's the general idea,' Henry said.

'Mm, OK. Another beer for you?'

Henry nodded. 'Cheers, Bill.' He indicated for the two Cypriot detectives to seat themselves at the table.

'Have you settled in?' Georgia asked.

'Yeah. Slight hitch with the room size, but that's sorted now.'

'Oh, I'm sorry.'

'Not a problem,' Henry beamed.

DI Tekke leaned forward. 'Can I say I'm

117

pleased to meet you, Mr Christie?'

'I'm pleased to meet you, too.'

'I've done some research on you.'

'Oh,' Henry said, withdrawing slightly.

'You've had an interesting and varied career.'

'You could say that.'

'So how come you're acting like a bounty-hunter now?' The question stung Henry, for it was one he had asked himself. He was sure that Tekke did not mean to offend, so he took it on the chin and in the spirit in which it was intended.

'There's a few wanted people who needed catching,' he said simply.

'And you were chosen for the job?'

'Yep.'

Bill returned with the drinks from the bar and distributed them, then slumped down and instantly sank half of his new Keo.

'What about you, Andrew?' Henry took the opportunity to deflect the question.

He shrugged modestly. 'Work hard, follow procedure, stick to the letter of the law, get results, that's me.'

It was at that point that Georgia laid a hand on Tekke's arm and Henry caught a quick glance between the two that gave him a very incisive insight into their relationship. 'He's being modest,' Georgia said. 'He has one of the best clear-up rates of any detective in the force.'

'Not, you understand, that we have much crime. Not like Britain. Ours is a very low-key-crime country. Nicosia has its share of organized crime and the bigger resorts do have a drug and

118

prostitution problem, but our main crimes are usually Brits killing Brits. Usually easy to solve.'

'And every so often we get someone like Scartarelli in the mix,' Georgia added. 'Which is why we'd like to get him, catch him for you and deport him, never to come back.'

'It'll be a pleasure to take him off your hands,' Henry said. 'But I'm presuming you'll want to have a long talk with him first? He may be implicated in a murder and the serious assault of a policewoman, I believe.'

'Yes, when we arrest him, we will interview him,' Tekke said. 'But the consensus is that we would rather have him off the island than on – and unless he immediately confesses his involvement in the matter you refer to, then let's get rid of him.'

'But first things first,' Henry said.

'Yes, we need to arrest him ... which is why I suggest we talk about how we hope to achieve that before too much alcohol is imbibed. And then, when we've done that, I am going to treat you to the best Greek mezze this side of Nicosia,' Tekke said. 'But business first – before you stay awake all night with a distended stomach.'

There was no particular theme to the mezze they consumed that evening. It was a heady combination of fish, meats and vegetables and Henry lost count of the number of dishes they ate after the eighth course. On reflection he estimated there could well have been fifteen dishes brought out to them, each one tasting wonderful. These,

119

combined with more beer and wine, had a very stretching effect on his stomach. Bill, on the other hand, did not seem too affected by the amount of food and drink. It just seemed to disappear into a hollow container.

The meal concluded at eleven, having taken about three hours.

Bill and Tekke had fallen into a long-winded conversation about guns, whilst Henry and Georgia made very small talk.

Their bill came with a complimentary brandy for each of them that tasted like rust.

Bill and Tekke were discussing the merits of the H&K machine-pistol. Two firearms buffs together.

Henry clinked glasses with Georgia. It was her first taste of alcohol that night.

'Can I just ask something?' he said hesitantly.

'Of course.'

'I got the impression that your informant was known only to yourself, from what you told me.'

'Only Andrei knows of him.'

'Ahh. I know what it's like to lose an informant, one who's been with you for a long time,' he said. 'I won't patronize you to say I know how you feel, but I've been there very recently and found it hard to deal with.' Henry explained his recent experience and she listened carefully. 'The difference is that I put my informant in a dangerous situation. You didn't.'

'They put themselves into dangerous situations. They're usually in dangerous situations to begin with,' Georgia said philosophically. 'Situations that can easily go wrong.'

120

Henry thought about it. 'Maybe.'

Tekke picked up the bill and slapped a wodge of euros on it and waved at a passing waiter. He had not been as alcohol-free as Georgia and was slightly drunk. Bill was suddenly very drunk. Henry was just about right, but bloated by the food.

They all stood up and left the restaurant, tumbling on to Coral Bay's main street.

'I parked outside your hotel,' Georgia said. She and Henry walked ahead.

Bill and Tekke were loudly discussing the merits of the Glock pistol. Apparently it was light, well constructed, reliable, had hardly any recoil and was therefore a good weapon for putting bullets into villains' chests.

'Great double-tap,' Bill slurred, eight pints of Keo swishing about inside him.

'One of the best,' Tekke concurred, two bottles of wine in him.

Henry and Georgia had put about twenty metres between them and the firearms argument. The street was fairly quiet now, many of the restaurants starting to close up for the night, all the shops having done so an hour and a half earlier. A few cars drove past.

'Live locally?'

'Pafos.'

'That's why you're sober – designated driver.'

Georgia nodded.

Henry yawned. 'Been a long day.'

'Could be a long day tomorrow. Will Bill be all right for an early start?'

Henry laughed. 'In the best traditions of the

Lancashire Constabulary, he'll be bright-eyed and bushy-tailed.'

They stopped at the kerb.

Forty metres away, Bill and Tekke were loudly disagreeing over the best sniper rifle available.

'What about your inspector?'

'I'll make sure he's up.' She glanced quickly at Henry, confirming his guess about them.

'Good.'

'That's my car.' She pointed diagonally across to another Terrano and took a step off the high kerb.

Henry heard the acceleration of a car, the deep growl of an engine, a crunch of gears. His head twisted quickly to the right. Headlights on main beam glared at him, four of them on a bull bar, and a huge four-wheel drive vehicle hurtled towards them. Georgia had left the kerb and was now a metre and a half into the road. She spun to face the noise, stunned momentarily in the beam. The vehicle was maybe twenty metres away to her right. Not far. Maybe two seconds away from ramming into her.

A roar emanated from Henry's throat.

He saw the vehicle, two figures in it, driver and passenger, the passenger leaning out of the window, in the hand the dark but unmistakable shape of a gun.

He saw Georgia in the road.

And he had four pints of beer slushing inside him and a huge mezze, neither, either separate or combined, designed to make him the most efficiently operating human being on the planet.

He reached out and grabbed Georgia's forearm

and violently dragged her back to the footpath, the force of his strength making her go like a rag doll. The vehicle swerved in towards them, front wheels mounting the pavement. Henry yanked her as if they were in some kind of brutal dance, still twisting her away. Both of them staggered until the back of Henry's knees hit a low wall surrounding a cafe terrace and they fell over it, falling through spiky bushes and smashing into tables and chairs, landing hard on the concrete-paved floor.

Henry looked up from their embrace.

The vehicle had stopped.

The passenger was leaning out. The weapon he held was aimed at them – and he fired.

Georgia screamed.

Henry, still holding her, gripped tight and rolled them over and over across the terrace, crashing into the furniture, hearing shots fired, bullets whizzing just over them, all the while expecting to be hit. Then the vehicle accelerated away, and there were three more shots and shouting.

He had rolled on top of Georgia.

She pushed him roughly off and clambered to her feet, drawing her own weapon, which Henry didn't even know she had in her possession to-night. She scrambled back over the wall and ran into the road.

Suddenly Bill Robbins was standing over Henry.

'You OK, boss?'

Henry picked himself up very gingerly. He'd clattered a few parts of his body – the backs of his legs, his elbows, his sore ribs and his head, but all in a minor way. Bill assisted him to his feet and they were joined by Georgia and Tekke, both now with weapons drawn.

'I got three shot shots off at them,' Tekke said, still dangerously waving his gun in the air.

'I thought you said you didn't have much crime on Cyprus,' Henry said accusingly.

EIGHT

The noises coming from the bathroom were awful to behold, almost inhuman, making Henry Christie feel queasy himself. He stood by the door, listening, his face a mask of horror. Then, with a guttural moan, the sounds stopped suddenly and there was a worrying silence. Henry put his ear to the door and tapped gently with his fingertips.

'Bill, are you OK?'

There was no response.

Then immediately the noises began again, moans, retching sounds, unbelievable farts and groans, then a 'Jesus Christ!' then the flush of the toilet, the third in about five minutes.

Henry knocked again, this time more urgently. 'Bill – you OK?' he asked and wondered whether his claim about being bright-eyed and bushy-tailed would come back to haunt him.

The lock slid slowly back. Bill opened the bathroom door and stood there, his head peering round, looking at Henry who had not seen a human being looking much worse this side of the grave.

'Hell fire,' said Henry, taken well aback.

'Something I ate,' Bill explained.

'You look bloody dreadful.'

125

'You want to feel what my guts feel like.'

'It couldn't be something to do with that local beer, could it?'

'Prob'ly a combination of things,' Bill said, evidently not wishing to put his state down just to the beer. 'The long flight, dehydration, that mezze, and maybe the beer ... and tiredness – they all go into the mix, y'know?'

'There was a lot of food, admittedly, but I'm not sure copious amounts of beer helped matters.'

'Nah, definitely not just the beer,' Bill insisted. 'Anyway, need to get dressed.' He pushed past Henry and padded towards his bedroom, Henry open-mouthed at the naked form of his new flatmate. 'By the way,' Bill said over his shoulder, 'it's not for the faint-hearted in there.'

A single manned patrol car had been parked up outside their hotel for the night, a paltry but well-received gesture designed to reassure Henry and Bill and dissuade anyone from trying anything further. Henry had actually argued it wasn't necessary to tie up a cop all night, but Georgia dismissed his protestations with a wave.

'It's the least we can do,' she insisted.

'Well, it's kind of you,' Henry relented.

The night had panned out without further incident and after the surge of police activity at the scene of the shooting, Henry had slept like a baby stuffed with Calpol. He could only guess from the loud snoring in the other room how well Bill had slept. The sleep of the drunk, the waking of the very poorly, as it happened.

126

The two men emerged from their ground-floor apartment into the bright sunlight of a Cypriot morning. Bill shielded his eyes and complained of a terrifying headache. Henry felt OK, glad he hadn't drunk too much and not only because of his lack of a hangover. If he had been drunk, and slower to react, he and Georgia could well have been dead.

They walked past the police car which had been on guard all night and gave the officer behind the wheel a wave of appreciation. He had been there since the shooting, hadn't been relieved even yet and looked only marginally better than Bill.

They had been told to make their way to a particular cafe on the main drag that offered a full English breakfast, starting at three euros. Georgia and Tekke would meet them there.

After finding the place, not far from the scene of last night's incident, Henry felt well enough to devour the 'Gut-buster' but Bill contented himself with a coffee and croissant, which he nibbled like a sparrow. He had become surly and uncommunicative, his mouth twisted as though there was a bad smell coming from somewhere. Henry didn't mind the silence because as he ate he ran through the shooting, and the implications behind it, with a clear mind.

His first instinct was that there had to be some connection with Scartarelli, otherwise it didn't make sense. He took his musings backwards a stage further. DS Papakostas had been given information by a trusted source about a new operator on the block, one Paulo Scartarelli, a guy who was evidently muscling in on the snout's territory. The snout, Haram, had gone whining to Georgia, his controller, and told her about Scartarelli, giving her details of when and where he could be located – i.e. moving prostitutes around who happened to be illegal immigrants. Then it looked as if Haram had been set up, fallen for the bait, then been eliminated for his trouble. He had been assassinated in broad daylight and Henry, despite liking Georgia, did tend to think she hadn't done everything she could to catch the offenders. In his experience, a daylight killing was usually quickly bottomed, but the police here didn't seem to have got their act together in terms of a full-blown professional investigation. But maybe that's the way it was over here and Henry tried not to judge by his own standards.

So, Haram was executed and then an attempt was made on Georgia's life.

Going for a cop was a very serious move indeed, not one that any criminal would take lightly, even one in Cyprus.

Henry couldn't even begin to guess why she had been targeted, yet he accepted he knew very little about anything that was going on here.

Haram's desire to let Georgia know how to catch Scartarelli smacked of a fallout between crims. Henry would have happily laid odds that he and Haram were into something together that had gone wrong, resulting in a fatal disagreement. And Georgia didn't know about it.

Still, he thought, not my business. My job is to lock up a fugitive and take him back to face justice.

His mind reverted to the shooting itself: Bill and Tekke in heated discussion about the merits of particular firearms, some forty metres behind him and Georgia. The bright lights of the car mounting the pavement, shots being fired, him and Georgia probably saved by toppling over a low wall.

The additional shots were Tekke's, apparently firing wildly at the fleeing vehicle and missing.

Henry gulped drily as he thought he could so easily have been a victim.

Yet ... they weren't particularly good shots...

'You not want that sausage?' Bill asked, coming to life.

Henry looked at his plate and realized he hadn't made any significant inroads into his Gut-buster breakfast. 'Yes I do, so fuck off. And anyway, do you actually remember anything about last night?'

'Which bit?'

Henry regarded him as though he couldn't believe his ears. 'The shooting?' His voice had a hopeful tinge to it. 'You know, me nearly being killed, having to go home in a body bag in the belly of an aeroplane?'

'Nah.' He rubbed his eyes.

'It's a bloody good job I like you, Bill.'

Robbins fluttered his eyelashes that were attached to eyelids sliding over bloodshot eyes. 'I like you too.'

Henry concentrated on his breakfast, which he was finishing with a large white coffee as Georgia and Tekke arrived in her Terrano. They sat at

129

the table, shaking hands. Both were dressed in jeans and windcheaters and neither looked the worse for wear, unlike their professional British counterparts.

'How are you feeling?' Georgia asked.

'I'm OK,' Henry said.

'Me too,' Bill said. Henry squinted quickly at him and saw that, all of a sudden, he did look quite well again, as though someone had just inserted new batteries. The appearance of a beautiful woman he wanted to impress probably had something to do with it, so instead of being totally catatonic, Bill was now semi-catatonic.

'How about you?' Henry asked.

'Shaken, but OK.'

Henry looked at Tekke, whose dark, sunken eyes were even more bloodshot than Bill's had been. On closer inspection, he looked like hell on legs. Tekke simply breathed out heavily and said nothing other than, 'I need an espresso.'

'Well, if you're having something, I feel like I could down a proper breakfast now,' Bill said. 'Not a Gut-buster, maybe, perhaps that Belly-buster.'

'I think I'll join you,' Tekke said. 'Greek yoghurt and toast is only so good.'

Whilst Bill and Tekke tucked into their breakfasts, Georgia and Henry seated themselves out of munching distance over coffee.

'Anything from the crime scene?' Henry asked.

Georgia shrugged. 'Our people are looking at it. Don't hold out too much hope, though.

130

They're good, but...' She shrugged again.

'OK,' said Henry briskly, 'to business, then. I was pretty much under the impression that you had Scartarelli's location and as soon as I arrived we'd bc able to make an arrest and get proceedings underway ... is that the case? Because if it isn't, Bill and I may have to return home empty-handed because as much as we'd like to make a holiday of this, I'm not sure my bosses would approve of us staying for a fortnight.'

As Henry spoke, Georgia was nodding seriously. 'I can see your point, but we do have Scartarelli's location, kind of.'

Henry's mouth skewed sardonically. 'Kind of?'

'As a result of that second piece of paper Haram gave me, we know that he returns frequently to a villa on the edge of the Akamas, not far away from here. We've been keeping a surveillance operation since...' Her voice broke slightly. 'Since Haram was killed ... but we don't have enough people to keep a tail on him.'

'The villa.' Henry tried to get it right in his head. 'That's the address Haram gave you.'

'Yes.'

'And how long is it since he was murdered?'

'Over a week ago.'

'How many times has he used the villa since then?'

Georgia blanched. It was time for her mouth to twist. 'He's been seen once,' she admitted, 'but managed to get away before we got to him.'

Henry sighed, scratched his ear and gave a short laugh.

131

'What's so funny?' Georgia said, irritated.

'Nothing, nothing,' he assured her – except there was always that disparity between expectation and actual events. He'd arrived thinking that trussing up Scartarelli would be the proverbial piece of piss, but the reality was a completely different kettle of fish. Basically, and as far as he could see without over-egging the pudding, it was a shambles. It was made much more palatable by the presence of Georgia, but in reality even that pleasure was tainted by the fact that he'd nearly been riddled with bullets on his first night on a holiday island.

'Why are you a target?' he asked her bluntly.

'I don't know. Maybe it's because I'm so close to Scartarelli and he doesn't like it, or maybe it has nothing to do with him at all. Maybe it's someone else I upset, maybe it was a mistake. Lots of maybes, but I'll only know for sure when I arrest the guys with the gun – which I will do,' she concluded confidently.

'Yeah, it's best to keep an open mind. But it seems a hell of a coincidence to me, and you need to be extra-careful, Georgia.'

'I will be.' She sipped her coffee. 'Just how long *can* you and Bill stay?'

'Maybe three days at most – unless we make a quick arrest and then we'll stay as long as necessary to complete the processing – unless of course it drags on. Lots of unlesses,' Henry said.

Across the cafe Bill and Tekke had finished their Belly-busters, were wiping their lips and generally coming to life.

'Let's go for a drive,' Georgia said.

Georgia explained that the Akamas, a designated national park, was a beautiful region of valleys and rocky shorelines and was the westernmost extremity of Cyprus. One of the beaches, called Lara, she said proudly, was where loggerhead turtles came to lay their eggs. She also said that there was very little development in the area, but a lot of building was taking place right up to the boundary and it was there they were going.

She drove out of Coral Bay and turned northwest along the E701.

Henry and Bill were in the back of her Terrano, windows open, enjoying the warm rush of wind on their faces. Georgia and Tekke occupied the front seats.

The heat of the day was building and Henry loved the effect it had on his bones.

She drove to an area called Agios Georgios, Henry noticing quite a lot of holiday villas being built, many standing unfinished like monstrous insects. Many were finished, however, and looked big and comfortable causing Henry to wish ... if only he'd been a millionaire instead of a cop.

Henry saw a sign for the Akamas and Georgia veered off the main road by a pleasant-looking restaurant called the Sunset, and on to a side road which cut through a development of villas in various stages of build and occupation.

'Straight on is the Akamas,' Georgia said, slowing down and pointing to where the tarmac ended abruptly and became a dusty, pitted road. As she turned right, Henry saw a snake slither

133

across the road and disappear into a banana plantation. Next she turned left into a cul-de-sac, villas either side, again in varying stages of development. She turned into the driveway of one of them – a completed one – and the Terrano lurched as it instantly dropped sharply into an underground garage. 'Pretty neat, huh?' she said climbing out and indicating for Henry and Bill to do the same. The garage was spacious enough to house another 4WD, which it did, and a fun buggy.

She led them through a door into the villa itself, explaining as she went, 'It's built on three levels. Underground, ground and first floor. It's just been completed for some buyers in Germany, but the contracts haven't been exchanged as yet ... hence...' She gestured.

'Her uncle is the builder,' Tekke said sourly.

'Wow,' Henry said, looking at the magnificent villa appreciatively.

'How much is it worth?' Bill asked with his traditional bluntness.

'About a million.'

'Euros?'

'Pounds sterling.'

'Oh,' said Bill as though this was OK.

'Her uncle's very rich,' Tekke said, still sounding sour.

Georgia scowled fleetingly at him and he shrugged. 'He's built all these on this road and when I found out Scartarelli had been using an address nearby, my uncle was happy enough to help out. Want a guided tour?'

'Yeah,' Bill said enthusiastically. It was

134

Henry's turn to scowl at him. He didn't feel this was the time for house viewing.

Georgia saw Henry's reaction, hesitated for a moment, then gave him a cheeky smile. 'Underground we have the garage, obviously,' she began as though she was an estate agent. Henry clamped his mouth shut as he was led unwillingly on a tour of a fabulous house with an infinity pool, superb fixtures and fittings and a roof terrace giving magnificent views towards the village of Agios Georgios and the shimmering sea beyond, then to his right, the bays and hills of the Akamas. He was suitably impressed. 'And if you turn that way,' Georgia said, 'we can see a villa right on the edge of the Akamas. I won't point to it, but it's the one not part of any development, surrounded by a high hedge.' Henry got it. 'And that is where Scartarelli is supposed to be visiting. Let's go back downstairs.'

Henry took a good look at the villa, then followed the trio back down the stairs and Georgia opened the door to a bedroom they hadn't inspected on their tour, inside of which was the police observation point. It consisted of a lone, smelly cop, cooped up with a thermos of strong coffee and a pair of battered binoculars, pen and notepad. He was sitting in an uncomfortable chair, probably with backache, keeping observations on Scartarelli's villa through slats in a blind.

The cop turned slowly and Georgia introduced him as Detective Piali, one of her team.

He was young, dark and handsome and Henry

135

hated him instantly, though the BO issue was an issue. 'Hi, I'm Henry Christie,' he shook the officer's hand, 'and this is Bill Robbins.' Bill extended his hand, too. 'How's it going?'

Piali shrugged. 'Nothing so far. Place is empty.'

'Who owns it?' Henry's question was directed at Georgia.

'An Englishman from London, but he's not there at the moment.'

'Are you assuming Scartarelli has permission to use the place?' Henry frowned.

'I'm assuming nothing.'

Henry pouted now, his mind jangling and thinking, 'Connections?' Scartarelli had been operating in England, albeit in the north; after committing the murder, he flees and ends up using an Englishman's house in Cyprus, if the information is to be believed. 'Do you have the guy's name?'

'I do, and he's been checked out and he's clean as far as we can tell.'

'Clean, as in not on a computer clean, you mean?'

Georgia nodded, but Henry saw her eyes register what he meant by these words. 'I'll give you his details,' she said. Turning to her detective, she asked, 'Anything you need?'

'Fresh coffee, a croissant – and a shower.'

'I hope we haven't wasted your time,' Georgia said. She and Henry were seated on the veranda and under the shade at the Sunset restaurant, the one they'd passed on the way to the OP at her uncle's villa.

'I'm sure you haven't.' He sipped his iced tea and winced at the unfamiliar but pleasant taste. It was refreshing, just took a bit of getting used to. The day was alrcady too hot to drink coffee, his usual upper. The restaurant was by the roadside, right on the junction that led towards the villa development and the Akamas. It was a good position from which to observe the comings and goings of the traffic for a short time. The road was fairly quiet, but a stream of quad bikes and fun buggies throbbed past them, heading for the Akamas, which was a popular off-road destination.

Tekke and Bill were sitting inside the restaurant itself, Tekke busily chatting up a young waitress.

Henry was still thinking out loud about last night's drive-by shooting, which had rattled him. 'Crims don't usually go for cops, whatever the provocation – and I'm not including drunks who fight with cops in that statement. I would've thought that if Scartarelli was involved in Haram's shooting – and again, there's nothing to say he definitely was. Haram, by all accounts, had his fingers in many pies for many years. Anybody could've been after him.' He rolled his shoulders. 'But if he was involved, then killing Haram should be enough and to go after the cop who was handling him seems very extreme. To me, anyway. If he thought Haram's death wasn't enough, I would think he'd be more inclined to run again, rather than stand and slug it out with the local law.'

'That's what I would think too.'

'Unless what he's into here is too profitable to leave?'

'Only Scartarelli will be able to tell us that, I guess.'

A silence descended between them. A huge buzzing wasp flew past Henry's head, making him duck instinctively. 'Jeez, that was a big one.'

Georgia laughed, then stopped suddenly. 'You saved my life last night,' she said seriously. 'I'd like to thank you. I wasn't very gracious about it at the time.'

Henry dipped his head. 'Heat of the moment. You seem to have recovered well.'

'They were rotten shots.'

Both smiled, locked eyes and a moment of connection passed between them. Inside, Henry told himself to beware of the look that could lead to lust. Not long ago, he would have liked to believe he had the skills and abilities to drag this woman, kicking and screaming orgasmically, to bed – despite the proximity of her partner. Thinking of which, Henry said, 'How was your inspector about it last night?'

'Angry that he wasn't the one to save my life, angry that his shots completely missed the men in the car, and other stuff,' she said.

'It's lucky he didn't kill any of the bats flying around. Guns and booze don't mix.'

She laughed. 'He'll get over it. He's a bit of a dinosaur now. Very gentlemanly and very sexist at the same time.'

'I know the type.'

138

Her face changed into one of affection as she glanced at Tekke who was back to discussing firearms with Bill. 'He's OK.'

A flurry of vehicles passed, several turning towards the Akamas. Henry glanced up, not really paying them much attention.

His mobile phone rang, irritating him. It was tuned into the local provider, charging a horrendous rate for both making and receiving calls. He picked it up from the table and answered it, his eyes still on the traffic. A few minutes earlier he had placed a call through to Jerry Tope, his tame – but angry at being left behind – intelligence officer and computer hacker. Tope was still rumbling because he was sitting behind his desk and computer, not on a sun-drenched restaurant terrace on a jolly. Henry indicated to Georgia that he would take the call away from the table, so he stood up and moved from under the shade of the veranda into the sunshine which hit him like a furnace.

'It's Jerry ... that name you gave me?'

'Walter Corrigan?'

'Yep. I've been on a trawl through numerous databases on your behalf, most of which I'm not supposed to have access to.' He made it sound as though he was doing Henry a great favour, rather than just doing the job he was paid for. 'And there's pretty much no trace.'

'Pretty much?' Henry queried. 'Either is or ain't.' He was shading his eyes with his free hand, watching traffic and surreptitiously glancing at Georgia, who was now sipping a Greek coffee. The light filtering through the slatted

139

veranda roof dappled across her and made her appear even more attractive. Henry stifled a shudder of appreciation, deciding that watching the road was the more sensible option.

'Well, there is a mention of him in one database I looked at.' Tope had seemingly decided to keep Henry dangling on the end of a hook.

'Look, Jerry,' Henry began testily, 'I promise if there's any more jollies coming up, you can come with me. How about that? Now just effin' tell me.'

'OK, the guy who came up isn't English or British for a start. He's a Yank.'

'How did you find that out?'

'I'd rather not reveal where I've looked. Y'know – satellites have ears? Needless to say it's a database belonging to a company from across the pond.'

'Jerry, just tell me, eh? Let's live dangerously.'

'Call me on a landline and I will,' he said stubbornly. 'I really don't want to chance it.'

'Right, whatever.' Henry grunted and turned to face the road as two vehicles shot past him, coming off the main road and heading towards the Akamas, putting up dust behind them. It was one of those moments for Henry, and he'd had a few in his career, when he needed to keep his calm. To ensure he did not stare open-mouthed or show that anything was different in any way whatsoever. The only thing he allowed himself was the usual hidden contraction of his ring piece and it was only a doctor conducting a rectal examination at that exact moment who could have determined that Henry Christie was

140

excited. 'How's the weather across there?' he asked nonchalantly, still shading his eyes but not allowing himself to turn his head at all, or allow his non-verbals to betray, in any way, the fact that the driver of the first car was none other than Paulo Scartarelli.

'Pissing down.'

'Good.' Henry snapped his phone shut and walked slowly back up the steps of the veranda, then found it impossible not to dash the last ten feet to Georgia's table and blab.

She leapt to her feet. 'You certain?'

'Hundred per cent.'

'But you've never seen him in the flesh.'

'Seen mugshots. I'm sure.'

She indicated urgently to Tekke and fished out her police radio from her bag. 'Piali – are you receiving?'

The radio crackled a reply. 'Yes.'

'Target One en route, repeat, Target One en route.'

A few seconds passed. Henry guessed Piali was pulling his wits together.

'OK, received.'

Henry heard footsteps behind the voice meaning the detective had probably quit his OP and had been caught lounging about somewhere else in the house, half-asleep.

Tekke and Bill joined them. Georgia quickly told them the situation.

'What do we do?' Henry said, the excitement now showing in his body language, more widespread than his arsehole.

'Sit tight,' Georgia suggested. She raised her

141

eyebrows at Tekke who shrugged and looked desperately pissed off.

'Your case,' he said, bouncing the ball back into her court.

'OK, we sit tight and just make sure he goes to the villa. If he does, then as soon as he's settled, we hit him.'

'Just us four and Piali?' Henry asked.

'I'll arrange for uniform backup.'

She sat down at the table, biting her bottom lip, her eyes darting around nervously as she worked out the moves. Henry sat, too, letting it all happen. He had no jurisdiction here and was happy to let others make the decisions.

'DS Papakostas?' It was Piali on the radio.

'Yes.'

'He's arrived – at least a Range Rover has pulled into the drive of the villa and driven under the awning. Two males got out and entered the house. Could not ID either.'

'Thanks for that.'

Henry had a sudden thought, recalling that two vehicles came off the road, the lead one a Range Rover, the one behind a Nissan Patrol, another four-wheel drive. He frowned. Could they have been together? It was his gut feeling that maybe they were. He leaned on the table. 'I might be wrong, but it's possible there was another vehicle with Scartarelli. They both came off the main road at speed, as if travelling in convoy. Just a feeling, nothing else.' He jerked his fingers tightly. 'Not sure.'

'But only one has turned up at the villa,' Georgia pointed out.

'True.'

'I vote we get to Piali and take it from there,' Tekke said.

'It's just that...' Henry began weakly.

'Second vehicle could be a lookout, or something,' Georgia said.

He shrugged. 'Who knows?'

Georgia thought about it. 'Just me and Henry go,' she decided. Tekke looked crestfallen and his dark eyes shot between her and the English detective, suspicion in them. 'If we go, all four of us in one vehicle, and the second car is somehow connected and is watching Scartarelli's back, four of us in a car could cause them to jump.'

'OK,' Tekke said reluctantly.

'Come,' Georgia said to Henry. She brushed past him, down the veranda steps and into the tiny car park where she climbed into the Terrano. Henry was just behind her, feeling that great surge of cop-juice, the drug that had kept him going for almost thirty years. One day it would kill him, he thought, but he could not help from keeping a smile off his face as Georgia forced the car into reverse, swung it backwards in an arc out of the car park, then hit the gas.

The dusty road bore slightly left, after which was the turn-off right into the estate on which the villa was situated. Just beyond this junction on the road to the Akamas was the car that had been behind Scartarelli's Range Rover. The Nissan Patrol was parked up by the roadside, exhaust fumes belching from the tail pipe, the engine therefore on and idling.

'The second car,' Henry confirmed to Georgia's sideways glance.

'So they are together,' she concluded, then turned right on to the estate.

'If they clocked this car on the car park when they flew past, we could have blown it,' Henry warned.

'We'll see ... but this country is filled with brown Terranos, you know?'

'I've noticed.'

Georgia pulled into the steep drive of the OP villa and drove into the underground garage, the car lurching on its suspension as it jarred to a stop. She got out, Henry in tow, rushing through the villa, literally clambering over the fun buggy into the villa itself, then up the stairs to Piali who was now eagerly glued to his binoculars, watching for any activity at the target premises. He didn't even look around when Georgia and Henry barged in.

'Anything?' Georgia asked, panting.

'Nothing.'

She exhaled unsteadily and flicked back some invisible wisps from her face.

'No, something,' Piali corrected himself. 'They're getting back into the Range Rover.'

'Shit.' Georgia wrenched the binos from him and took over. 'Damn it,' she uttered. 'Tekke,' she said into her radio. 'They're on the move again.'

'OK.'

Henry lifted one of the blinds a quarter of an inch and peeped out to see the Range Rover drawing out of the driveway. As it pulled away from the villa, it went out of sight but Henry knew it was travelling along the cul-de-sac parallel to where he was, then back on to the road which was the spine of the estate.

Georgia forced the binoculars back into Piali's hands and said to Henry, 'Front bedroom.' She tugged at his T-shirt and ran through the house to the main bedroom, opening the French windows and stepping on to the balcony. The vista was as Henry remembered – the sea, the village and to the right, the Akamas. The Range Rover flashed down past the end of the road, then out of sight again, but a few moments later was back in view. They watched it, with the Nissan Patrol, travelling west along the gritted track into the national park. Then, because of trees and geography, it went out of sight.

The detectives looked at each other.

'I think we should follow,' she said.

'Me too,' he agreed. There might not be another chance of nailing Scartarelli.

'But if we use the Terrano, it could give the game away.' She regarded Henry thoughtfully. 'Ever been in a fun buggy?'

'A what?'

'Tourists hire them all the time,' she said, dragging Henry back down to the garage where the buggy was parked. 'They're all over the place. This one belongs to my uncle, but I use it lots.'

Henry looked doubtfully at the two-seater buggy, recalling that even in the short time he'd been on the island, he'd seen several. He thought they looked pretty dangerous.

'We'll blend in perfectly, more or less – and

145

they're ideal for the Akamas.' She looked at their garb. 'I suppose we'd look better in shorts,' she said. Both were dressed in jeans. 'What've you got underneath your jeans?'

'Marks and Spencer Y-fronts.'

'Not boxers?' she asked astounded. 'I thought all men wore boxers.'

He glared at her. She giggled. 'Jeans'll have to do, I guess.'

'What've you got on under yours?' he demanded to know.

She gave him a quick wink. 'That's for you to find out.'

Actually he already knew she was wearing a thong because he'd seen the top when she'd bent over earlier and her T-shirt had ridden up, exposing her back. Henry's eyes could not tear themselves away from the tanned skin and the butterfly tattoo at the base of her spine.

She jumped into the driving seat of the buggy and strapped herself into the bucket seat like a fighter pilot.

Eyeing the hazardous-looking contraption with trepidation, Henry swung into the other seat and fumbled inexpertly with his seat belt.

'Perhaps we should just wait here for them to come back.'

'They may not necessarily come back this way. The Akamas is criss-crossed with tracks and they could even get across to Polis. It's rough, but easy in a four-wheel drive. My guess, though, is that they're eating out, meeting someone, perhaps. I can't think of any other reason for him to go into the park. It's not as though

146

he's a tourist.'

'Eating out?' Henry said.

She fired up the 250cc engine. 'I'll explain ... now hold on.'

She drove up the steep drive and on to the road where they came across the sturdy figures of Bill and Tekke making their way to the OP villa on foot. Georgia stopped the buggy and shouted over the noisy 'phut-phut' of the two-stroke engine. 'You guys follow slowly in the Terrano. Keys are in it. Arrange for backup to be ready,' she added to Tekke, who gave her a mock salute and still looked severely pissed off. He was sweating, his jacket was slung over his shoulder and a cigarette dangled from the corner of his mouth.

With that, she gave a quick wave. Henry shrugged helplessly at Bill as if none of this was his fault – and they were off.

'If nothing else,' she shouted into Henry's ear, 'it's a great way to see the Akamas.'

They left the tarmacked road behind and bounced in a lively way on to the track, which was, in essence, the main road through the park. Behind the buggy rose a huge cloud of dust from the road surface.

Georgia put her foot down. Henry braced himself for a rough ride.

NINE

The ride was bouncy and spine-jarring as the little vehicle, nothing more than an engine on a frame, crashed over the pitted track. Even though he was tightly held in and there was a roll-cage for protection, Henry had little doubt that at the speed they were travelling, they would flip over sooner rather than later.

Georgia seemed intent on going as quickly as possible, picking out all the ruts and boulders and glancing sideways at Henry to witness his discomfort, laughing each time the buggy smashed down and made him gasp for the air that was forced out of his lungs. It was like being taken on a wild safari.

Despite all this, Henry could see that the Akamas was a harsh, beautiful place, with large tracts of impenetrable-looking bushes, some pine trees and lots and lots of dust, most of which billowed out behind them. It would have been hard being a close-following car.

'I take it you're a bit of an expert at this,' he shouted hopefully.

'When I was younger I hired buggies regularly to come out here with friends, down to the beaches to swim.' She jerked the steering wheel sharply down, avoiding a particularly large and

148

jagged outcrop of rock in the trail, sending stones and gravel skittering out behind them in a shower. 'I love it,' she shouted.

Suddenly the road veered down to the right and they passed a restaurant at the foot of a steep valley. Henry noticed two large fat pigs sleeping in the shade of a tree. Then they climbed up the other side of the valley and emerged on the flat, Henry mesmerized by the crystal-clear sea out to his left. Next the trail dipped sharply down and Georgia slowed the buggy to a crawl as the size of the boulders grew and the buggy had to pick its way, lurching, over a dried-up river bed. Then she gunned the willing engine and accelerated away with a whoop.

'Well, they weren't at that restaurant,' she said after she'd calmed down. 'They might be at the next one, but if they're not there, they could be making over to Polis ... if so, better hold on tight.'

'How far is the next restaurant?'

'Not far now.'

After another quarter-mile, Georgia skewed the buggy to a stop at a T-junction, allowing all the brown dust behind them to catch up and envelop them in a choking cloud.

Henry wafted it away disgustedly after breathing in a lungful and coughing and spluttering like a smoker.

As it cleared it revealed a rustic signpost in front of them which simply pointed to The Last Castle.

'Whatever happens,' Georgia said, 'if we get a

149

chance, we'll come up here for a meal before you leave. It's fantastic.' She pointed ahead, up a rugged hill. 'The food's simple, but good, and the position and atmosphere – stunning.'

Henry peered up, seeing the track rise to what looked like the old stone wall of a castle.

'Was it once a castle?' he asked stupidly.

'Yep – that's why it's called the Last Castle.'

'I'll have that,' Henry said, then groaned as the buggy bounced and landed hard.

'Unfortunately the car park is at the back of the restaurant, so we'll only know for sure if he's here when we arrive.'

Henry had to admit it was a great spot, perched on the top of a steep hill with tremendous views across to the sea. They were driving along the foot of a steep gorge and the road split, the left fork taking them up to the restaurant, the right one disappearing into the wilderness, he guessed.

Henry's mobile phone rang. It was Jerry Tope, who had been waiting impatiently for Henry to call him via landline.

'Something came up,' Henry snapped. 'Speak soon.' He closed the phone. 'Don't let me forget to call him.'

'Call who?'

'My colleague.'

The road curved under the wall of the restaurant. Peering up, Henry could see diners sitting under a vine-covered trellis. Georgia drove up and around the back of the restaurant on to the car park on which sat the Range Rover and the Nissan Patrol, amongst a half-dozen other cars

150

belonging to customers.

Problem was that two salty-looking men were lounging in the shade by the Nissan, smoking. They were young, mid-twenties, dark-skinned, wearing jeans and T-shirts. Henry clocked them straight away and sussed them as hired help. This observation was confirmed when they came erect and watchful as the buggy came on to the car park and pulled in a few cars away. Georgia had parked right on the edge, overlooking the gorge behind the restaurant. It was a beautiful view.

The men watched them, feigning indifference, but Henry felt their eyes burning into him. He smacked his seat-belt release and turned to Georgia so his face was only inches from hers.

'They're watching us.'

She looked into his eyes. 'I know.' Her eyes were clear and gorgeous. Henry knew his were old and bloodshot.

'What do you want to do? It's your play,' he said.

She released her seat belt and contorted towards him. Her right hand snaked around his neck. The touch made him quiver.

'Better make it look convincing.' Her fingers opened on the back of his head and she tilted him down gently, angling his face slightly so they could kiss. It was as though a charge of static had seared through Henry's whole being, finishing up with a lightning strike somewhere around his balls. The first kiss more like a peck, just sizing up each other's lips. The second one, however, was very different.

151

Henry drew away, breathless, from one of the most wonderful kisses he'd ever experienced, even though there was the faint taste of tobacco in there somewhere. That addition made it even more delicious, although he could not recall Georgia actually smoking.

She looked at him, lips parted.

'For an Englishman you're a good kisser,' she acknowledged.

'That's very kind of you. Normally we're such a cold-hearted race ... that doesn't completely answer our current predicament, though.'

'Fuck that.' She grabbed him again. This time it was a long, slow, exploratory kiss and Henry, two thousand miles from home in a hot country and on expenses, just went along with it.

'We need a plan,' he said when she eventually drew off him, a little groan of ecstasy escaping from her throat.

'Those guys have relaxed,' she said, sneaking a glance over Henry's shoulder. 'And I've very nearly climaxed, yeah? I think we should go eat, get the reinforcements in place and then pounce. How does that sound for a plan?'

Henry pretended to consider it. 'As a plan it's as good as they come,' he conceded.

They disentangled themselves from each other, dismounted from the buggy and, holding hands – just for effect – they strolled past the two henchmen, who eyed them under dark, suspicious brows.

'What if Scartarelli knows you?' Henry asked.

'No reason he should.'

'But Haram was murdered straight after a

meeting with you. And you've been shot at.'

They stopped and turned to face each other before they walked down the side of the restaurant to the vine-clad terrace at the front. She had put on big sunglasses and she shook her hair loose, like a black-maned lion. 'I'll take a chance. The worst he can do is run and we chase him and if he doesn't recognize me, we sit, eat and wait for the cavalry. And I've got my gun in my bag, just in case it turns nasty – and I'm not afraid to use it.'

'OK.'

She grabbed the front of his T-shirt and yanked him towards her, rising up on her toes, kissing him again.

Then they walked to the front of the restaurant and Henry was stunned by the setting, the panorama, the coolish breeze wafting through the vines and the simplicity of it all. There was just a series of rustic benches and tables cut from rough-hewn wood. The place was busy but not packed and the meat was being cooked on a barbecue, emitting a wonderful aroma.

They were shown to a table and Henry slid in opposite Georgia, who kept her back to Scartarelli. He was sitting at a bench at the far end of the terrace in deep conversation with another man.

'I don't recognize the other guy,' Georgia said. A waiter appeared and took their drinks order. There was no choice with the main menu – you simply got what was on the grill, chicken and pork, together with a baked potato and salad. Georgia called Tekke on her phone. 'He's at the

153

Last Castle,' she told him. 'Can you arrange for the ERU to be ready on my command? Have them on standby on the Akamas. Yeah, that's it.'

'What's the ERU?' Henry asked.

'Emergency Response Unit.'

He nodded, then said, 'Tactics? I assume they'll be arriving in liveried vehicles, which will give matey the chance to do a runner as soon as he spots them.' He looked down the gorge to the sea, noting that the drive up to the restaurant was clearly visible most of the way from the coastal track.

She matched his gaze. 'I see your point.' She stared thoughtfully at the view.

Henry estimated even at speed over that terrain, it would take at least five minutes to get from the mouth of the gorge up to the restaurant. Time enough for Scartarelli to flee in the opposite direction.

'Perhaps we should wait for him to finish and leave?' Henry advised. 'Get him on the way out?'

'He could be here for hours.'

'Then so could we. I assume the ERU has the capacity to bide its time?'

'Good idea.' She laid a cool hand on the back of his. Henry saw that Scartarelli and his companion were being served their food. 'We'll just sit back.' She phoned Tekke again, told him the plan, hung up. 'Not a happy man,' she muttered.

'He's got Bill for company. What's not to be happy about? They can chat about bullets and stuff.'

* * *

154

As promised, the meal was substantial, simple and superb. The conversation between Henry and Georgia flowed well and once again he found himself thinking what it would be like if things between them progressed further. His imagination ran riot, but he curbed it by being one hundred per cent certain he would not act on his impulses, even if the situation arose – so to speak. He'd learned too many hard lessons and would content himself with flirtation and laughter. No longer would he put himself in a position where he hurt Kate and the girls. And there was always the slightly menacing figure of Tekke on the sidelines, a guy he wouldn't trust as far as he could chuck him, which was an amendment of his initial assessment of him.

Georgia's phone rang continually, Tekke insisting on regular updates and informing them the ERU was ready and waiting at the mouth of the gorge.

Henry kept a beady eye on Scartarelli, who dawdled over his food.

Henry flinched when the man's companion stood up, but relaxed when he walked to the toilet block.

'They could be getting ready to move,' he warned Georgia.

'I could stay here all afternoon,' she replied dreamily.

'I could, but business first.'

He leaned in close so their foreheads were nearly touching and looked into her eyes. Her pupils dilated.

'I'm only doing this because Scartarelli's

155

friend has reappeared from the toilets and he's on his mobile.'

'I understand,' she breathed, her eyes playing over his face. 'You're very handsome.'

Henry guffawed. 'I've got bags under my eyes, skin tags popping up all over the place, a neck like a scrawny chicken, bloodshot eyes, hair growing in places it shouldn't...'

'Distinguished, then?'

'I prefer handsome,' he said. For a moment his eyes were directly looking into hers – at the exact moment they shouldn't have, because Scartarelli's friend suddenly veered by and sat down next to Georgia in a flash, catching them both by surprise. In his hand was a gun, hidden from other diners, which he jabbed hard into Georgia's belly, angled up under the ribcage.

He shot a warning look at Henry. 'One move and I'll kill her here and now.' He pushed his face right up to the side of hers and spoke into her ear. Henry watched, terrified. 'All you have to do is sit here with me and don't move.'

Scartarelli stood up slowly from his table, tossing a wad of euros on to his plate. He sauntered unhurriedly across to the trio, then leaned with both hands on the end of their table, his eyes taking in both detectives, a smile playing across his features.

'I don't kill cops unless I need to,' he growled at Georgia, then looked at Henry, then back at Georgia. 'This is your first and final warning. Do not ever come for me – understand?'

His greaseball mate twisted the gun harshly under her ribs, making her squirm. 'Do you

156

understand what he said?'

She nodded, but there was no fear in her eyes, just defiance.

'Otherwise I will kill you,' Scartarelli said viciously. He moved away from the table, eyes on them like a panther.

His friend moved the gun from underneath Georgia's ribcage and both men sauntered towards the car park, leaving the duo shocked and speechless, but only for a moment.

Henry felt something primitive build inside him. A rage, an anger. His eyes burned and his nostrils flared and his teeth grated while he gripped the edge of the table, knuckles pure white.

'Are you going to let him get away with that?'

'No way.'

She picked up the phone, dialled Tekke.

As she spoke, Henry leaned over the wall and watched the two vehicles that had brought Scartarelli's party heading back down the dusty track, the Nissan leading, the Range Rover driven by Scartarelli following. He pulled Georgia to her feet while she spoke and they ran back to the buggy, jumping in and strapping up.

'He's going to get a good reception,' Georgia said triumphantly, snapping her phone shut.

'Let's make sure we're there to witness it.'

She slammed the buggy into reverse and skidded backwards, a massive cloud of gritty dust enfolding them in the moments before she selected first and raced off the car park. The trail snaked back down in front of the restaurant wall and she hit it fast, the suspension throwing the two occupants around like crash-test dummies. Henry held on for dear life, his whole being jarring, his internal organs feeling as though they were loose inside him, up in his throat, then in his lower belly. He clung to the roll cage.

Having run to the buggy at the back of the restaurant, they had lost visual with the two cars and even when they bounced on to the track along the bottom of the gorge, they still could not see Scartarelli's transport. Henry assumed they had met the ERU by now – so it was a huge reality check when, as they skittered around a rock-strewn corner, they came face to face with Scartarelli's Range Rover bearing down on them like a charging bull.

Obviously they *had* met with the ERU but had managed to do a U-turn and evade capture and were now tearing away in the opposite direction. It looked as though the Nissan and its occupants hadn't been quite so lucky.

An expletive, coupled by a blasphemy, came out of Henry's mouth. There was going to be a head-on crash.

The Range Rover was almost on top of them – and if there was a collision, there would be only one winner. And it wouldn't be the buggy. Henry and Georgia would be crushed and mangled and the Rover would clamber over the wreckage.

Georgia screamed.

An impact was inevitable.

She wrested the steering wheel down to her right and the light buggy jumped off the track out of the way of the big 4WD at the last possible moment. However, the trackside wasn't an even, tarmacked hard shoulder. It rose steeply and immediately. The buggy ran up it, but flipped over and suddenly Henry and Georgia were in the drum of a washing machine as it rolled twice, both of them screaming, then incredibly landed – crash/bounce – on all four wheels, the engine still running.

They were covered in dust.

For a second, Henry was disorientated, then his equilibrium came straight back. He was astonished to find that not only had they flipped three times, but they were back on the main track and facing the direction taken by the Range Rover, miraculously undamaged.

He and Georgia exchanged looks. They knew how lucky they'd been.

Her brown face had gone ashen, but though shaken, she was unhurt and determined.

'You OK?' he asked.

She nodded, said nothing, struggled with the gear lever, then they were moving in pursuit of the Range Rover, a bit like a whippet chasing a tiger.

Henry looked over his shoulder. 'No signs of reinforcements.'

'The Nissan's probably blocked the track.'

'Will the Range Rover have to go back up to the restaurant?'

'No – the road splits below it. He can get away by heading further up the gorge. There are many tracks crossing the Akamas which a car like that could use,' she shouted over the din of the two-stroke as she floored the gas pedal and went for it with grim determination.

When they reached the split in the road below the Last Castle, the rising dust along the right fork indicated the route the Range Rover had taken – powered straight on, going deeper into the gorge.

'I know these trails well,' Georgia went on, not hesitating. 'He could easily lose us if he gets too far ahead, but his options are limited in that basically there's only two ways to go, left or right. Going left he could get across to Polis, but I guess he'll be going right towards Pafos. It's easier going, but I won't assume anything.'

They reached another split in the track – left, right? – but the rising dust indicated right. She swerved in that direction without stopping.

She stuck doggedly to the trail of low dust, the springy buggy bouncing with delight over the boulders and rocks, skidding through corners, and judging by the height of the dust trail they followed, they were closing in on the Range Rover. Tantalizingly, though, it remained out of sight.

During the chase Georgia managed to pass Henry her mobile phone and shouted for him to call Tekke.

He looked at the display and saw it was set in her native language. 'It's all Greek to me,' he shouted in her ear, eliciting a laugh from her.

However, the buttons on most phones throughout the world do the same thing and Henry managed to connect to Tekke with the phone clamped tightly to his ear to eliminate as much of the sound of the buggy's screaming engine as possible.

'Where the hell are you?' Tekke demanded urgently.

Henry looked at Georgia. 'Wants to know where we are,' he yelled.

'Heading in the general direction of the E709 – that's the road leading over to Prodromi,' she shouted grimly, concentrating on driving and not killing them.

Henry relayed that to Tekke, who made some sort of response, but he could not tell what. Then the phone went dead and he looked crossly at it. No signal bars showed.

The buggy careened around the next corner where the track narrowed and rose steeply for fifty metres before opening on to a barren plateau of rocks and harsh shrubs. But slewed across the track, barring any further progress, was the black Range Rover. Scartarelli and his companion stood ready to confront their pursuers.

Scartarelli's arms were folded across his chest. His henchman had a gun in his right hand. He was crouched in a marksman's stance, left hand supporting the gun in his right. At the moment the buggy slapped on to the flat, his hands rose and he fired.

Henry heard the crack of the shot. He jerked instinctively to his left and felt the disturbance of air as the bullet whooshed past his face, narrowly missing him and passing between the two detectives, out of the back of the buggy.

Henry cowered as best he could, there being no protection afforded by the open-fronted buggy. Georgia fought for control, won, and

161

once more rammed her foot on the accelerator, changed down a gear and aimed the buggy at the two men.

The man with the gun dropped into a crouching combat stance.

Georgia twisted the wheel and zigzagged towards him, making aiming tougher and tougher for him – but not stopping him loosing off two more shots. Henry saw the muzzle flash, heard the bangs. The bullets went somewhere, but not into Henry or Georgia.

She continued to bear down on the men until they realized she was not going to stop, meant business and they had better move fast. At the last moment they parted like synchronized swimmers, diving away either side, their faces a picture of disbelief and horror.

Georgia slammed the brakes on hard. The buggy skidded and slithered on the gravel, and angled to a halt near the Range Rover. As it stopped, she smacked the quick-release catch of her seat belt and leapt out of the bucket seat, smoothly drawing her own weapon from her handbag as she rolled over. It was as though it was a move she practised in training: the lady draw, perhaps.

As she jumped right, Henry went left, in the direction Scartarelli had scrambled. The man himself had rolled into the dirt and was rising to his feet, frantically trying to draw a weapon from his leather jacket. At least that's the impression Henry got.

Henry dived for him at the same moment as he heard the discharge of a gun from the other side of the buggy. But with no time to check this out – *Scartarelli was pulling out a pistol* – Henry had to move decisively.

He threw himself at Scartarelli, smashing his right hand away, then following this up with a shoulder barge into the solar plexus, driving himself hard and forcing all the air out of the man's lungs with a noise like a deflating football.

The gun windmilled out of his fingers.

Henry, now in his own world of determination, fixated on keeping himself alive whilst at the same time flattening and overpowering his opponent, continued to force him over. He landed squarely across him, then rose up like a demon and crashed his right elbow into Scartarelli's cheekbone. He followed this up with a hammer-like blow to the temple with a fist, sending all the fight out of him.

Henry was back on his feet in an instant, trying to see what had happened to Georgia – but Scartarelli, dazed and battered as he might have been, launched himself for the discarded gun. Henry also went for it, seeing it was a snub-nosed, six-shot revolver of some type, not a pistol as he'd first thought. He reached it first, kicking it away, then scooping it up and pointing it unerringly. Scartarelli sat up groggily, but Henry decided to take no chances. He flat-footed him in the chest, sending him sprawling and hearing a satisfactory clunk as his head connected with a rock.

Only then could he find out what was happening on the other side of the buggy.

Henry smiled. Georgia was dragging the henchman across the ground by his collar. A flower of bright-red blood blossomed around the man's left shoulder where she had shot him. She threw him down and returned Henry's winning smile before flicking a few strands of hair away from her flawed, but beautiful face, and blowing out her red cheeks.

TEN

As Henry Christie had always suspected, it was very unlikely that the wheels of justice would spin quickly in the case of Paulo Scartarelli. Not because it was Cypriot justice. It would not have mattered where in the world Scartarelli had been detained, there was no way he would be extradited from anywhere, no matter how willing the authorities, within the promised two days. It just didn't happen – such was life – but he was surprised that it took only four weeks, in itself a miracle. The problem, as ever, was defence lawyers and Scartarelli wasn't going to be taken to the UK without a legal battle of some sort.

And just to draw out the process, he hired and fired a series of quite capable lawyers until a high court judge said enough was enough. Twenty-eight days after his arrest, Scartarelli was ready to be handed over to the British authorities – Henry Christie, in other words.

Since the arrest in the Akamas, Henry had been involved in shuttling back and forth to Cyprus because there was no way he would have been allowed to remain on the island for that length of time, despite pleas that fell on deaf ears. By the time Scartarelli was ready for collection, Henry was heartily peed off with

165

travelling backwards and forwards on cramped planes. He was glad, in some ways, that the episode was drawing to a close.

And as his final journey to Cyprus ended and he and Bill Robbins clambered down the steps of the easyJet Boeing 737, hopping on to the bendy bus to take them to the terminal building at Pafos, Henry did have one big regret that this was all soon going to be over.

It was like being sardined into a packed Tube train, swaying and bumping into other people as the bus lurched across the tarmac on its short run.

'You must be well used to this,' Bill Robbins said.

'Yeah – and pissed off with it all.'

'Yeah, right,' said Bill sarcastically. He had not been back to Cyprus since the first visit. 'I really hate coming to nice, hot countries,' he mocked.

'Just eff off, Bill,' Henry said quietly. It had been another tiring journey, beset by unexplained delays, crap food, shrieking kids and simmering air rage inside him.

Bill pulled his face and shut up. 'Whatever,' he did manage to say.

For once, Henry's bag was one of the first to come along the conveyor belt and he left Bill fuming because his was nowhere to be seen.

'See you out front,' Henry said.

He passed through customs and into the arrivals hall and the reason why Henry was filled with such mixed emotions was standing there waiting for him.

DS Georgia Papakostas.

166

Henry literally felt himself go weak at the knees and they approached each other and kissed formally on the cheek.

'Where's Bill?'

Henry jerked his head backwards. 'Still waiting.' He looked at her, mesmerized, unbelievably ecstatic to see her again even though it had been only a week since he last visited the island. She smiled widely, her eyes playing over his face; she, too, was overjoyed to see him.

'Where's Tekke?'

'At the police station in Pafos. We'll meet him there.'

Bill appeared through the door of the baggage hall, lugging his suitcase behind him, a big smile on his face at seeing Georgia. After an effusive greeting they were taken out to the Terrano and Georgia drove them from the airport.

'What's the plan this time?' Henry said, rubbing his hands together.

'I've booked you into a hotel in Pafos – separate rooms.' She eyed Henry. 'Tonight we'll chill. Tomorrow is paperwork day, then the day after he's all yours to take back – and that's the last we'll see of you,' she concluded wistfully. 'But,' she went on brightly, 'I do have some news of my own, kind of mixed.'

Henry waited.

'Promotion – detective inspector.'

'Oh, well done,' he said genuinely.

'Yeah, brill,' Bill perked from the rear.

'What's the mixed bit?'

'Tekke is being moved and I'm taking his place. He's being posted to Protaris on the other

167

side of the island.' She gave Henry a short smile that said an awful lot.

Henry and Bill didn't see Georgia or Tekke that evening. They went out for a meal in Kato Pafos, down at the harbour. Henry was eager to see the spot where Haram had been murdered and the Pelican, though they didn't dine there. However, they ate and drank too much as usual, then hit the sack. Both were exhausted from the long flight and the delay.

As soon as Henry's head hit the pillow, it was lights out.

The morning after, a uniformed cop picked them up after breakfast and took them to the main police station in Pafos where they met a strained-looking Georgia and an extremely grumpy Tekke who spent the time communicating with them in monosyllables. They were clearly not a happy couple, but Henry tried to ignore it as much as possible and get on with what they were there to do – complete the file-checking with the Cypriot lawyer who was representing the police.

Scartarelli's fate had been sealed at a hearing two days earlier and this was the final run-through of the extradition papers. It was certain his lawyer would be engaged in the same activity and if anything was found out of place, it had to be spotted and dealt with.

Eight hours after starting, the task was complete.

Henry, Bill, Georgia and Tekke sat back and watched the lawyer leave. Then there was a collective sigh of relief.

All that needed to be done now was to arrange an escort for Scartarelli from the prison in Larnaca in which he was lodged and for that to tie in with the scheduled flight back to Manchester the next day. Henry also needed to be met at Manchester with a further escort to take the prisoner to the cells in Lancashire.

The four looked at each other.

'Mine's a pint,' Bill ventured.

'Mine's a red wine,' Georgia continued the theme.

'I'll have whatever's going,' Henry said manfully.

Tekke grimaced, stood up and left the room, saying nothing.

The three of them, showered and changed after a clammy day inside, walked on to the harbour at Kato Pafos and ate a meal at one of the waterfront restaurants. As the sun dropped, the heat fell a little, but it remained warm and pleasant. Bill decided on a lone stroll after the meal, leaving Henry and Georgia sitting across the table from each other, slowly and thoughtfully spinning their wineglasses by the stems, inspecting the ruby liquid as it rolled around.

'How's the guy you shot?' Henry asked to break the ice.

'Well enough to face trial.'

'And what's eating Tekke?' Henry asked eventually.

'Mm ... he asked me to marry him last night. I said no.'

'Bit of a bummer for him,' Henry said, realizing this must have been the reason for their no-show the previous evening.

'Add to that his unexpected departure from Pafos.'

'That, too.'

'And the fact I'm taking over his job.'

'And that.'

'And he simply doesn't want me being a cop – especially after our little shoot-out in the Akamas. Not a woman's job. He thought it would have dawned on me after that, the drive-by shooting, and the chase after Scartarelli, and Haram's murder – still undetected, incidentally. A woman's place, at least in the eyes of the men in our society, is still in the home, cooking, giving birth, screwing her husband. He's a through-and-through sexist and I think our relationship has come to a grinding halt.'

'I'm sorry to hear that. Deep down I'm sure he's a good man.'

Her face tightened. 'And there's the age difference.'

'That's not his fault,' Henry said reasonably.

'I mean – he's as old as you, Henry,' she laughed.

Henry sat back and surveyed her, a smile twitching on his lips. He had very much come to be obsessed with her and he knew she felt the same way about him. At least neither of them had done anything about it, other than flirt and enjoy each other's company. No harm done so far.

'You need to do what's right for you,' Henry

170

said in a very clichéd way. 'Sometimes you fall into things, relationships, that seem right but they turn very wrong and it's hard to pull yourself out of them, but it can be done.'

'There speaks the voice of experience.' She sighed deeply. 'But there is a part of me that thinks I should settle down and have kids, grow fat, feed an even fatter man. That is a big pull, believe it or not. But I know Tekke isn't the man for that side of me. Oh shit, Henry, what should I do?'

They made their way up from the harbour, spending a little time in a couple of bars before finding their way to the hotel where Bill and Henry were staying. They sat and chatted for a while in the bar, then Georgia excused herself reluctantly and left. Bill and Henry had a couple of nightcaps, ouzo and lemonade.

'You OK about tomorrow?' Henry asked.

'I'd be better with an MP5 slung across me and a Glock in my holster – but yeah.'

'Just make sure you're happy with everything, OK? Not that I'm expecting anything to go amiss, but you never know...'

Once again, Henry Christie's male ego and self-destruct button were working in parallel with each other – but only in his mind, fortunately.

His hotel room was pretty standard fare, two double beds side by side and air-conditioning blasting away, but even this comfort did not help him sleep that night. He tossed and turned on the wide bed, unable to drift away, until midnight passed. As the time approached 1 a.m. he rolled off the bed, had a much-needed pee, then did something he rarely did – raided the mini-bar. He took two mini-bottles of Bell's whiskey and a couple of chunks of ice from the freezer unit and went out on to the balcony overlooking the pool.

The whiskey hit his throat harshly, but felt great going down into his chest.

He was annoyed with himself.

He couldn't get Georgia out of his mind and he was annoyed with her too. Why hadn't she come knocking? Why weren't they making hot, passionate love?

But most of all – why was he bothered?

Why in the name of hell and his new marriage was he even thinking like this?

He sneered at himself, feeling his face darken with anger.

Would he never change?

Would he always be destined to feel the need to seek new sexual adventures for as long as he could manage it? Encounters which clearly had no rhyme or reason?

He felt pathetic and inept, both as a man and husband.

There was no doubt that he and Kate really had something going now, better and deeper than it had ever been, and here he was, two thousand miles from home, wishing a sexy, vulnerable woman would come knocking on his hotel-room door and fuck him.

'You pathetic shit,' he said aloud.

'I'm not sure that's the way you should be

talking about your travelling companion,' a voice called back from the next balcony along. Bill Robbins' head bobbed up over the dividing screen and held up his glass of double whiskey and clinky ice and said, 'Cheers. I hope these are on the firm.'

The knock came at 2.16 a.m., about three-quarters of an hour after Henry had finally managed to get to bed, having clambered across on to Bill's balcony and raided his fridge for another couple of miniatures each before calling it a night.

Henry was asleep, but the persistent light tapping eventually worked its way into his brain and switched him on.

He jerked awake, swallowing something hard, trying to recall a strange dream about being naked in a shopping trolley in Debenhams. What the fuck did that mean? He flipped off the single sheet and, pulling up his baggy sleeping shorts, padded to the door and peered through the spyhole.

His heart fell and soared at the same time.

He took a moment to compose himself, detached the security chain and opened the door to see a very distraught Georgia out in the corridor. She immediately stepped into the room and threw her arms around his neck, burying her face between his developing man-boobs, sobbing.

'Hey, hey, hey,' he said gently, easing her away from him. 'What's happened?'

'I told him,' she gagged, 'I told him it was over.'

'Ah. How did he take it?' Henry held back from saying, 'How did he *Tekke* it?' in a Lancashire accent.

'Badly.'

Henry stepped into the corridor and checked it both ways before closing the door and shuffling Georgia ahead of him into the bedroom. He sat her down on the edge of a bed. 'I'll get you a drink.'

He raided the minibar again, finding an ouzo for her and another whiskey for him. He poured both neat, handing her the ouzo.

Rubbing his eyes, he sat next to her.

'I'm sorry to bother you, I'm so sorry.'

'Not a problem.'

'It's just – my family are in Nicosia. I've no one else to go to. Just you, Henry Christie.'

'That's OK,' he said with a shrug of acceptance and a smidgen of dread now. 'Come on, take a deep breath, tell me everything.'

There were moments, Henry knew, when he could easily have taken advantage of the situation. He could have put his arms around her, held her tight, turned her face up to his and kissed her, but something inside held him back. Not long ago he would have done, but Kate and the girls were now his first loyalty and infidelity was no longer on the to-do list. It would have to remain within the confines of his cranium for the rest of his days.

Georgia told him how she had informed Tekke their relationship was over. He had exploded. She had never seen him so angry and dark. At

174

one point she thought he was going to attack her, but he held back – fist in the air – and at the last moment stormed out of their flat. He hadn't been seen since.

'He mentioned your name,' she said. 'He accused me of having an affair with you.'

A chill of fear swept through Henry's veins. 'I hope you put him right on that?'

'Yes, yes, of course, but I don't think he believed me.'

Henry exhaled long and hard, wondering how he'd got himself into the middle of this mess.

Eventually she calmed down and said it would be best for her to return home. Henry didn't try to prevent her from leaving and with a heavy heart he steered her to the door after pulling on a pair of jeans and a shirt. He accompanied her to the hotel foyer and on the steps outside she turned to him and kissed him.

'Thank you,' she said simply, and walked away. Henry watched her get into the Terrano and drive off. He turned glumly back to the hotel, knowing he would be unlikely to get any sleep now.

He failed to see the dark shadow, which then moved, revealing the brooding figure of Tekke.

Next morning, two bleary-eyed men and one delicately balanced woman met in the hotel foyer and had a breakfast together. They discussed the fine-tuning of the plans for the day, the main problem being timing. They had to ensure that the prisoner was picked up at the prison by an armed and properly briefed escort at the correct time; was taken to the airport to meet the plane due to fly him back to Blighty; was handed over to the British authorities on the tarmac (i.e. to Henry Christie and Bill Robbins, ambassadors extraordinaire of the British justice system); and was flown out of the country – and then the Cypriots could wash their hands of the bastard. Lots of bits of things depended on other bits being right and if the plane was delayed, the whole process would be thrown out of kilter.

As they reached the end of their discussion, Henry enquired about Tekke.

Georgia shrugged. She looked completely exhausted. 'He reported sick, but I haven't spoken to him. Don't even know where he is.'

Henry thought about that and felt vaguely uncomfortable. A man on the loose who thought he was having an affair with his girl was not a good thing.

Bill eyed the two of them, not understanding any of the subtext.

Henry looked at Georgia, sensing Bill's position. 'I think Bill should know what's happening.' She nodded. 'To cut a long story short,' Henry continued, 'Georgia has split up with Tekke. There are several private reasons for this, but the one you might need to know about is that he suspects Georgia and me of having an affair...'

Bill's eyes flicked from one to the other. Then he guffawed, 'You and her? An affair?' and suddenly burst into a huge, sustained fit of belly laughter, interspersed with the occasional word such as, 'You? ... Her? ... An affair? ... You!'

Henry and Georgia watched the display of mirth stony-faced, Henry because he felt affronted by the realization that Bill seemed to think it preposterous that he could even contemplate sleeping with Georgia and that Georgia would even fancy him at all.

'It's not that far-fetched,' he said.

'Yes it is.'

Eventually he regained some sort of control over himself, wiping his tear-stained eyes with his knuckles. 'Look, I'm really sorry you and Tekke broke up ... that's not what I find funny ... it's the thought that...' He gave a dismissive wave. 'Sorry, sorry.'

Georgia hung her head. Henry glared at the firearms officer and shook his head in disbelief.

'Totally inappropriate, Bill,' he said coldly.

'I said I'm sorry, and I mean it.'

Georgia checked her watch. 'Let's go to the airport, make sure everything's set there.'

The scheduled BA flight from Manchester touched down bang on time; 12 noon. There was a two-hour turnaround for refuelling and a fresh crew, then the boarding was due to begin at 2 p.m. for a 2.40 take-off. As the plane landed, Georgia was on her mobile instructing the escort to pick up Scartarelli and make their way to the airport.

Hopefully, everything was in place. The customs procedure would be carried out separately for the prisoner and then, before the embarkation of the normal passengers, Scartarelli would be driven out to the plane, still under armed escort.

177

He would be taken to the top of the steps and handed to Henry and Bill. They had arranged seats right at the front, and the plan was to keep him sat between them, cuffed to one or the other, throughout the flight.

By all accounts, a foolproof plan.

Georgia's phone rang. She listened and said a few words, then hung up. 'They're en route.'

'How long of a journey?' Bill asked.

'Forty-five minutes.'

The three officers were in the police room at the airport. It was hot and cramped, the air-conditioning ineffective and overworked. Henry checked his watch and rose from the plastic chair, his back and arse dripping with sweat. 'I'll get some fresh air,' he declared and went through the security door into the departure lounge, where he knew he could find an outdoor seating area overlooking the runway. He meandered through the duty-free shop and the bookshop, bought a coffee and went outside thinking the air would be fresher. However, everybody seemed to be smoking and it was fairly unpleasant in the heat of the day.

Even so, he found a seat and plonked himself down whilst contemplating life and this situation in particular. He ran through the plan in his head, which seemed pretty straightforward. It should be smooth as silk.

He gazed across the runway, the heat haze rising from the concrete. He thought about Scartarelli and how little he actually knew about the man, the criminal. He was the whole point of the visit to Cyprus in the first place yet he seemed to have taken second place to the relationship that had developed between him and Georgia – and Tekke. Henry knew he'd taken his eye off the ball a little where Scartarelli was concerned. He knew he mustn't forget what a dangerous man he was, well connected and needing to be watched carefully, hence the armed escorts here and back home. He seemed to have the ability to move from country to country and mix in easily with the organized criminal fraternity and as such it had to be assumed that someone might want him released by any means possible. Or even try to kill him.

Better safe than sorry.

He gazed around as Georgia joined him at the table. She too had a coffee.

'Bill has apologized to me about his outburst.'

'Good, he needed to.'

'Is it so outrageous that we could be lovers?'

'Not at all. The thought is very, very nice. But it's not going to happen, except in my dreams.'

'You're happily married. I understand.'

'Yes, I am. I wouldn't want to jeopardize that.'

'I was hoping you'd make love to me when I came to your room.'

Henry sighed. 'I almost did.'

'But you were very gallant.'

'That's something I haven't been called before.'

She leaned over and kissed his cheek. 'Well, you are.'

'Ta.'

'And the prisoner will be here in ten minutes ... we need to be ready.'

179

Since his arrest under the body weight of Henry Christie, Paulo Scartarelli had been held in custody in various locations in Cyprus, from the police station in Pafos to the jail in Larnaca. His background had been researched thoroughly and he'd been interviewed extensively but neither approach had really uncovered very much about him. He had some minor convictions in his younger years in Italy, mostly relating to violence and pimping. The last few years had not seen him come to the notice of the police very often. His name had appeared in a few intelligence bulletins across Europe on the periphery of gang-related activities in the field of human trafficking, but not much of great interest and nothing that could be formed into meaningful evidence.

His appearance in Britain had been a surprise and Henry had been doing some background checks. It appeared that Scartarelli could have been involved in prostitution rackets in the north of England, but he couldn't seem to unearth much more than that. It was always difficult with foreign nationals, even more so now that they could virtually come and go across borders as they pleased, legally or otherwise.

Henry spent some time going through the murder file relating to the girl Scartarelli had killed. She was an Albanian national, sucked into prostitution and ending up abused in England. But again, her background was sparse. Just another statistic, really. The assumption was that Scartarelli had been her pimp and had murdered her for reasons unknown. Henry had hoped to be able to take over and complete the murder investigation but had been told no, in no uncertain terms. His job was simply to bring him back and let others – namely Dave Anger and DCI Carradine – complete the investigation.

It had annoyed him. After all, the case had been virtually closed for almost a year, but he had come to expect the worst from those two. He was no longer an SIO, so he just shrugged it off, accepted his lot and began to speculate if he could get a trip to Australia to bring back the third person on his list. Might as well get all the jollies he could, he reasoned.

Whilst in custody in Cyprus, Scartarelli had been spoken to by Cypriot detectives, including Georgia, but they could get no admissions from him in relation to Haram's murder. In fact he said almost nothing and despite their best efforts, by the time the extradition proceedings were complete, Scartarelli still remained a bit of an enigma. An international man of mystery, no less.

But he wouldn't remain one for long, Henry thought while he waited at the top of the steps leading into the aircraft on the runway at Pafos airport. He knew there was good DNA at the scene of the murder in England and once Scartarelli was linked to that, he would, in police terminology, be buggered.

Henry waited patiently, Bill by his side, cabin crew nervously behind with very worried expressions on their faces. He gazed across the apron at the terminal building, checked his

181

watch again.

Scartarelli should have cleared customs by now.

Two vehicles drew away from the departure-lounge gates – a covered Jeep and a Fiat box van, similar to a Ford Transit.

The prisoner and two escorts were in the back of this van.

They accelerated towards the plane and screeched to a halt at the foot of the steps. Georgia jumped out of the lead vehicle, smiled quickly at Henry, then accompanied by two heavily armed cops they ran to the back of the Fiat, shouted a pre-arranged password to the occupants and the double doors opened. Another two uniformed cops sprang out, fanned away from the vehicle and Scartarelli appeared, blinking against the bright sun. His wrists were cuffed in front of him, a pair of rigid handcuffs provided by Henry. He dropped on to the ground and another officer came out behind him.

It was the first time Henry had seen Scartarelli since the arrest. He looked slim, but pale, his eyes more sunken than before. Even so, there was an air of arrogance about him. That would be knocked out of him by a life sentence, Henry hoped. Even if he only served ten years, he'd be knocking mid-forties when he got out and a big chunk of his life would be lost forever.

Henry watched Georgia walk up to him. She said a few words and he looked up the steps to Henry, who gave him a nice warm smile and wave.

Taking him by the arm, Georgia led him up the

182

steps. He offered no resistance. They walked up side by side, an armed officer a couple of steps behind them, until they reached the flat landing at the top of the steps before the plane's door.

Scartarelli looked blandly at Henry.

Henry kept his smile in place, then looked at Georgia.

'All yours,' she said.

'I'm grateful. The British justice system is looking forward to welcoming Mr Scartarelli with open, then closed, arms.'

'I'm sure he'll love returning to the UK.'

Henry stepped sideways so he was edge-on to Scartarelli, giving Bill enough room to move in and place a big hand on the rigid section of the handcuffs between the wrists.

Bill and the villain eyed each other.

'You behave yourself and we'll be fine,' Bill said. 'Misbehave and I won't be responsible for my actions...'

At that point Henry had his back to the door hinges, Bill and Scartarelli were facing each other on the threshold, Georgia was standing just one pace to the right of the prisoner's shoulder and behind her, on the top step, was a single armed cop who had his back to everyone else and was facing outwards. A machine pistol was slung across his chest and behind a pair of cool Ray-Bans he was surveying the terminal building and runway. The other cops from the security escort were milling about and chatting at the bottom of the steps, job done.

The sniper hit the cop on the steps.

The bullet slammed into his temple, the size of

a five-pence piece at one side, exiting the size of a side plate the other, toppling him over the railing and sending him plunging to the ground which he hit hard – and dead.

Although Bill's vision was restricted by Scartarelli, he was the first to react, but not before the second bullet slammed into the bulkhead just inside the plane, somewhere between Henry's and Scartarelli's head. Bill's hand was already on the cuffs, so he gripped tight and hauled Scartarelli violently through the door, wrenched him round into the aisle and threw him to the floor. Then he dived on top of him.

He did this quickly and efficiently and by the time he'd completed the manoeuvre, Henry and Georgia had reacted. Henry backed quickly into the plane, shouting for everyone to hit the floor (actually screaming, 'Down! Down! Down!'), whilst Georgia pirouetted and dropped into a crouch, drawing her weapon and crisscrossing the terminal with its muzzle. At the same time she yelled instructions to the cops on the runway. They, on seeing their colleague fall, had dived for cover behind their vehicles. They too yelled, shouted and got into a panic.

But it was over. As soon as a sniper has made a shot, the game is up and the job is either done, or it isn't. It's actually a luxury to get two shots off but to miss with both was not good. More shots could result in his firing position being revealed and no sniper wants that. They just want to melt away and live to fight another day.

So no more shots were fired.

There was just a dead cop on the tarmac and a bullet hole inside the plane.

And panic at the airport.

Henry and Bill found themselves surrounded by headless chickens, but were powerless to do anything about it because of language. English might well be the official language, but when the shit hits, Greek is the only thing anyone understands.

They had to sit tight, together with their prisoner, and allow it all to happen.

The police went into hyperdrive for about four hours and if it hadn't been so tragic, it would have been comical.

The airport went into lockdown. Huge numbers of police and military personnel were brought in and an emergency was declared. All flights in and out were cancelled or diverted and no one was allowed to enter or leave the immediate area without express police permission.

In the police room Henry and Bill waited patiently for things to level out and as the day progressed, a kind of order came from the chaos.

Scartarelli sat numbly in a holding cage, still cuffed, saying nothing even when he was carted off for 'interrogation'.

He came back having made no comment, a sneer of contempt on his face. Henry wanted to smack him.

Henry saw little of Georgia, other than in short bursts of breathless activity. She appeared to have taken some control over most of the response but Henry detected a lot of friction as

185

senior officers and the military appeared on scene.

Five hours later the ring of steel was removed and the airport reopened. A mass of hot and angry tourists surged into the small complex.

A wasted-looking Georgia reappeared then, everything askew. She looked completely drained.

'Nothing,' she said despondently. 'No trace of the sniper. We found his position, but nothing of evidential value. He was out by the seashore, hidden by tall grass. The bullet that hit the plane has been recovered, believed to be a 7.62 from a high-powered rifle. The dead officer hasn't been medically examined as yet, no autopsy. His family has been informed.'

'What do you make of it?' Henry asked.

'Hypothesis: someone didn't want Scartarelli to leave the island alive. A hired gun, I'd say. Probably from Turkey. The Turks are cheap and numerous, some are very good and all are willing to do something like this for the money.' She paused. 'However, this doesn't affect the extradition, if that's what you're thinking. The sooner that man is off the island the better.'

This time all the legitimate passengers boarded the plane first, leaving three seats at the front for the prisoner and escorts. Everything was accomplished safely in the dark of early evening. Henry didn't have time to say a proper goodbye and good luck to Georgia. Scartarelli was seated between the two cops, scowling and surly. Henry hoped he would kick off, so he could batter him. Take-off happened without incident and within minutes they were at 35,000 feet.

'So,' Henry said, turning to Scartarelli. 'Who wants you dead?'

The felon twisted his head to give Henry a look up and down. 'Who's to say it's me they wanted dead?' he responded.

ELEVEN

He was hot-desking again. In other words using somebody else's desk, a bit like a cuckoo but without any of the benefits. This time it belonged to the DI who ran the Intelligence Unit at headquarters. Henry knew he was on leave for a week, so that's where he parked his rear end whilst he worked out what to do with the remaining name on his wanted list, Jane Kinsella.

However, as he pushed papers around the pristine surface, he was unable to rid his mind of what had happened in Cyprus over the last month. Meeting Georgia – and Tekke, of course; being shot at, arresting Scartarelli; the legal to-ing and fro-ing and being shot at again. And a dead cop. He ran things continually through the mush that was his grey matter, eyes squinting as he tried to make sense of it all, then finding that he came to no real conclusions, although he was haunted by the words Scartarelli had spoken to him on the plane.

What in hell did he mean?

That Henry was a target? That Georgia was a target? Maybe the dead cop *was* the intended target.

Of course Henry could only speak for himself. There was no reason why he should have been the target, other than he was the cop charged with bringing Scartarelli back to face the British courts. Georgia said she was as puzzled as he was and could see no reason for her to be the target and the background of the dead cop had been investigated and he was found to have led a blameless existence.

And if Henry or Georgia had been the target of an assassin's bullet, it made no sense. Even if they'd been killed, it would have made no difference to the eventual disposal of Scartarelli. He would still be in custody and killing one or more of his arresting officers would have achieved nothing. If his underworld colleagues had wanted him free they would have been better to arrange a prison break, or an ambush on the way to the airport.

Which brought Henry full circle.

The target *had* to be Scartarelli. That was the only hypothesis that hung together. Someone wanted him dead.

And yet ... did the drive-by shooting have any connection?

Henry exhaled. Too many questions.

His brain hurt and none of this really mattered now. He was back on home turf and still had a third felon to apprehend. One who was supposed to be in Australia. He imagined a long – maybe three-week – chase across the outback, being guided by some cop who looked like Crocodile Dundee. Maybe not...

He looked down the office and saw Jerry Tope's back was towards him. Tope had been pretty aloof since he had returned full time from

189

Cyprus and Henry hadn't had much time to sop up to him.

Maybe now was the moment.

Henry picked up the desk phone and dialled Jerry's extension. He watched him answer his phone.

'Jerry, it's me, Henry.'

Tope twisted and half-looked over his shoulder down the office. 'What?'

'Can we be friends?' Henry said. 'Pretty please – or shall I just pull rank?'

Tope's shoulders rose and fell in a shrug. 'Whatever.'

'Come to my office, then.'

'Do I need to bring anything?'

'You can find out how much I've got left of my budget.'

'I also still have some information for you – but you never rang back or asked.'

'What information?' Henry wracked his brain.

'About a Yank living in Cyprus?'

'Oh, God, yeah.' Henry had a sudden recall and his face fixed in a shocked expression. But then his mobile phone rang. He hung up on Tope and answered it. Two minutes later, once again having put Jerry Tope completely out of his mind, he was striding through the corridors on the way to the chief constable's office.

Henry breezed into the office that housed the staff officers working for the chief and deputy chief constable. Both higher-ranking officers had offices accessible only from this kind of ante-office. It was a bit like stepping into a de-

190

pressurization chamber in a rocket before being flung out into space. The office was quiet, two secretaries tapping away at their keyboards, a space at the desk of the deputy chief's staff officer, but there was someone sitting in the desk once occupied by Chief Inspector Andy Laker.

Henry's breeze stopped abruptly two steps into the office. He halted in his tracks. Henry knew, of course, that Laker had been unceremoniously dumped and was presently causing havoc with the Special Projects Team, so rumour had it. Henry hadn't even given a second thought as to which fool Laker's replacement might have been in this office. It was a job Henry could not even have imagined himself doing. He would have hated it.

She swivelled on her chair and their eyes met across a virtually empty room.

And Henry Christie felt as though he'd been hit in the guts by a medicine ball.

He made a reasonable effort of giving the impression of being unfazed by the shock appearance of Jane Roscoe, a former detective with whom Henry had once had a sticky, tricky affair. It had ended, as most affairs did, with recriminations and bad feelings – particularly when Jane ended up working for Dave Anger on FMIT and Henry suspected her of colluding with Anger to bring about his own downfall.

'Jane,' he said. The word clogged his throat.

'Henry.' She stood up and crossed the office to meet him with a very stilted handshake.

'I didn't know you were...' He gestured at the room.

191

'Thought I'd have a go for it when it was advertised. Got it!'

'And a uniform to boot.'

'That too.'

'Never seen you in uniform.' He squinted at her, appraising. 'And a third pip – congratulations, Chief Inspector.'

'Thanks,' she smiled. 'Come and sit down at my desk. He'll be a few minutes yet.' She jerked her head at the big oak door leading to the chief's office. Almost on cue there was the sound of raised voices from within. The two secretaries jerked up and looked at the door, startled. They eyed each other with an 'Oooh!' expression. 'Mm,' Jane said, then headed back to her desk, Henry in tow. He sat on a chair positioned at the end of the desk, gave her a nervous smile and struggled for something to say. At least with Laker he could have traded insults.

'How you doing?' he asked.

'Good, good.'

Silence.

'How's ... er...?'

'My husband?'

Henry nodded.

'Not my husband any more.'

'Thanks to me?'

'Actually, no thanks to you.'

Another loud outburst from the chief's office caused everyone to look at the door again.

'What's going on in there?'

'None of your business.'

'Mm.' Henry looked at Jane. No one could have said she was a raving beauty, but she was a

192

very pretty woman and he had once thought her stunning. As he took her in now, he felt something stirring within. He could tell she was experiencing something similar. 'But you're all right?'

'As can be. You?'

Henry shoved his left hand towards her and wiggled his third finger.

'I'd heard,' Jane said mutely. 'How is Mrs Christie? You could never let her go, could you?'

He said nothing, just swallowed.

Fortunately the chief's door opened at that point and Dave Anger stormed out of the office. Henry turned to see. Anger gave him a poisoned stare, didn't stop, just flew out of the door and, had a pneumatic arm not controlled it, he would no doubt have crashed it shut.

'Not a happy bunny,' Henry observed.

Jane regarded him knowingly. 'I wonder why?' she asked primly.

Taken aback, Henry stage-whispered, 'So it was something to do with me! I haven't shagged his wife recently. He just can't be mad at me.'

'Maybe not you directly.' She raised her eyebrows, then looked over to the open door of the chief's office, where the rotund boss of the constabulary leaned wearily against the door jamb.

'Henry – in here, please.' He pushed himself up, a tight look on his face, and disappeared into his inner sanctum.

'Have you come to terms with your ethical dilemma, Henry?' FB asked as he slid round his

193

desk, tugged up his shirt cuffs and sat down heavily on the luxuriously padded leather chair. Henry saw the Rolex on his wrists, thick and chunky, and felt that familiar pang of envy again.

'I've reached an impasse, I guess.'

'In that case, can we move on from it?'

'Sure.'

'By the way, I heard about the ruckus in Cyprus. You did a good job there. Need any counselling?'

'Nah.'

'Good – counselling's for nancies.'

And with a quick change of subject, FB said, 'What do you know about the shooting of Jonny Motta in Liverpool?'

Henry blinked, pouted and said, 'Only what bits I read in the newspapers, seen on Teletext ... thank God it wasn't one of our jobs.'

'Yeah, thank God,' FB agreed. 'So what *do* you know?'

Henry considered a moment. He did not know much, as he'd admitted because it had happened during his there-and-back and back-again trips to Cyprus. 'A police firearms operation gone wrong, in as much as a weapon was discharged and someone, a shady guy called Motta, got shot. Happened in Liverpool – well, in the Merseyside police area, because it was a job in Southport, actually. Motta was a low-life, very gang-related and supposedly wanted for a shooting in Liverpool city centre, I think. So he was known to carry firearms...' Henry plundered his poorly functioning brain. 'Police raided a multi-occupancy block of flats ... They enter Motta's flat, he jumps up with a gun in his hand, fails to heed a warning and takes two in the chest. Dead gangster, no boo-hoo. Sounds like a straight-up job. The cop who fired the gun looks pretty watertight by all accounts. It's certainly not a Jean Charles de Menezes shooting cock-up,' he said referring to the debacle that faced the Metropolitan Police after gunning down an innocent Brazilian in Stockwell tube station, 'and that's as much as I know.'

FB hadn't interrupted, but as Henry had spoken, he'd moved out of his big chair, silently indicated for Henry to sit himself down on one of the leather settees, then sat opposite him, crossing his chubby legs. In passing, Henry had noted another sign of FB's wealth – the loafers he wore with Gucci tassels. Henry didn't like loafers, so wasn't troubled by any pang of envy on that score. But they did look comfortable and very, very expensive. FB nodded while Henry went through his meagre background knowledge of the case, which had been in and out of the north-west headlines for a few weeks.

'You obviously know a bit.'

'A bit.'

FB sat back and displayed his broad stomach. Although not as large as the Fat Controller from the Thomas the Tank Engine series, Henry was reminded of him. All he needed was a hat and a flag ... but having said that, FB was a much more dangerous character.

'Why, boss?'

'Well, like you say, it seems a pretty open-and-

195

shut case, but the IPCC investigation has stalled.'

Henry waited. The IPCC was the independent body charged with investigating any complaints against or alleged wrongdoing by the police.

'The lead investigator went and got, er, killed in a road accident ... not, obviously, connected with the investigation, just a tragic accident and coincidence. So,' FB took a breath, 'the IPCC are after somebody to pick up the whole thing and run with it, tie it all up into a little bow and get it filed.' He smiled grimly. 'They've asked me.'

Someone, somewhere, holding a scythe and wearing a hood and cloak, stomped on Henry Christie's grave. The feeling barged through him like a lead weight in his veins. Suddenly his mouth was parched.

'Really, it's a bit of a nothing job, Henry. An important one, don't get me wrong, but it's just a tidying-up thingy,' he finished weakly.

Henry thought FB would never make a salesman.

'Do you fancy taking it on, H?' he asked with a nice smile, now. 'All the work's been done, more or less.'

Ahh, the shortening of the name to a single letter, that sign of intimate affection. Henry was often referred to as 'H' by mates. The Grim Reaper started doing a sand dance on his grave.

'Why me?'

'Fuckin' good question!' FB rolled upright. 'Because you're a very good, nay excellent, detective who also happens to be brilliant at

196

tying up loose ends and pulling complex files together. Why wouldn't I choose you?'

'In that case, why am I not on FMIT as an SIO? Or doing other detective work, SOCA, maybe?'

The chief steeped his stubby fingers in front of his chest, more like a grain silo than a church tower, and said, 'I think we've travelled down that road before.'

'OK, then – but why me?'

'Because you are a good detective and I'd like you to do it – isn't that enough? Oh, and,' he added, 'Dave Anger doesn't want you to do it. Thinks you're not capable. I told him to go to hell, defended you.'

Henry's visions of death were suddenly replaced by a warm glow of contentment.

'Again – it's probably something of a nothing job,' FB said apologetically. 'Just dotting I's and crossing T's.' Henry caught him giving a quick look that actually said, *This is much, much more.* It was an expression that crossed his face briefly, but Henry was really too far engrossed in the possibility of getting one over on Dave Anger to take in the meaning properly. That must have been the reason Anger had given Henry such a terrible look when he left FB's office a little earlier, and maybe the reason for the loud exchange everyone outside had heard.

'I'd love to do it,' Henry said.

FB flipped his left wrist around and checked the Rolex. 'Best get on to it, then.'

As much as he tried, Henry could not prevent

197

himself walking cockily back through the corridors. Suddenly his stature had grown – at least in his own mind – and this fuelled a rolling-shoulder, balls-of-the-feet gait, reminiscent of someone who might have won the lottery.

'Henry!'

He was on the ground-floor corridor, the narrow one which basically ran the whole length of the building, with one or two dog-legs in it. He had just passed the crossroads in the middle, turn right to go to the garage, left to the front exit, straight on to the Intelligence Unit, and the voice came from behind.

It was a sharp, barking noise, one he knew well.

He stopped sharply, hoping the smug, supercilious look adorning his face wasn't too extreme, as he turned to face the person who had called his name: Dave Anger, Detective Chief Superintendent, Head of FMIT – and Henry's recurring living nightmare.

'Dave!'

'Did you take it?'

Henry didn't feel like playing games by saying, 'Take what?' Instead he simply said yes, knowing exactly what Anger was talking about.

Anger stood there, a file under his arm, his hair cropped tightly to his skull, his national-health John Lennon-style spectacles making him look like a fully paid-up member of the secret police. His head nodded as he considered Henry's response.

'Thought you would. Did FB tell you I didn't want you to take it?'

'He alluded to it.'

'Did he tell you why?'

'Nope.'

'I'll tell you.' He pointed a warning finger. 'A job like that needs a delicate touch, some finesse, sensitive handling – and someone like you,' Anger stood in close to Henry, 'a bull in a fucking china shop, is not something that's needed.'

Someone walked behind them. Anger stepped back, his snarl turning into a bright smile.

Henry was puzzled for a moment. Then it dawned. 'What you mean, Dave, is that you don't want anyone upsetting your old chums in Merseyside.' He saw the quick, almost hidden flinch and knew he'd hit the spot. 'Why's that? Surely they won't have anything to hide, will they?'

The two men – who hated each other so much it almost devoured them from within with the virulence of Ebola – stared at each other, until Henry stepped back and grinned. 'In that case, I'll do my very, very best. Rest assured.'

Henry's cocksure walk turned into one of determination as he made his way to the Intelligence Unit and let himself in, brushing all thoughts of Dave Anger aside. He stopped at Jerry Tope's desk. The DC looked up, searched for something and handed Henry a piece of paper. It was the balance of the Operation Wanted budget, which Henry scanned quickly, not really taking it in, but seeing it had been depleted even further, mainly, he guessed, by the cost of the flights back and forth to Cyprus. Even so, it seemed to have gone down an awful lot more than it should, but he wouldn't be certain how much until he checked it against his receipts.

'Hey, guess what?' Henry said, glancing up from the numbers.

Tope drummed his fingers on the edge of his desk and pretended to think. 'Er, you're being transferred back on to FMIT ... Oh, sorry, pigs ain't got wings yet, have they?'

'Not even remotely amusing, Bung,' Henry said, emphasizing Tope's nickname. 'No, remember I said I'd take you along on my next jolly?'

Tope visibly brightened and sat upright, doing his puppy-dog impersonation again. 'The Australia job?'

Henry raised his eyebrows in half-confirmation of this.

Tope's mouth sagged in disbelief. 'Honest?'

'No, the nothing job, actually. How does Merseyside sound?'

Tope's whole body sagged in disbelief. 'You rotten git – sir.'

'Best I can do under the circumstances.' He flashed the budget printout and shook it. 'Not enough cash in the account to go halfway there, I'm afraid.'

Tope said, 'Yeah, something peculiar there...' His voice trailed off when his eyes caught the movement of someone being shown through the door into the Unit.

'I'm going to have to take a closer look at this,' Henry said, looking again at the printout,

200

but not noticing that Tope wasn't even looking at him any more. He, and everyone else in the long, narrow office, particularly the women, were watching the progress of a tall, well-built and extremely handsome, in a clean-cut sort of way, man as he walked towards Henry, who he stood behind. In a pleasing American accent, the man said, 'Someone in this office has been real naughty.'

The two men sat across the table from each other in the headquarters dining room.

'The problem for y'all, as I see it,' the American said, 'is that every day – *every day* – up to two million people attempt to hack into our computer system.'

Henry gave a low, appreciative whistle.

'Of that number, about six are successful. Our firewalls are two steps ahead of the state of the art.' He moved and winced as though he had a pain in his chest.

'Six out of two million. Pretty good protection.'

'Out of those six, maybe three get one step further before they're stopped and two get two steps further inside and one, maybe, gets through. These six people, who are not the same six every day, are serious hackers. Some professional, some terrorists, some amateurs trying their luck, just to show they can do it.'

Henry watched his American friend, Karl Donaldson, speak. He'd known him for a dozen or so years, having first met and become friends when Donaldson, then an FBI field agent, was investigating American Mob activity in the north of England. Since then their professional lives had crossed several times and they had become firm friends, although this friendship had been damaged fairly recently and had been repaired by a great deal of effort from both men. Donaldson was now an FBI legal attaché based in the US Embassy in London and he was married to an ex-Lancashire policewoman who now worked for the Met.

'Just recently, though, our firewall has been breached by a very gifted hacker,' Donaldson went on. 'One who had the opportunity to do a lot of snooping before being tracked and ejected by our IT guys. The hacker was so good our technicians decided to go after him. He was very, very clever, but they stayed with him and because he wasn't quite clever enough, we nailed him.'

'That's really good news, Karl – but why tell me?'

Donaldson reached inside his jacket, extracted a folded sheet of paper and opened it. 'Because the hacker is right here' – his index finger pointed down to the floor – 'in this building and this is the computer ID.' Donaldson gave the sheet to Henry. 'Thing is, pal,' he continued, 'the hacker looked at only one file and then extracted himself, followed by our posse. And that's the reason I'm here. There's been a lot of ass-twitching down in Grosvenor Square over this and some people down there want to make a big noise about it – but I've stopped all that shit for two reasons...' Henry waited. 'One, I want

202

to meet and congratulate him and two, I want to know why he was looking at a particular file.'

'You're saying your computer system was hacked into by someone working for Lancashire Constabulary?'

'That would be the assumption. To me, pal, the first step would be to find out where the computer is situated.'

'When you say "here",' Henry wanted confirmation, 'do you mean "here" as in this building, or on this campus or within the force?'

'My techs say this site.'

To Henry that meant the HQ building, the SOCA building, the training centre, the comms room and the ICT department. The latter seemed to be the logical starting point to trace the wrongdoer.

Henry reached over his shoulder and picked up the internal phone on the wall of the dining room. He dialled a number then asked for the internal number of a specific person in ICT, then redialled that.

'Bob, Henry Christie ... I wonder if you could do me a favour?' Henry then gave Bob the task then asked to him to call back on that extension. As he was talking, Donaldson was acquiring two more coffees from the machine.

'What can you tell me about the file the hacker looked at?' Henry asked.

'If I told you, I'd have to kill you.'

Henry tried to laugh that remark off, but a quiver of apprehension skittered through him. He suspected Donaldson of being much more than just a legal attaché. Much more. 'No, go on.'

'Because it's you and I trust you,' Donaldson relented. 'The file related to an American by the name of Corrigan...'

As good as Henry thought he was in covering up his body language or the look in his eye, there was no way he could cover up the effect this name had on him. Donaldson saw the twitches right away.

'A name that obviously means something to you,' Donaldson said.

Henry stood up. 'Come with me.'

As they left the dining room, the phone on the wall started ringing. Henry ignored it.

'Bugger,' Jerry Tope said. He, Henry and Karl Donaldson were sitting in the DI's office in the Intelligence Unit. Henry was behind the desk, the other two occupying the seats opposite. 'I knew I was being chased. I thought I'd shook the bastards off.'

'You almost did,' Donaldson said with a tinge of admiration, 'but you slipped up in a server in the Far East, apparently.'

'Hong Kong,' Tope said. 'Shit!' He looked pleadingly at Henry. 'Am I in it?'

Henry's eyes flicked to Donaldson. 'Over to you.'

Donaldson paused, adding to the tension, then ruefully said, 'Nah ... but you're on a major warning ... and if you ever try it again...'

Tope grinned. 'If I try it again, sir,' he said, 'with all due respect, you won't catch me next

204

time.'

'Jerry – don't annoy him, he might change his mind.'

Tope shrugged. 'I was only doing it for you, sir, anyway. On your orders.'

Henry's eyes momentarily flickered past the two men in front of him, out through the glass window of the office, into the Intel Unit. Two female admin assistants were in a girlie huddle, giggling and taking sneaky peeks into the office. Henry bridled. They were not trying to get a look at him, but at the big Yank, who was good looking beyond belief, something Henry openly despised him for. Henry leapt up and ripped the door open. 'Have you two got work to do, or not?' he demanded. The women shot him looks that could have nailed him to the wall before slinking back to their workstations. He closed the door, returned to his chair, muttering something.

'OK,' Donaldson said, 'let's cut to the penisbone here. Why, DC Tope, were you hacking into confidential FBI files? And why were you interested in Walter Corrigan?'

'I'm afraid only my boss can answer that one. I was just doing his bidding, as is my lot in life.'

Four eyes turned expectantly to the DCI.

Knowing he had nowhere to go with this now, he came clean. 'In a nutshell, this man's house was being used by a criminal on the run from the UK, a guy called Paulo Scartarelli, who was wanted for murder over here. He turned up in Cyprus and I went over to pick him up.'

'Without me,' bleated Tope.

'Without him ... The police in Cyprus had info he was using a villa owned by a guy called Corrigan, who they thought was English. They couldn't find anything about him on their systems, which is why I asked DC Tope to have a dig.' Henry paused, looked at Tope. 'And by the way, may I say you should get out more? You are a serious nerd, pal.'

Tope puffed up. 'Thanks,' he said genuinely.

Henry shook his head sadly and closed his eyes. He opened them and looked at Donaldson. 'Over to you. That's all I know. Scartarelli was arrested and that's pretty much the end of it as far as I'm concerned. Didn't really follow up the Corrigan angle.'

Donaldson sat back. 'Could you and I have a little chat?'

'He's Mob-funded.'

'That's why you're being so lenient with Tope?'

'It's worth it for us to back off, so long as you share information with us about Corrigan.'

'And if we don't?'

'I'll go back on my word. We'll go for Tope and Lancashire Constabulary.'

'We being the FBI?'

'Yup.'

'Won't go anywhere.'

'I know that, but it'll ruffle feathers and tighten assholes.'

'He was just doing what I required of him – getting information.'

'And he's so good, we're interested in having

206

him for a big fat fee.'

'Let's keep that on the back burner, shall we?'

'Out techies are very impressed with him.'

'He's mine, and I love him,' Henry said petulantly. 'Hands off.'

'Corrigan,' Donaldson said, bringing them back to the topic in question.

'Mob-funded, apparently.'

'Did you know there's more money to be made trafficking people across Europe than bringing Mexicans across the border to the US? That's a non-starter, these days. Old hat. Big business is over here. People, hookers and drugs. There's a big mind-shift by the Mob. They see easy profit and they're willing to chase it.'

'Corrigan?'

'He's an organizer and a good one. But I don't necessarily want him, I want what's behind him.'

'And what's behind him?'

'Miami, Atlanta, New York, Detroit and LA. The Tantini family. Big, brutal and very rich. They stop at nothing in the pursuit of wealth and won't leave any stone unturned to get to sources of wealth.'

'Somebody tried to kill Scartarelli, by the way.' Henry told him about the fun they'd had in trying to get the fugitive on board a plane.

Donaldson considered this. 'Interesting.'

'I nearly get my arse shot off and you call it interesting,' Henry said. 'Mm, anyway, that's all pretty much in the past for me. I did my job, Scartarelli's in custody and I have other plates to spin.'

Donaldson shrugged. 'Fair enough.'

'All we're interested in doing is getting him charged with murder.'

'I'd like to interview him.'

Henry stifled a terrified chortle. He was more than familiar with Donaldson's interview techniques and their effectiveness.

'All above board,' the American reassured him. 'Intelligence-gathering. Just doing my job.'

'I'll see what I can do.'

But Henry's mind wasn't on Scartarelli. As soon as he had finished with Donaldson, having arranged to see him later in a social setting, Henry's attention spun to his computer. He logged on to the Internet and typed the name Jonny Motta into Google and pressed Search. That was as far as his hacking skills went.

From the results he entered the BBC News website and scanned the items relating to the police shooting of this man. His brief recounting of his own knowledge of the incident to FB seemed to fit very well with what was written in the news reports.

Jonny Motta was a known gangster, an Italian with Albanian connections, who was supposedly involved in people-trafficking, particularly young women who would become prostitutes for him. He was known to be violent, carried weapons, and was suspected of carrying out a shooting in Liverpool where a man was callous-ly gunned down outside a club in the city centre. The man was supposedly one of Motta's rivals.

The police raid, organized by a detective

superintendent called Paul Shafer, seemed to have been executed by the book. It was only when Motta was challenged and responded by producing a handgun did he get two 9mm Glock bullets drilled into his chest. Every indication was that the firearms officer adhered to procedure, shouted several clear and unambiguous unheeded warnings and only then opened fire. The officer was now suspended from firearms duties as per normal procedure, but was carrying out an admin role in some back-room office somewhere. This suspension was pending the result of the investigation, inquest and any CPS recommendations, but it seemed that, from what Henry read, the officer had nothing to fear – except the thought that he'd killed a man and that would be with him for all his life.

He spent about an hour tabbing through a lot of fairly repetitive reports, then after checking for any news updates on the Rolling Stones he logged out and sat back.

Straight up, he thought ... then his brow furrowed as an image kicked into his brain. He logged back in, found a grainy image of Motta and felt as though he was vaguely familiar. Then again, maybe not. He logged out and sat back for a moment before picking up the internal phone and dialling the chief constable's number.

Jane Roscoe intercepted the call. 'Chief Constable's Staff Officer, Chief Inspector Roscoe ... can I help?'

'It's me, Henry.'

'Henry who?'

'Henry Christie.'

'Oh, hello. Can I help?'

'Can I speak to the chief, please?'

'About...?'

'The investigation he's asked me to do.'

'I'll see if he's free.' She sounded cold and distant. The phone clicked and MOR music started playing softly in his ear. Then she came back on the line. 'I'm afraid he's busy right now.'

'Can you ask him to give me a bell?'

'Will do – bye.' She hung up. No chit-chat.

Henry hung up slowly. Their relationship was well over and he had no desire to rekindle something that could have been terribly destructive. It was also a long time since he had had any contact with her, but he still felt annoyed that she had curtailed the call so abruptly. But who could blame her?

His thoughts were cut short by the phone ringing. This time it was his mobile, which had a Rolling Stones tune as a ring tone. Previously it had been 'Jumpin' Jack Flash', now it was 'Satisfaction' – that thing Henry didn't seem to get much of. The call was from a withheld number.

'Henry Christie.'

'DCI Christie? May I introduce myself? I'm Detective Superintendent Paul Shafer from Merseyside Police.'

For a second, Henry did not recognize the name – but then he remembered. He smiled when he said, 'Hello there, can I help you?'

Shafer sounded pleasant, youngish and efficient. 'Just thought I'd touch base with you. I

210

believe you're taking on the Motta shooting, just tying it up et cetera?'

Henry hesitated. 'I'm taking it over, yeah.'

'Well, I think you'll find it's pretty much done and dusted by the IPCC. I just want to say that we're waiting for your arrival and you can count on us to be as helpful and open as we can be, though there won't be much investigating for you to do. As I understand it, it's just a read-through and recommendations.'

'You know more than me, sir.'

'I should do.'

'Could I enquire how you found out I'd be taking over? I only found out myself a short while ago.'

Shafer chuckled amiably. 'Jungle drums.'

Henry's mouth tightened sardonically. His disquiet was that he immediately suspected Dave Anger to be the drummer in question – and how professional was that, to ring up his old mates and warn them of Henry's impending arrival?

'When can we expect to see you down here?'

'Day after tomorrow, I expect,' Henry lied. He'd planned for tomorrow but didn't feel inclined to share that with Shafer, pleasant as he might be.

'Look forward to meeting you in person.'

'You too.'

Henry didn't have time to consider the meaning of the phone call before the desk phone rang again.

'FB – you were after me, Henry,' came the brusque, no-shit voice Henry love-hated so well.

211

'Quick question – this shooting enquiry? Can I take a couple of people down with me?'

'Anyone you like.'

'And if I feel it necessary, can I start from scratch with it, or at the very least do some digging? I don't want to take everything at face value, you know me.'

'As far as I'm concerned you can do anything you want with it. If you're happy to close it down with what's already there, then OK; if you're not happy, dig away.'

'Just the news I wanted to hear.'

TWELVE

Although not technically a murder investigation (even if someone had been shot to death), as far as Henry was concerned he would be running the enquiry into Jonny Motta's demise as if he had been put in charge of one that hadn't been completed or solved. He believed it would be remiss of him not to be thorough and professional in his approach, make sure he didn't accept anything at face value and, basically, do the job FB expected of him as an SIO and maybe wind up Dave Anger into the bargain.

He decided that his approach would be to spend time reviewing the case as it stood, seeing if there were any obvious gaps that needed plugging and revisiting witnesses where necessary. In other words, do all the things he would have done on a genuine murder enquiry. He knew that by following the accepted model, the first stage being 'Think murder until the investigation proves otherwise' and sticking to the problem-solving formula of 'Why + When + Where + How = Who', he couldn't go too far wrong. He knew he had the 'Who' bit – the poor sod who'd pulled the trigger twice and was now working in an office somewhere – but unless the file showed that he had all the other bits, then there was still somewhere to go with the job.

The rain lashed across the River Mersey as the famous Liver Building came into sight and Henry negotiated his way across several lanes of traffic as he drove along Dock Road, Liverpool, and towards the Albert Dock, passing some of the great historic buildings that made the city famous.

Henry had not been to Liverpool all that often. Work had rarely taken him there, but he'd had occasional family jaunts and found the city vibrant and lively with a lot of attitude, mostly positive.

He was driving a Ford Mondeo from the police pool. He glanced to his left and then over his shoulder at the two people in the car with him – his team.

'So that's the plan, guys. Any gaps in it you can see?' he asked. 'Jerry? Bill?'

Jerry Tope shrugged indifferently. 'Sounds OK to me.'

In the back seat, Bill Robbins also shrugged, too. 'Whatever.'

Henry shook his head in disbelief at the hot enthusiasm of his crack investigative team. Bill had been brought along for his firearms experience and Jerry for his attention to detail, both of which would be crucial if this job was to be done right.

He reached the dual carriageway alongside Albert Dock, opposite which was Merseyside Police headquarters. Rather than trying to get a space in the small car park there, he turned in to the large one next to the dock and paid for a day

214

instead.

The three of them trudged across and entered the building. It was nothing fancier than an office block, nothing special other than the signs singling it out as police premises.

They couldn't get any further than the reception desk, where they signed in and were given visitors' badges, then were told to wait and someone would come to collect them.

Bill looked extremely bored. He preferred being on a shooting range or part of a team bursting into houses, brandishing weapons and trying not to shoot innocent members of the public. The thought of checking statements appalled him, but at least it was another jolly and saved him from having to go out and patrol a division.

Jerry Tope hummed and tapped his fingers on his laptop. He actually liked reading statements and analysing data in whatever form. He was eager to get going, although he was still annoyed about not being able to go to Cyprus.

Henry paced the foyer, his mind clicking over, wondering what lay in store for his band of merry men.

A young crew-cutted man strode through the security doors. He was expensively suited and booted, an air of efficiency surrounding him. Henry came upright, alert and pegged him instantly.

'DCI Christie?'

Henry extended his hand. 'You must be Detective Superintendent Shafer?'

They shook. Henry turned to his mini-team

215

and quickly introduced them. Shafer's sharp grey eyes took them in and assessed them, as they had done Henry – and found he did not like what he saw, particularly in Henry's case. He beckoned them to follow him, and using his fingerprint and number combination on the key-pad opened the big glass doors leading into the HQ building. Uncharitably, Henry thought they were stepping into the lions' den.

Shafer herded them into the lift.

'A day early,' Shafer said, looking down his nose at Henry. 'I was expecting something like this,' he smirked as the doors hissed shut and the lift jerked upwards. 'Henry Christie,' he said, 'we meet at last. Your reputation precedes you.'

Henry narrowed his eyes suspiciously and like Clint Eastwood once said in a film he could not recall the title of, said, 'What reputation is that?' Henry was sure that Eastwood had received a reply that summed up his hard-boiled, flawed character, but Shafer wasn't playing the game. Instead he just shook his head and continued smirking, sending a shiver of annoyance through Henry's backbone. He already wanted to swipe it off his face.

As the lift jolted to a halt on floor eight, and before the doors opened, Shafer answered, 'Nothing to write home about,' then, his timing perfect, he stepped out of the lift into the cor-ridor before Henry could collar him and demand to know exactly what he meant. He glanced quickly at Bill and Tope and they dropped their eyes quickly, embarrassed for him.

'This way,' Shafer said brightly.

216

Henry gritted his teeth, already seething, his nostrils flaring so widely he could have fitted king marbles up them.

They followed the brisk be-suited superintendent along the corridor, left-turned and stopped outside a door which had no markings or number on it. Shafer produced a key and slid it into the lock.

'This is the office we provided for the IPCC to conduct their investigation. They've also got a small room at Southport nick, Southport being where the incident took place, as you'll know,' Shafer explained, unlocked the door and pushed it open.

'Ahh, the broom cupboard,' Henry said glancing into the tiny, dim office which seemed to have no natural light coming into it. Inside two small desks were crammed in, back to back, and three plastic chairs.

'Office space is always at a premium,' Shafer said. He stepped in, then let Henry and his team filter past him. Henry appraised the room and found it wanting. There was a half-sized filing cabinet which looked as though it could have been jemmied open at some time in its life, and nothing else other than a Formica-topped table tucked in one corner. There was a kettle, two mugs and some milk in a bottle on this table. By its looks, the milk could have already become cheese.

A box file sat on the back-to-back desks.

'This is where the IPCC investigator worked from and that's his stuff.' Shafer indicated the box. 'Everything he collected is in here. And this is his key – the only one for the room, apart from the master.' He handed the key with which he'd opened the door to Henry. 'OK? I'm sure you'll want to get started.' He turned away.

Henry screwed his nose up. 'There's a big list of things we'll need, actually.'

This stopped Shafer. 'Why would that be? I understand that your task is simply to...'

'Dot and cross?'

'Exactly ... shouldn't take too much. Not, you understand, that we won't be as helpful as possible.'

'It's just basic things,' he said, pleasantly enough, not wanting to get off too far on the wrong foot. Although he wanted to spell out what he saw his task as being, he could imagine how vulnerable the force would be feeling and then to get a snotty detective to come along from another force and start nosing around again did not help matters. He glanced at the room and saw computer access points. 'It'd be useful to get a computer in here, for example,' he said innocently with a deprecatory shrug. 'We'll need ease of access to the building, to know where we can photocopy stuff ... that sort of thing.'

Shafer looked slightly relieved. 'I can get those things sorted.'

Henry went on, 'But I will have to go through everything, you can understand that.' He pointed at the box file on the desks. 'Then take it from there. May even need to interview or re-interview people again.'

'Yeah, sure.'

'And try to live up to my reputation,' he added

slyly, his face set, his eyes levelling with Shafer's. They locked, then broke.

Shafer handed Henry a business card with his internal phone number on it. 'I'll let you get settled.'

He spun on his shiny heels and left the office.

The three Lancashire officers watched him go, remained silent for a few moments, then Bill said, 'Don't know about you guys, but I've got a bad feeling about this already.' He shivered.

'Yeah, me too,' Tope said. 'Didn't like him.'

'At the end of the day,' Henry said magnanimously, 'we are investigating them and they will feel just a bit jittery. Understandable. However,' he levelled his gaze at Bill and dangled the office key in front of him, 'nip into the city centre, will you, and buy a padlock and an electric screwdriver from a hardware shop. I think we'll take the unilateral decision of putting our own security on the door. I'll lay odds there's more than one key circulating and I'd like to keep our little room to ourselves. Some coffee, milk and another mug might not go amiss either...'

'And biscuits,' Tope said.

'Can you manage that?' Henry asked Bill.

'I'm the gofer?'

'If the cap fits.'

'Short simple steps,' Henry explained. He now had a mug of cheap coffee in his hands which tasted like treacle, but had a kick like a mule. He was feeling refreshed and ready to rock and roll. 'Let's take this whole thing from start to finish.

219

To me that means going back to the shooting Motta was supposed to have committed, then through all the intelligence-gathering after that up to the point where Motta was pinpointed as a suspect and then located. An operational order must have been drawn up for the armed arrest. Then we go through everything relating to the raid and the shooting. See how it all flows. I know there's gaps, but we'll fill 'em as we go along.'

'Shall I just fix doors and coffee,' Bill asked.

Henry fixed him with a contemptuous stare, then turned his attention to the box file that should contain all the things Henry had just described. He opened the lid for the first time and said, 'Dig in, chaps.'

It was a long, tedious, caffeine-fuelled day, as once they sat down to their task they diligently worked their way through the file. It was an orderly and well-put-together piece of work. The IPCC investigator had been assisted by members of the West Midlands Police who had, seemingly, professionally investigated, interviewed and made recommendations.

On the face of it, Henry could see very little wrong with what had been done.

Based on what he read, the story of Jonny Motta and his demise was one of those unfortunate but inevitable incidents and if the police hadn't pulled the trigger, then it was quite likely that someone else would have done so, sooner rather than later.

There wasn't much background on Motta, but

it seemed he had been a fairly low-level hood in Italy, then Amsterdam, where he was suspected of pimping and running brothels; then he turned up in Merseyside and tried to muscle in on some nefarious but established criminal operations in the city. These included illegal immigrants, drugs and gang-mastering. There was some hint he had been involved with the gangmasters who ran the Chinese cockle-pickers who tragically died in Morecambe Bay. Motta got involved in arguments and fights, and was eventually suspected of killing a guy whose business interests he'd tried to move in on.

The murder enquiry, run by Paul Shafer, pinpointed him as the prime suspect and an arrest operation was pulled together. When his flat was raided, he pulled a gun and was shot dead for his trouble by a firearms officer because he didn't put it down when requested. It was one of those split-second decisions, yet it seemed the officer had acted lawfully and reasonably in the circumstances.

There would be no prosecution.

The officer would get his old job back.

A bad man had been taken off the streets.

And all was right with the world of policing in Liverpool.

'Observations?' Henry asked at last.

It was 4 p.m.

Bill stretched and yawned.

'Bill? Firearms perspective?'

'Looks sound. Good risk assessment on the operational order. Well-briefed team. Looks as if the officer did everything right and reacted

221

according to the situation.'

'Thanks, Bill. Jerry, your take?'

Tope nodded. 'Looks fine to me, too. The work's been done for us here, I'd say.'

'Huh hum,' Henry guggled as Tope spoke. 'Yep, yep ... cut and dried ... not many witnesses, though.'

'There wouldn't necessarily be many on a job like that,' Bill said. 'Multi-occupancy flats, early-morning raid silently done. Most folk wouldn't even be awake.'

'True,' Henry conceded. He ran his fingers over the stack of statements in front of him, let his mind do some wandering. 'It would be nice to have a couple more independents, though. This is all very police-heavy. However...' He winced.

'I wonder where all the photos are?' Tope said. 'Crime scene, dead body, all that sort of stuff. There's nothing in here like that. Is that odd?'

'Good point. Let's ask to see them. Should be available ... OK!' Henry clapped his hands and made them jump. 'From what we've read it's all pretty done and dusted? Agreed?'

His team regarded him as though he was losing his mind. He allowed himself a grin. 'Good – I'm glad we're on the same wavelength, guys. We start from scratch and work through it, because that's the only way I'll be satisfied that all bases are covered.'

They both nodded.

'In that case we do what we're best at. Jerry, the intelligence side, Bill, you make more coffee ... only joking. Honest!' he said in reply to Bill's warning look. 'You need to pay the firearms team a visit and start chatting about the guy who pulled the trigger. Look at his record, all that sort of stuff. I'll leave that with you. Jerry – intelligence and statements. Once we get logged into their computer system, will you be able to access their intelligence files?'

'I should think so.'

'Do that and dig up anything related to Motta ... you know the score.'

'And what will you be doing, boss?' Bill asked.

'Just messing about. I'm the boss, I delegate while you plebs do the work. Now, about that coffee, Bill...'

Henry called it a day at 6.30 p.m. After securing the office door with the padlock that Bill had bought in town, the three of them piled gratefully into the Mondeo in the Albert Dock car park. Henry asked Tope to drive and he sat in the back, Bill being up front with Tope. He tilted his head back and closed his eyes. But he didn't sleep. He found himself thinking through the day.

Suddenly, he shot forward.

'You two guys in a rush to get home?'

'To my wife and kids? Hardly,' Bill said.

'Jerry?'

'So-so ... going out for a pint with Dave Rooney and his missus. Why?'

'Something's bothering me, just a nagging up here.' Henry touched his forehead. 'How do you fancy having a look at a gunshot victim?'

'I'd rather have a pizza,' Bill chirped.

'I'll treat you to one later,' Henry promised.

Instead of taking the A59 which would have taken them back up to Preston, Jerry slotted on to the A565 and headed out towards Southport. To keep her happy, Henry gave Kate a ring on his mobile to say he'd be late, then sat back again and sighed deeply, pleased with himself at having done his duty by her. By the time they reached the outskirts of Southport he was so drowsy he almost regretted the diversion. He pulled himself together and stretched, slapping the back of Bill's head because he had nodded off.

'The mortuary is at Southport General. Just follow the signs,' Henry told Tope.

'OK.'

Ten minutes later they were following a hospital porter down a long corridor. The porter was a lucky find because he was manoeuvring a gurney with a black body bag on it containing a dead patient for sliding into a fridge.

'Fourth one today,' he moaned. 'Must be a bug going round. Dropping like flies.'

'Remind me not to get ill here,' Henry said, looking worriedly at the other two.

'I think they came in with it,' the porter said defensively, virtually ramming the trolley through a set of double doors and into the hospital mortuary that was on the lower ground floor, often called a basement. The walls were lined with body fridges, most of which had labels on their doors. The place almost had a 100 per cent attendance.

'You need him,' the porter said. He pointed to a man sitting in an office to their right. Rock music blared from a CD player and Henry recognized the group as the Cure, ironic based on the fact he was standing in a place where people came who were beyond a cure. Henry thanked the porter and leaned against the office door. He flashed his warrant card.

The mortuary attendant had sleepy eyes, crooked teeth and skin so pale and waxy under the artificial light he looked like a moving cadaver.

'Help ya?' he asked dreamily.

'I want to have a look at a body you have stored here.'

'Got loadsa bodies stored here.'

'How many have two bullet holes in them?'

The sleepy eyes opened a little more. Henry saw how bloodshot they were. 'Ah, that one.' He rocked up on to his feet, surprising Henry with his height – or lack of it. He was about five feet tall, but when seated looked average. Obviously an optical illusion. 'Follow me.'

Without checking Henry's ID properly, or asking to see Tope's or Bill's, he led the three officers down the mortuary, nodding at the porter, who was leaving after having put the latest visitor in the fridge.

The fridge doors were stacked four high and there were thirty rows of them and the body they wished to inspect was down at the far end, two up from the floor.

'These are our longer-term residents down

here,' the attendant said. 'The ones without homes to go to. Two tramps, someone who died in hospital we haven't ID'd yet and your chappy.' He grinned. 'Old mates.'

'You need another hobby – seriously,' Bill said, bringing a broken-toothed laugh from the man.

'I'm dating one of the tramps. She's a lovely lady, tangoes like a Latino once she defrosts.' He pulled the lever down on the door and opened it. A blast of icy air gushed out. 'Why d'you want to see this guy?'

'Morbid curiosity,' Henry said.

'I can go with that,' the attendant said. He slid out the tray on which lay the muslin-covered body of Jonny Motta.

The three cops took up positions from which they could see the body clearly and, like a magician revealing his latest trick, the attendant folded back the material.

Everyone remained silent, until, inevitably, Bill had to say something: 'Good shooting.'

Henry raised his eyebrows at him and though he didn't agree verbally he did so mentally. Despite the post-mortem mess in which the body was, sewn up with no finesse whatsoever, the two places where the bullets had entered the body were still clear to see – grouped side by side over the heart.

'Great shooting under stress,' Bill added.

He would have been dead before hitting the floor of his flat.

Jerry Tope gasped. He had managed to keep it in, but the sight of the murdered man got to him

226

and he staggered drunkenly away, then out of the mortuary doors, groaning and retching.

The body wasn't a very nice sight, but Henry had seen much worse in his time. In fact Jonny Motta looked in pretty good condition to say he'd been shot to death and kept in a fridge for a few weeks.

'Good double-tap, that,' Bill said admiringly again.

'OK, thanks for that.' Henry now looked at Motta's face, twisting his own head so he could inspect it from a variety of angles. Motta had been a good-looking man, that was plain. Dark eyes, a hooked but imperious nose ... and there was something about him he couldn't quite figure. The problem was that during the course of the post-mortem, Motta's scalp had been pulled down over his face like a balaclava so that the top of his skull could be removed and his brain inspected. Standard procedure in all PMs. But when the skin had been pulled back into place it hadn't been stitched with as much tension as originally and the features had sagged slightly.

'Can I borrow a pair of latex gloves?' Henry asked the mortuary attendant.

The man came back a minute later from his office, handing Henry a pair which he slid on, then twiddled his fingers.

Bill and the mortuary attendant watched with interest as Henry leaned over Motta's body, placed his thumbs on the hairline on either side of the head and eased the skin upwards, pulling it tighter over the skull and redefining the

227

features, even if the mouth became a sickly grin which dribbled with something disgusting.

Henry kept his thumbs in place, reared back slightly with his head to get a better view of the face, angling his head again, squinting at Motta.

Then he looked carefully at Motta's neck and right arm and muttered, 'Mm – recognize him, Bill?'

Bill shrugged. 'Should I?'

'Go get Jerry, will you?'

Bill retreated from the mortuary and found Tope in the corridor, bent double, hands on knees, whiter than a shade of pale. He looked nauseous in the extreme.

'Never been good with dead bodies,' he admitted to Bill, wiping flecks of spittle from the corners of his mouth and sucking in.

'Then I don't have good news for you. Boss wants you back to have a gander at Motta. He's given him a facelift.'

'Oh God, I'd rather be searching a database.'

'Sorry, pal.' Bill slapped him hard between the shoulder blades. 'Needs must.'

Tope took a deep breath and pulled himself together, brushed his trousers down and re-entered the mortuary with the unwillingness of a pupil entering a headmaster's study for a sound thrashing.

He averted his eyes all the way, keeping them firmly on a blemish in the paint on the wall behind Henry.

'Do I have to do this, boss?' he bleated. He dropped his eyes a few degrees and looked directly at Henry, over the body.

228

The DCI frowned, but refrained from making the remark he really wanted to make and instead said, with as much genuine empathy as possible, 'Just look at the fucker, will you?'

Jerry swallowed something wedged at the back of his throat, then cast his eyes downwards, trying to control his breathing and not vomit.

'Recognize him?'

'No,' he said quickly and looked away.

'Take a proper fucking look,' Henry said, getting angry.

Tope bit his bottom lip, steeled himself and looked at Jonny Motta's face, which was still being manipulated to look as natural as possible by Henry's thumbs.

'Not sure.'

'Keep looking. I know you've been doing a bit on that double murder in Preston ... what d'you think?'

'Bloody hell – yeah!'

'Go on,' Henry encouraged him.

'Spitting image of the guy caught on the CCTV tape.'

Bill butted in. 'You mean that murder you turned out to? The one where you drove around with the body in the boot?'

'The very one,' Henry confirmed with a cold stare. 'A mistake anyone could have made.' He turned his attention back to Jerry Tope, who seemed to have forgotten his adverse reaction to dead bodies and was now looking at Motta's face from all angles as Henry held the skin tight.

'Looks like the guy on the CCTV,' he said. 'Not a hundred per cent certain, though, but he

229

isn't far off.'

'It is him,' Henry said.

'How can you be sure?'

'Well,' Henry began and released Motta's skin. His face suddenly slid gruesomely downwards like some horror-movie special effect. His face distorted and Jerry Tope was once again reminded of exactly what he was looking at.

'Oh, Jeez,' he cried, and spun away from the table, unable to contain his sickness any more. He hurled the contents of his stomach across the tiled mortuary floor, splattering vomit up the wall.

Tope was given a mop and bucket, floor cleaner and disinfectant. He diligently slopped up his mess, an activity that made him feel even more ill until the majority of it had been wiped up and was in the bucket. Some colour seeped back into his cheeks as he sprayed the area with bleach and water.

Henry watched him dispassionately and without much interest, his mouth pursed and his bum very much mirroring that shape, twitching to a beat as his mind whirred.

Perhaps he was just being picky, but he could not for the life of him work out how Jonny Motta could not be identified as the murderer of two poor girls in Preston city centre.

Unless, of course, he was completely wrong, which wouldn't be a first. Maybe the two forces had liaised and Motta had been discounted as a suspect despite the similarity of appearance.

Henry's main problem was that he was now

230

out of the detective grapevine and could not keep abreast of what was going on in investigations any more. That sort of thing happened when the head of FMIT cut you out – not many other people wanted to spend a lot of time with you, either, lest they received the same fate.

He needed to find out – because he was certain of one thing: the man in the fridge was the same man he had come to blows with in a back alley in Preston and had escaped his clutches.

'Finished.' Tope rose creakily from the vomit-clearing task and shoved the mop into the bucket with a squelch.

'It is clean?' Bill asked patronizingly. He'd been watching Tope without helping.

Tope shook his head and brushed past. Henry followed the two of them out of the mortuary, giving a nod and a wave of thanks to the mortuary attendant, who had retreated to his office. He was now playing a song by Doctor and the Medics. It seemed he had a self-burned CD with tracks on it that were in some way related to the world of medicine and death.

In the car Henry suddenly felt drowned by weakness. He gave Tope, now fully recovered from his bout of illness, the instruction to get back to headquarters and not to spare the horses. Henry wanted to get home, sink a couple of JDs and then collapse into bed with Kate.

As the three officers sauntered out through the hospital, neither noticed the diminutive figure of the mortuary attendant tiptoeing after them. He opened double doors quietly, peeked down corridors, seeing the three cops turning right at the far end of another corridor in the direction of the exit. He followed silently, his shoes making no sound on the polished surfaces. He managed to follow them out of the hospital and watched them struggle to find the change to pay at the pay station, then walk across to where their car was parked.

Happy they'd gone, he came back inside and sauntered up to the reception desk, where he used the phone.

'It's me ... You said you wanted to know if anyone came to see Motta ... Well, someone did ... Three of 'em ... Cops, yeah ... Don't know, I was casual about it, didn't want to freak 'em out ... Only one ... The guy was a DCI ... Yeah, I'm sure ... Positive ... His name was Christie, Henry Christie.'

THIRTEEN

Henry had a restless night, more through the intake of too much Jack Daniel's than anything else. He never really slept well after too much alcohol, but often kidded himself he did. And though he was feeling pretty wrecked, he rolled out of bed at seven, fixed the shower, because for some unfathomable reason Kate had unscrewed the shower head from the pipe, and was on the road by seven thirty, still damp.

He'd arranged to meet the 'A' Team at headquarters at nine, when they would decide on the plan of the day before shooting down to Merseyside.

There was something he wanted to do before actually going into headquarters, hence the early start.

He took the A563 from Blackpool to Preston and pulled up at the new police operating centre in the city just before eight. This was where the investigation was being run into the deaths of the two women who'd been stabbed to death by – he now believed – Jonny Motta.

The Major Incident Room was strangely quiet. In fact, as Henry peered through the glass panel in the door, it was deserted. He checked his watch to make sure the clocks hadn't gone

233

backwards or something. To say the least, he was surprised verging on shocked to find the room wasn't buzzing with activity. For a double murder, unsolved as far as he knew, he would have expected to have had to push his way through a throng of cynical but eager detectives.

He tried the door and found it locked. With a 'Harumph' of annoyance he spun on his heels to find a key, returning a few minutes later with a cleaner who was grumbling about having orders to let no one in other than DCI Carradine, the SIO, who would then decide who came in after him.

'I'm really not supposed—' the cleaner began in protest.

'Open the door,' Henry said flatly. Then added, 'Please.'

With a sigh she did as bid and allowed Henry access. He ran the side of his hand down the bank of switches and the fluorescent lights clicked and hummed on reluctantly.

Henry walked slowly around the room.

The walls were plastered with charts, which he fully expected to see, but nothing else. No photos of the deceased and none of the suspect caught on camera which, again, he found odd. Unless of course the offender had been caught and he didn't know anything about it, or the enquiry was being scaled down and he didn't know about that, either.

His hands were thrust into his pockets, his face screwed up in a puzzled way.

Behind him the door of the MIR opened.

He turned.

Jack Carradine entered and was immediately on the offensive.

'What're you doing in here?'

Henry pouted, unfazed. 'Just bobbed in to see how things were progressing. Y'know – showing some interest.'

Carradine said, 'Attention unwelcome ... you're not on this investigation and only I have access to this room, so you shouldn't even be in here.'

'Actually it's a bit more than passing interest,' Henry said.

Carradine posed with disbelief. 'What?'

'A line of enquiry for you.'

'Wouldn't be anything to do with Jonny Motta, would it?' he sneered.

'Actually, yes,' Henry said dubiously.

Carradine gave a snort of derision. 'He's not the man.'

'But he...'

'Looks like the guy in the CCTV, admittedly,' Carradine finished the sentence for him, 'but it's not him, trust me.'

'OK, no probs,' Henry said. 'Still, do you have any photos of him I could have?'

'Why?'

'Just humour me. OK?'

'Henry, the world has been humouring you for too long. I don't have any stills and if I had you wouldn't be having one. I expect you to accept my word that the Merseyside connection has been checked out thoroughly and there is no connection.'

'So how's the enquiry going?'

235

'It's a tough one. The victims haven't even been properly identified yet. Maybe when that's done, we'll take a major leap forwards. Y'know, find out how they lived, find out how they died?'

'Any leads at all?'

'Possibly Albanian prostitutes plying their trade up here. OK?' he concluded shortly.

'Right, OK, fine,' Henry said. 'Just trying to help out.'

Carradine's face softened, but not genuinely. 'Appreciate it. Honestly. Sorry I was a bit – terse – pressure and all that.'

'Whatever,' Henry said.

'You back down to Merseyside today?' Carradine said conversationally.

'Yeah – ruffle some feathers,' Henry said maliciously and watched the shadow cross Carradine's face which he wasn't sure how to interpret. 'You were in Merseyside once, weren't you?'

'Briefly, years ago.' It was a dubious answer.

'Probably meet some of your old mates, then. D'you keep in touch?'

Carradine's mouth twisted into a cruel grin. 'Henry, they'll chew you up and then spit you out.'

'Guess I'll just stick to the bottom of their feet, then.' He gave Carradine a short nod and made to leave the MIR. At the door, he stopped and turned. 'One thing, though.'

'And what would that be, Henry?'

'Jonny Motta *is* the guy I chased on the night of that double murder.'

'And how can you be sure of that?'

236

Henry's eyes narrowed. 'He just is, and I know it.'

He went out of the room, and on the corridor outside he picked up pace and by the time he left the operating centre he was almost doing the four-minute mile as he legged the two hundred or so metres to the multi-storey building which was once the main police station in Preston.

His swipe card still allowed him access to the basement garage. He ran past the closed, locked and inaccessible cell complex, jumped in the lift and took it up to the floor on which the CCTV room was situated, the one he'd visited the night he'd turned out for the girl's murder.

And, with shift rotas being what they are, and it being such a small world, he found the same wheelchair-bound CCTV operator on duty, the one with whom he'd had a major fallout for her lack of vigilance. As he pushed through the door, breathless, she looked up from the screens, saw him and her face dropped even further than the one on Jonny Motta's corpse.

Because Henry wanted her on his side, he gave her one of his world-famous lopsided grins that he egotistically believed was one of his greatest keys to a woman's heart. However, this particular wheelchair-bound lady did not seem too impressed. He perched the corner of his bum on the desk in front of her and said, 'Hi.'

She gave him a curt nod. Today, it seemed, he wasn't faring too well in the popularity stakes.

'Can I help you?' she asked.

'Remember our meeting a few weeks ago?'

'How could I forget?' She sounded hurt.

'Good ... could I get a copy of said CCTV tape on a disc, please? The bit with the man.' He didn't add, 'The man you neglected to see,' because it might not have been helpful in furthering his cause. But he did add, 'Please,' because even if he wasn't Mr Popular, he was always polite.

'The DCI running the murder has a copy.' She didn't look at Henry as she spoke, but kept her eyes glued to her monitors giving her pigeon's-eye views of the city.

'I'd like a copy, too, please.'

'I'm afraid I can't do that. I've been told I can't release any more copies to anyone without that DCI's authority.'

Henry digested this. 'I'd really like you to get me a copy,' he insisted.

'Sorry, can't.' This time her eyes rose to his, defiantly, triumphantly, mockingly. I must really have upset her, he thought.

'It's not an option,' he told her. 'I want a copy.' He smiled dangerously. 'Because it's more than your job's worth to refuse to do it.'

'I'll sue you for disability discrimination,' she warned him. 'You'll be at an employment tribunal before you know it.'

Henry leaned forward so his face was on a level with hers. He recalled reading somewhere that it was always good practice to get down on to their level. 'And I'll get you fuckin' sacked. I don't have time to arse about, young lady.'

The woman's face set hard and it was clear that the cogs were churning in her mind. Was he bluffing? Was he full of bull? Did he mean it?

238

Did he have the power?

'You've already made one faux pas and got away with it,' he said, adding on the pressure he didn't really want to. 'So just do it.' His eyebrows raised and lowered quickly.

'My relief comes in at eight thirty. I'll do it then,' she caved in, not realizing that Henry *was* actually bluffing and *was* full of BS. 'I wouldn't want to leave the place untended, would I?'

But what really was bothering Henry was why Carradine had stopped anyone else getting hold of a copy of the tape. It wasn't as though any evidence could be contaminated because the original should be stored safe and sound in the system somewhere and if it came to court proceedings, then that original would be produced, not copies.

'I'll get a coffee and come back in twenty minutes,' Henry told her. 'Then we can be friends.'

'I don't understand it,' she said worriedly, almost verging on hysteria. Henry's face was now granite.

'Explain,' he snapped.

'I checked the hard drive storage to run a copy off for you and it wasn't there.'

Henry could easily have barked, 'It wasn't there! What do you mean, it wasn't there?' It's what he wanted to do and would have made him feel good – i.e. blowing his stack. Instead, with a furrowed brow he said, 'Does that mean it's been wiped clean or something?'

She looked helpless, 'I guess so.'

'And is that the whole of that particular tape,

or just the section I want to see?'

'It's the file with the bit you want in it. Each file is four hours long, running from midnight onwards. The four hours after midnight on that night aren't there.'

'Who sets up the files?'

'The computer.'

'Does it also back up automatically?'

She nodded.

'So there's a chance there is a backup file. Can you access that and give me a copy from that?'

She neither nodded nor replied.

He said, 'You can't, can you? Because the backup tape's not there, is it?'

'No,' she squeaked.

'Who has access to these files, these computers?'

'Us, the operators, our supervisors and if the police want to see them, they can and we do the copies for evidence if necessary.'

'And you're sure DCI Carradine has a copy of the incident?'

'Yes. I did it for him.'

'Thank you.' Henry stood up, then turned back. 'You must not tell anyone that I've been here this morning and found this out, OK?' He smiled. 'Our little secret – for the time being.'

After briefing his team at headquarters and arranging a pool car for each of them, they went their separate ways on their allotted tasks. Henry, deciding to claim mileage for his own car, went to Liverpool in it.

Before setting off, though, he popped along to

the accounts department and checked how much money was remaining in the Operation Wanted fund. He managed to speak to Madeline about this and after some flirting, she told him the news: three hundred and twenty pounds. Not enough to get even halfway to Australia, even by bike, should he have decided it was necessary to recapture the third felon on his wanted list.

He mentioned about being disappointed that he'd probably never get to Australia and she blurted, 'I'm going to Florida with John in a month. Disney and Key West. Taking the kids – his two from a previous marriage. Three weeks, sun, sea and scary rides and swimming with dolphins.'

'Phew – that'll cost a packet.'

'Yeah,' she smiled, 'but it's worth it.'

Henry told her he hoped she had a good time, then bade farewell, walking out of the HQ building via the garage at the rear in which the chief officers were allowed to park their vehicles. He could not help but notice the top-of-the-range Jaguar parked in the chief constable's slot. He knew it was definitely the chief's because it was displaying FB's personalized number, which he'd had for a few years. Shaking his head with envy – everybody seemed to be spending money like water, except him – he walked out to his second-hand Rover 75. Squinting at it, and with a bit of imagination, it could look like a Jag, but the truth was it was a rubbish car and he regretted trading in his Mondeo for it, God rest its soul. He wished he'd bought another Ford instead.

A minute later he was on the A59, heading towards Merseyside.

He'd fixed up a swipe card and fingerprint ID to get into their headquarters and breezed in as though he'd been working there for years: Henry Christie, Merseyside DCI. No one gave him a second glance as he stepped into the lift and then stepped out on to the floor where his tiny office was situated.

When he reached the door he almost burst into laughter.

The door was open. It had been smashed open and the lock that Bill Robbins had fitted had been jemmied off with a crowbar, from the looks of the marks on the door jamb. The door itself was virtually hanging off its hinges.

Henry fought the hysteria and stood on the threshold looking at the devastation within.

The office had been on fire and the place was a blackened, burned shell and quite obviously the files that had been left locked and secure in the office had been destroyed.

He took a step inside. The smell of smoke hung and clung.

There was a noise behind him. It was Detective Superintendent Shafer, who said, 'You're in for a bollocking, Henry.'

'Why would that be?'

'Almost burning down Merseyside Police Headquarters – or at least almost ensuring that it almost burned down by affixing an unauthorized lock to the door, thereby delaying entry into the office by several minutes, several vital minutes when the fire alarm went off. If access had been

242

immediate there would have been less damage to the room and, quite possibly, your precious files could have been saved. As it is...' he shrugged, 'they haven't.'

'How did it start?'

'A faulty socket where the kettle was plugged in, we think.'

Henry turned back to the room, his jaw doing its crunchy rotation.

'Staff were able to force an entry – eventually – and using a hose, stopped the fire spreading.'

'Did the Fire Service attend?'

'Not necessary.'

Henry's eyes tried to pinpoint the source of the fire. He'd been to enough arsons to have some idea what he was looking for.

'This is bollocks,' he said, treading carefully into the office and, taking care not to disturb anything, he peered closely at the offending plug socket and kettle. To him, both seemed pretty unscathed. He sighed, said nothing and looked at the box file on the desks containing the investigation into the shooting of Jonny Motta. He blinked. The fire had destroyed it easily. It was just a charred mess of brittle, black paper.

'Bit of a setback, eh?'

Henry screwed up his nose. 'These were just copies,' he said. 'We have the originals up at Hutton. Seemed like a common-sense thing to do, copy the whole lot.' He looked daringly at Shafer, who tried his best not to respond visually or verbally in any way, but Henry could almost imagine steam coming out of the man's ears, especially when he said, 'But it wouldn't matter one way or the other, because we'd decided to start the investigation from scratch anyway.'

There was nothing to salvage from the room and a few minutes later Henry left the building, having been warned to expect more than a telling-off for adding the lock to the door. He dashed across the dual carriageway to the Albert Dock complex where he seated himself in a café overlooking the inner dock and ordered a latte with an extra shot of espresso. He needed the kick without the bitterness.

The rain started to tumble and he found his mood darkening with the clouds as he tried to think logically over the events of the last twenty-four hours. He hoped his conclusions were not based on the fact that he disliked certain people and they disliked him.

First of all, he didn't really expect the local plods to fall over themselves in helping him. That was only natural, and so long as they didn't blatantly obstruct his investigation he had no real problems with reticence or bad feeling.

Secondly, was he reading too much into what happened in the CCTV room this morning? Sometimes things got wiped. Shit happened, and usually in connection with the things you happened to be working on at the time.

It didn't mean there was a conspiracy.

Carradine had not hidden the fact that Jonny Motta had been put forward, then eliminated, as a suspect for the Preston murders.

It just happened that Henry was one hundred per cent certain that Motta was the guy he'd had

244

a rumble with on the night of the murders and that put him right up there in suspect number one place.

And the fire in the office?

Just bad luck?

Maybe. And Henry wondered what was to be gained if the fire had been intentionally set. Anyone coming into the investigation would probably have copied the paperwork anyway. The only thing was, if someone in Merseyside was trying to hide something, perhaps they thought Henry had already uncovered something new and incriminating and therefore worth destroying. And putting a new lock on the door was a bit like flashing a red cape at an angry bull – it just had to charge.

He knew he had to keep an open mind about everything, whilst at the same time keeping his focus on the task, which was to close the IPCC investigation into a police shooting ... which took him by the nose to his next thought...

He had been through everything left behind by the IPCC investigator – the statements, interviews, and all the things he would have expected to find – except photos, of course – but with one other glaring exception.

Henry pulled out the mini-ringbound reporter's notebook he carried around with him in which he'd jotted a few notes and telephone numbers. One was the mobile number of the dead IPCC investigator. Henry looked at it for a while, pursing his lips, wondering whether or not he should.

Phoning a dead man was perhaps not the best

thing to do.

Still, Henry Christie was not noted for doing the best things.

Henry had often been around people who had lost loved ones. However they dealt with the loss – hysterically, angrily, philosophically, calmly – there was always something in their eyes that made him feel sad for them. There was no exception to this when the door he'd been knocking at opened and a woman about his age with sharply styled grey hair and handsome but tired features stood there.

'Mrs McKnight? I'm Henry Christie ... I phoned about half an hour ago?'

'On my husband's mobile,' she nodded. 'I still don't get why I keep it on and charged up.'

'I'm very sorry to trouble you at this time and I'm very sorry for your loss.'

She smiled pleasantly and her face became pretty. 'Come in, it's no problem. I need to talk to people.'

He took tea and biscuits, but didn't offer any more sympathy. She looked to be a strong woman, dealing with a tragedy in her life with dignity and resolve. Henry could tell she didn't need any soppy words. She'd probably had her fill of them. She looked tired and drawn, though, from lack of sleep and Henry promised he would be as quick as possible.

'As I explained...' He sipped the Earl Grey tea. 'I've been given the job of completing what Mr McKnight started in relation to the police shooting in Merseyside. From what I can see, he did a very professional, thorough job. It's just that when he died, the job wasn't finished and that's why I'm doing it.'

'In your phone call you said he might have left some paperwork at home, but to be honest, as far as I know everything he did was left in Liverpool. He was a workaholic and often brought documents home, but I'm sure there's nothing here.' She waved a hand loosely at the house.

Henry scratched his head. 'There's a full box of statements and stuff like that, but I think I would have expected a notebook of some sort and a policy book which he would have been required to keep. They don't seem to be there.'

She pouted thoughtfully, then drifted off momentarily before dragging herself back. She looked at Henry. 'I'm not really thinking straight ... I think I've let you come on a wild-goose chase ... Now I remember that what work stuff he had here, I've already handed over. I'm really sorry. One of your colleagues must have it.'

'Who did you hand it to?'

'A police officer, not someone from the IPCC ... With everything that's happened, all the things you have to do when someone dies, it just went out of my mind. I don't recall who it was, though.'

'Not a problem, Mrs McKnight. I understand. I imagine it'll turn up.'

'My mind's a bit of a mess,' she sighed.

'I understand ... but could you describe the person. I'll probably know who it is.'

Henry's mobile vibrated silently in his pocket.

He ignored it as Mrs McKnight gave a faltering, half-remembered description to him. He nodded as she spoke, memorizing what she said.

'Thanks for that,' he said, then rising and finishing the tea. 'You've been a great help and I'm sorry to intrude.'

'You're welcome.'

'I don't suppose there's anything else? I mean, did Mr McKnight mention anything to you about the investigation at all?'

'He rarely discussed his work. Much of it was highly confidential and he was very conscientious.' She and Henry walked to the front door. 'But on reflection,' she added thoughtfully, 'he did seem troubled by the investigation. It seemed to be a weight on his shoulders.'

Henry fought the urge to give her shoulders a good shake. 'In what way?' he probed gently instead.

'Hard to say.' She opened the door for him. 'He was just more withdrawn and distracted than usual, even more so on the day he was killed. I don't know. I could just tell. Even though he didn't discuss work, I could tell when things weren't going well and on that day he was acting quite strangely...' Her voice trailed off wistfully. 'But then again, hindsight makes all things significant, doesn't it?' She looked as though she was about to break into tears.

'Thank you,' he said, touching her shoulder gently. 'I won't take up any more of your time.'

What was left of the McKnight family lived in Ormskirk, the pretty little market town just inside the Lancashire border, so it was easy for Henry to pick up the A59 and he was back at Lancashire Police headquarters within half an hour. He strode through the Intelligence Unit and collected Jerry Tope on the way, who was sitting at his desk working at his computer.

They commandeered the DI's office and closed the door behind them. Henry invited Tope to take a seat and said, 'What've you got?'

'For most of the morning I've been trying to get into the Preston City Centre CCTV system and I've managed to succeed, but haven't managed to recover the file you're after. I can see where it's been, but I can't access the hard drive to recover it. I probably need to be physically in the CCTV room itself, but I have a program at home that might help. If I had that I might be able to get what you want. I'm sure the file will be there, even if it's been deleted. It's just finding a route to it.'

'I thought you were a computer nerd.'

'I am,' he said with pride. 'But not all things get done at the flick of a finger.'

Henry rubbed his eyes, tapped his fingers on the desk, then lifted a bum cheek to allow wind to pass: a great detective at work.

'Would it help if you worked from home?'

'That's where all my stuff is ... my unofficial stuff, that is.'

'I want you to have a look at some other things, too.'

'Will I get into trouble?'

'Only if you disobey my orders.'

'OK.'

Henry then told him about the mysterious fire in the office in Liverpool. It made Tope's jaw drop.

'Hell,' he said, 'what do you make of it?'

Henry opened his hands. 'Something and nothing. If it's a genuine fire, nothing. If it's arson, something.'

As he spoke the words, he spotted Bill Robbins sauntering through the Intelligence Unit, then enter the DI's office.

'Some bastard set the office on fire in Liverpool,' Tope blurted.

'Really,' said Bill unconcerned. He took a seat, looked at Henry after the incident had been explained to him. 'What d'you make of it?' he repeated the question.

'I'm told it was a faulty socket. From my experience of fires, it doesn't look like it.' He folded his arms. 'Deliberate,' he said firmly.

Tope and Bill exchanged worried looks.

'From now on we work from here – or home – and we ensure everything is backed up and secured from prying eyes and fingers. And, whilst I don't want to sound dramatic, we watch our backs, too. The fire might be genuine, who knows, but let's be careful when we cross the border because I get the impression they don't like us very much down there. Better safe than sorry...'

Bill took in the order, an unflustered look on his face. Tope seemed worried and said, 'The IPCC investigator got murdered, didn't he?'

A chilled pause descended on the office.

'What makes you say that?' Henry asked.

250

'Unexplained hit and run.'

Suddenly Henry felt very foolish. 'Unexplained hit and run?' – things were being repeated quite often in the office that morning. 'But I thought he'd...' Henry's voice trailed off because he was going to say something stupid like, 'been involved in a road-traffic accident.' He had made the assumption, a killer of a thing to do for any SIO worth his salt, that McKnight's death had been a car-to-car bump, a tragic accident with a fatal outcome. Head through the windscreen thing. He had made the error of not checking things out.

'From what I recall, he was hit by a stolen car which ended up being burnt out,' Jerry said. 'That comes under "unexplained" to me. It was on the Internet.'

'But not necessarily murder,' Bill pointed out.

'Admittedly not.'

Henry pulled himself together, kicking himself. 'And you didn't feel the need to mention this to me? Anyway, let's not jump to conclusions.' He said that even though he knew that a big part of the job of an SIO was to jump to conclusions and then test them out. 'Bill, you've been to Merseyside's Firearms Department this morning ... anything of interest?'

'Nahh, not really...'

But Henry's mind wasn't completely on what Bill had to say. It was on what Tope had just revealed ... plus the fact that the description Mrs McKnight had given him of the officer to whom she'd handed her husband's files matched Detective Superintendent Paul Shafer to a 'T'.

251

FOURTEEN

'Look, pal, all I want is ten minutes with this guy.' Karl Donaldson was pleading with Henry as they walked through the doors of the Tram and Tower, Henry's local pub, presided over by his favourite landlord, Ken Clayson. They approached the bar and already Ken, having spotted Henry, was pulling him a pint of the finest Stella Artois. The duo leaned on the bar. 'I don't wanna go through a loada bureaucratic shit, I just wanna get in and talk, that's all. Not even on the record.'

'Which is probably what worries them.'

Ken placed the drink on the bar and smiled at Donaldson. 'A water for you, sir?' He knew from past experience that the American could not take his liquor, despite his size. Two pints and he was anyone's, to quote a phrase.

Donaldson thought about it. 'I'll try a pint of that ... what is it? Bitter.'

'Good choice, sir.'

Donaldson had remained up in the north-west since last meeting Henry and had tried to get in to see Paulo Scartarelli, who was being held on a remand to police cells. He was at Leyland police station, Lancashire's highest-security nick.

252

'I've been on the phone, seeing people ... You name it, no deal. I keep getting referred upwards, sideways and up people's assholes.'

'Who have you spoken to?' Henry sipped his beer.

'Your pal, Dave Anger, from whom I got a flat no. His was the final say-so.' Donaldson's pint arrived. He allowed the head to settle before taking a sip and wincing at the taste. 'Folk drink this shit?'

'The second sip gets better, the third even better. Trust me.'

'You're right,' he said, wiping a foamy moustache from his top lip. They retreated to a corner table, Henry subtly furious that the ladies present, without exception, were watching Donaldson like predatory hawks. It also annoyed Henry that Donaldson, simple soul he was, did not even seem to know he was the centre of so much attention.

'Your fan club is in,' Henry said scathingly as they seated themselves.

'Come again?' the Yank said dumbly.

'Nothing,' Henry muttered darkly and scowled at the women who were openly gawking. Then he said, 'Am I being paranoid, or what?' as an opener for the discussion relating to his own problems of the moment.

'How do you mean, pal?'

'I've been asked to take over the investigation into this police shooting in Liverpool, as you know. Only been doing it two days and not even done anything yet, really. The natives aren't friendly. Which I expected. But the office we were allocated to work in has been set on fire and there's some unconfirmed rumour going about that the IPCC investigator died in mysterious circumstances. When I say mysterious, he was flattened by a hit-and-run driver in a stolen car.'

'Not much to go on there,' Donaldson said, taking a further swig of his drink and nodding approvingly.

'Supposing he found out something he wasn't supposed to and – bam! Splat!'

'Far-fetched.'

Henry leaned forward. 'And it turns out that the guy who was shot by the police is the same one who killed two prostitutes in Preston – but I've been told it's none of my business and to get lost.'

'Definitely the same guy?'

'He looks similar.'

'Can you prove it?'

'Well, I had an altercation with the guy and during it I dug my fingernails into his throat and clonked him with my PR on his arm. I've had a look at the dead body and he's got those injuries still. Faded, but definitely there.'

'Have you told anyone this?'

'Not at present.'

'Is there any other way of proving it's one and the same guy?'

'Possibly. I think some partial fingerprints were recovered from the car in which one of the prostitute's bodies was found and as far as I know, there was never a match. If I had a set of prints from a corpse lying in Southport, then got a friendly fingerprint guy to cross-check 'em ... that would be something to go back with, wouldn't it?'

'So that's you sorted out ... Now what about my problem?'

Henry stared at his friend over the rim of his beer glass. 'Scartarelli's in Leyland now, yeah?' Donaldson nodded. 'And he's up before the magistrates tomorrow for a remand hearing? If I scratch your back and you scratch mine ... how does that sound?'

'So long as you don't touch my ass ... What're you thinking?'

'I'm thinking that Scartarelli will be handed over to a private-security firm in the morning. That will effectively take him out of the police system – which means I might be able to get access to him, maybe. And I'm also thinking something else ... There's no time like the present to get a set of fingerprints from a dead man.'

No self-respecting detective would be found without a portable fingerprint kit in the back of their car. And although a few people in the organization that was Lancashire Constabulary had set out to make Henry Christie look a fool, he had never lost his professional self-respect. Which was why he always carried an inked strip, a tube of fingerprint ink, a wooden roller, a wooden block with a shiny metal strip on it, several blank fingerprint forms and many pairs of latex gloves in the boot of his car.

He and Donaldson walked quickly back to

Henry's house after finishing their pints. After a brief verbal joust with Kate, they jumped into the Rover and headed for the motorway. They came off the M6 south of Leyland and crossed the southern edge of the county to Southport. Henry, although he had only had one pint and was well under the legal limit, still drove like a Formula One Grand Prix driver.

They pulled into Southport General after about half an hour's nippy travel.

Henry collected his go-anywhere fingerprint kit from the boot, which he kept in a plastic Asda bag, and he and Donaldson entered the hospital.

The corridors were quiet as they plunged into the depths of the building. It was after visiting hours and hardly anyone was moving about.

The mortuary was staffed by the same mini-attendant as on Henry's previous visit, still playing medical/death-related tunes on his CD player. Henry was pleased to hear a familiar riff emanating from the attendant's office. It was the Rolling Stones' track 'Dancin' with Mr D', highly appropriate for the task he was about to undertake.

There was a surprised expression on the attendant's pasty face as Henry poked his head round the door and sang, 'Dancin', dancin', dancin' with Mr D,' in the style of Mick Jagger, his idol. It was obvious that his pint of beer as well as making him desire to travel faster had also removed his inhibition barrier.

Scrambling to his feet, the attendant blurted, 'You're back!'

'Yeah – brought a new friend.'

'Uh ... what d'you want?'

Henry held up his plastic bag and fleetingly in his mind's eye he saw the image of himself as the great comedian Eric Morecambe, who used to leave the stage wearing a long raincoat and flat cap and carrying a plastic bag. He coughed to clear the image, let his hand with the carrier drop to his side and said, seriously, 'I need another look at Mr Motta, please.'

'Why?'

'Police business.' He gave the attendant *the look*, hoping it would quake him in his tracks.

'Sure, sure.' The CD clicked on to the next track, one Henry did not recognize but had the words 'Dead, dead, dead' in it. 'You know where he is. He hasn't moved.'

Henry tilted his head in thanks and indicated for Donaldson to follow.

He slid out the drawer and as he snapped on the latex gloves, Donaldson folded back the muslin sheet covering Jonny Motta's nicely chilled corpse.

On seeing the bullet holes in his chest, he said, 'Good shooting,' admiringly, as Bill Robbins had done previously.

Henry got to work on the fingers, twisting out the hands, selecting the digits and rolling them on the ready-inked strips, then transferring the prints on to the blank sheets as best he could manage in the circumstances. Motta wasn't particularly compliant, but at least he wasn't fighting, as some of the people Henry had taken prints from had been.

At the far end of the mortuary, neither Henry

nor Donaldson noticed that the attendant was watching their activity discreetly and making a call on his mobile phone.

Henry completed his creepy task, then produced a digital camera from his pocket. He got Donaldson to lift up Motta's chin whilst he took a couple of snaps of the marks on his neck. Then he took a shot of the inch-long injury on his right forearm which could have been caused when Henry hit him with a police radio. Henry then recovered Motta with the sheet and slid him back into the fridge.

Donaldson slammed the door into place as Henry put his gear away in the Asda bag, then peeled off his gloves. They walked out past the attendant, who gave them an uninterested wave and turned up the music.

As the mortuary was on the lower ground floor it was a choice of going up the stairs or using the lift to take them to the ground floor. The lift won hands down and after pressing all the lift-call buttons they stood patiently at the doors of the three elevators that served the main spine of the hospital.

Two lifts descended almost simultaneously, one slightly ahead of the other.

The doors of the first one creaked open and the two men stepped into an empty lift just as the second one arrived and the doors opened slowly. As Henry pressed the button inside the lift to take them up a floor, a man stepped smartly out of the other lift and walked in the direction of the mortuary.

As the doors closed, Henry did a double-take

and managed to ease his foot between the doors to prevent them from shutting.

'What's the matter?' Donaldson said.

Henry placed a forefinger to his lips. 'I thought I recognized that guy ... in fact, I do.'

'Who is it?'

'C'mon,' he said. He stepped out of the lift, closely followed by Donaldson, and ran to the double doors at the end of the corridor that led to the mortuary. He crouched down and, like a naughty schoolboy, peeped through the strengthened-glass panel in the door and watched the man turn into the mortuary. Henry scuttled after him, Donaldson in tow and mystified. They reached the mortuary doors and, peeking again, Henry saw the man from the lift talking earnestly to the mortuary assistant, who was gesticulating defensively as he responded.

'Who is he?' Donaldson whispered over Henry's shoulder.

'Paul Shafer, the Merseyside super I told you about.'

'Ah,' Donaldson said as the dime dropped.

Shafer was pointing angrily at the attendant's chest with his right forefinger and the attendant was backing off, clearly afraid. Although Shafer's voice was raised, it was impossible to hear what he was saying because of the thick doors and the fact the CD player was still blasting out grim-reaper music. Then the tirade stopped, Shafer's shoulders sagged and his hand went into his inner jacket pocket, extracted his wallet and eased a twenty-pound note out of it. He folded it into the assistant's grubby hand.

'He's coming out,' Henry ducked back sharply and stood on Donaldson's foot. He gave a muted howl of agony and began hopping about on one leg. Henry dragged him down the corridor, almost at a run, through the next set of double doors, which they dropped down behind. Both men saw Shafer emerge from the mortuary and stalk away in the opposite direction to the lifts. Henry and Donaldson stood upright from their hiding place.

'What's the plan?' Donaldson asked. He was still hopping a little.

'Dunno.'

'Good plan ... Do we follow him, or not?'

'To what end?'

'Dunno.'

'So that's a good plan, too,' Henry said sarcastically. Glancing to his right he saw a set of stairs which he moved towards, saying, 'But it's a plan I like. Let's see if we can beat him to the car park.' Henry took the steps two at a time. He emerged slightly breathless on the ground floor and trotted towards the exit, only realizing he would have to pay for car parking before getting to his car. He searched his pockets for change as he reached the pay station just outside the main entry doors, ahead of Shafer he hoped. He slotted in a couple of coins, which fell straight through and out into the change dispenser with a metallic clatter. 'Shit.'

'Nice one,' Donaldson commented drily. 'He'll be in the queue behind us if you don't pay soon.'

Henry's thick fingers fumbled for the change

260

again which he stuck in his mouth to douse with saliva in the hope the money wouldn't just drop through again. The first coin registered ... and so did the second. Henry grabbed the ticket and both men ran hard to the Rover.

By quickly re-parking and getting a better view of the hospital entrance, they were able to watch Shafer join the short queue at the pay station then walk across to his car, which was parked dangerously near to Henry's. They ducked low. Shafer didn't even glance up. He was deep in thought as he unlocked and then drove off in his BMW.

The small amount of alcohol had now left Henry's system. He was clear-headed, even if the inside of his mouth tasted like the bottom of an oven.

'What the hell's going on?' he said out loud – and with the instinct bred of almost thirty years of being suspicious of everyone and their motives, never trusting a damn soul, Henry followed Shafer out of the car park in the direction of Southport town centre.

Donaldson remained enigmatically silent, thinking, until he said, *Something*'s going on.'

With a scowl of derision, Henry looked sideways at him. 'The great G-man has spoken,' he said with mock-reverence. 'Americans can sleep safe in their beds knowing guys like you are protecting them.'

Donaldson punched Henry very hard on the shoulder, numbing his arm.

Henry gritted his teeth and held his arm tightly to prevent it from spasming. For a further few minutes he followed Shafer driving with one hand.

Shafer drove along Lord Street, Southport's main shopping street, which at that time of night was buzzing with good-natured revellers. He drew into the car park of a large Victorian-style hotel and Henry drove on, parking a hundred metres north on Lord Street itself.

'That explained why he managed to turn up so quickly ... if he was here.'

'And if the creepy mortuary attendant called him,' Donaldson said.

'I'd make that assumption.'

'You know what happens when you assume?'

'All right, hypothesize then!'

'Anyway, I'm still not sure what we're doing here,' Donaldson said. He checked his watch. 'Time's winged chariot and all that.'

'It's just...' Henry's fingers tensed as though he was strangling somebody. 'Just ... like you said, G-man, something's not right.'

'I said something's going on.'

'Yeah, but what?'

'The Merseyside cops are twitchy because a real detective's investigating them and maybe their procedures were lax or something and they managed to fox the other investigator...'

'It's a theory ... and thanks for the compliment.'

'Aw, shucks, y'all know I didn't really mean it,' Donaldson drawled.

'Whatever,' Henry said, his mind now somewhere else. 'Why don't you sneak into the hotel and see if you can find out what's going on in there. Might be nothing, who knows?'

Donaldson sighed heavily. 'OK.' He smacked the dashboard with the flat of his hands. Something sounded loose inside it.

'I'll stay here, for obvious reasons.'

The bulky American rolled out of the Rover, pulled his jacket around himself and set off swiftly back to the hotel, passing Shafer's parked car and trotting up the steps into the spacious foyer, off which were several doors and a wide, sweeping staircase dead ahead.

Donaldson peered into a large restaurant, in which a few people were still at tables. No sign of Shafer. Next he checked a large lounge fitted with a variety of comfy chairs and Chesterfields; still no sign of Shafer. As expected, Donaldson found him in the bar. He was alone, being served. Donaldson glanced around the room. There was no obvious companion for Shafer, but he looked like a man who didn't drink alone. Donaldson crossed to the bar as Shafer paid for two shorts and mixers. He collected the drinks in his hands and retreated to chairs and a table in an alcove.

'Yes, sir?' the bartender asked.

Donaldson ordered a mineral water, leaned on the bar and picked at a bowl of nuts, able to keep an eye on Shafer in the mirror behind the bar.

The Liverpool detective looked ill at ease, constantly readjusting his seating position, fiddling with the crease in his trousers.

A well-kept middle-aged lady sidled up to the bar next to Donaldson and gave him a dry smile. He raised his eyebrows. 'Ma'am,' he said

263

respectfully, bowing slightly.

'Ooh, an American,' she giggled delightedly.

'Yes, ma'am,' he said, broadening his accent and making her quiver visibly. She seemed suddenly out of breath, especially when Donaldson flashed his white teeth and raised his square chin so she could see his handsome profile better. She placed the palm of her hand across her ample bosom, her eyes a-twinkle. 'May I buy you a drink?' he asked.

'That would be most ... Martini,' she gasped.

Donaldson crooked a finger at the barman and whilst he ordered, kept a watchful eye on the uncomfortable Shafer via the mirror.

'That'll be four-twenty,' the barman said, placing the single drink in front of the lady, who must have thought that all her Christmases had come at once. Donaldson pulled out a fiver – then two things happened almost simultaneously.

A man appeared behind the woman, glaring angrily at her and Donaldson.

'Esther, what the hell are you playing at?' This was the husband, Donaldson guessed, groaning inwardly.

'Why, darling, I don't know what you mean,' Esther flushed guiltily.

'I mean fucking flirting with strangers.' The husband squared aggressively to Donaldson. 'She's a fuckin' married woman, pal.'

Donaldson noted that Shafer, as well as everyone else in the bar, was now looking in the direction of the incident. He flicked the fiver on the bar and said, 'No harm done,' and started to turn

264

away from the couple. That was when he caught sight of another man entering the bar. A man he recognized and who he knew would be able to recognize him.

He was about to spin away and scuttle out of the bar, head down, vainly hoping he hadn't been spotted, but his planned exit was rudely curtailed when the angry husband grabbed his right bicep and tried to hook him round.

In a swift, blurred move, Donaldson twisted to the man, who was probably ten years older than the American, and though well built was no match for him in any respect. Donaldson pinned him discreetly to the bar and jerked him tight, causing pain to appear in the man's face. Donaldson peered into his eyes, his breathing shallow.

'Don't,' Donaldson said quietly, and nothing else. He released the man, who for some unaccountable reason had to hold himself upright on the bar, maybe because Donaldson's forefinger had touched a point somewhere behind his ear and caused some sort of shock wave to course through him. Donaldson then exited as speedily as possible, leaving the flirty wife to assist her husband remain upright on rubbery legs.

He hoped he managed to succeed to get out without being spotted, as out of the corner of his eye he saw Shafer rise and greet the man who had entered the bar, then shake hands.

So concerned was he about getting out unseen, he almost rammed face-to-face into another guy who was striding in the direction of the bar. At the last possible moment, Donaldson sidestepped with a muted apology, managed to avoid a collision and missed the man by a matter of inches.

For Donaldson that would have been the final insult. To have crashed in the hotel foyer whilst doing his level best to remain invisible.

He scurried out of the hotel and ran up to Henry's car, slotting in beside his friend.

'That was quick.' Henry looked at him. 'What happened?'

Donaldson eased out a long sigh, then gave Henry a worried look. 'I got hit on by a sex-starved woman.'

'That's a bad thing?'

'But her husband intervened.'

'That's a bad thing.'

'I did spot Shafer. He was alone in the bar until someone joined him.' A beat. 'Brace yourself ... Dave Anger. He didn't see me, incidentally.'

The name hit Henry like a demolition ball, but then he thought quickly, So what? Two old mates having a drink. He expressed that thought.

'Well, up to that point I might've agreed. Maybe your suspicious mind is seeing conspiracies where there are none.' Donaldson kept Henry's gaze, a serious expression on his ruggedly handsome features.

'What changed your mind?'

'The man I almost bulldozed into the ground as I left the bar in a hurry...'

Henry waited for the punchline, not even able to hazard a guess who he was talking about.

'Walter Corrigan.'

266

Henry then blinked. 'As in the Mafia fix-it guy?'

Donaldson nodded.

Stunned, confused, Henry's head tilted back and hit the headrest, only to jerk forwards again before he spun around as the rear passenger door was yanked open and an uninvited guest dropped into the seat with a cheery, 'Hi, guys.'

FIFTEEN

Georgia Papakostas immediately realized that there would be no quick solution to the murder of an innocent policeman on the steps of an aeroplane. But she also knew, as did all detectives, that the first seventy-two hours of any murder investigation are crucial. Maybe ninety-six hours in the case of a murdered cop ... but the fact remained that if a breakthrough wasn't made within either of those times, then the likelihood of solving the crime would lessen considerably.

That is why she did not allow the grass to grow under her feet and, exhausted though she was, as soon as the plane taking Henry Christie, Bill Robbins and Paulo Scartarelli rose into the air from Pafos airport, she got down to the business of tracing a killer.

The last thing she needed, or so she thought at the time, was the appearance at her elbow of DI Tekke, her former lover and, for the moment, her current supervisor.

She had set up an Incident Room at Pafos police station and was pulling together a murder team. She was very much aware that the crime was one of the worst in living memory on the island and had been reported internationally and there was every chance she would quickly be sidelined or even ousted from the job once the big guns shouldered their way into it.

That much she accepted. After all, despite her record, she was still just a lowly detective sergeant, albeit on the brink of promotion. But she was conscientious and knew things had got to be moving quickly. Contacts had to be spoken to, favours had to be called in and at the very least she could do some real initial groundwork for the investigation before the rug was pulled from under her. Sadly she believed that the police in Cyprus were not really up to the task of running such a high-profile murder enquiry, especially once the high-rankers moved in.

Following her hunch about a sniper possibly being a hired gun from the Turkish side of the island, the first thing she had to arrange were checkpoints on all the main roads north, particularly at the border in Nicosia which was a route used regularly by the underworld. Then she needed to alert every detective on the island to get into the ribs of their informants and get an information flow coming in. Then she needed to do some personal phoning – at the same time as setting up a properly functioning Incident Room.

If she could achieve these things before she was booted, she would be, if not happy, at least satisfied she'd done the best she could.

She was on the phone cajoling some action out of a particularly lazy detective in the capital when Tekke trudged into the office she was using. He looked hangdog and very dishevelled.

Georgia's heart missed a few beats as she resisted the temptation to tell him to fuck off out of her life – in Greek, of course.

She concentrated on the phone call, aware of Tekke's brooding presence. 'Yes, I know you've got some superb contacts,' she smarmed up to the lazy Nicosian detective. 'Yeah ... really interested in gunmen, riflemen...' She continued to schmooze him and got him to promise some action. All the while Tekke hovered, hands thrust deeply into pockets, continually sighing. Eventually Georgia replaced the phone and turned her attention to him. She was cold-faced and certainly did not want this complication.

'What?' she demanded, rubbing her eyes wearily.

'I've come to say I'm sorry,' he began falteringly. His eyes were stuck to the floor, but then he raised them. 'It was silly to accuse you about that English detective...'

'That was the least of our problems.'

'I want us back together.'

She snorted and shook her head. 'Won't work. Especially now that I'll be taking over your role. Too much friction, too much ... bah! You just can't stand me being a good detective, can you?'

'I could try.'

She told him to fuck off.

Six hours later, as refreshed as she would ever be after three hours' sleep and a long bath, she was back at work.

Much to her surprise she was allowed to pull the murder squad together and run with the

270

investigation – and she was promoted there and then to DI to do it. She was, in fact, astounded by the faith her superiors put in her and her view of them changed somewhat. Maybe they weren't as dumb as they seemed?

This gave her an extra surge of energy and she was even more invigorated when the lazy detective from Nicosia called her and asked her to make to the capital *pronto*. An arrest had been made.

Two hours later she was driving through the gates of Nicosia.

'I hear you and Tekke have split?' the detective half-enquired of Georgia. 'Sorry to hear that.'

'News travels fast,' she said stiffly.

The detective was in his mid-thirties, but was already sporting a Greek moustache and had the florid complexion of a drinker and the moth-eaten looks that reminded her sharply of Tekke. He was also, like many other Cypriot cops, always on the lookout for a score, even though he was married and had two daughters. Georgia could read it in his eyes.

'Don't,' she warned him. His face fell abruptly. 'I'm here to work, to solve the murder of a colleague, not to flirt or make dates – OK?'

He held up both hands defensively. His mouth became a thin, unpleasant line under his overgrown moustache.

'Now what have we got?' she asked brusquely.

Pulling himself together the detective said, 'This young guy was in a dirty fight last night. He ended up in hospital semi-conscious, drunk

271

too. Head injury, but not serious. Uniform cops went to speak to him and he pulled a gun on them, held them at bay for half an hour before he fell over and shot out the ceiling of the emergency room.'

'And?' she demanded. 'What's the connection?'

'Says he knows something about a cop being shot at.'

Georgia made her way to the cells in the police station where the man was now detained. Accompanied by the detective, she flung open the heavy metal-framed door and stepped into the oppressive space that was the cell. It – he – stank badly. She took two strides over to the prisoner, who was sitting propped up in a corner of the bench bed. The man looked sneeringly up at her, his face a mass of cuts and bruises from the scrap he'd been involved in.

His mouth moved into a painful smile, revealing a gap where a front tooth had been slammed out, but his eyes still glowered at her. Georgia knew a bit of his background, knew of him from her time in the city, but had never met him before. He was very low down the criminal food chain, a dealer, a gang member, a low-level enforcer, pretty much living hand to mouth. But like all punks he wanted to be the leader of the pack, hence the previous night's fracas, which was gang-related, albeit at a low level.

'This is funny,' he chortled as he looked at Georgia.

'Actually, nothing's funny ... I'm investigating the murder of a police officer, so nothing's funny, get me? You said you knew something about a cop being shot.'

'Nah.' He hacked up horribly, swallowed back. 'Being shot *at*, not shot dead ... big difference.'

'Meaning?'

He looked at her derisively, a half-smile on his face. 'I could've killed you, but I didn't.'

Georgia took a pace back, unsure, but with a very cold feeling inside her.

'Don't you remember me?'

'Why should I?'

He raised his right hand, pointed his first and middle fingers at her and used his thumb to simulate a hammer. 'Bang, bang, you're dead.'

'What?'

'Check the gun you took from me and the slugs you found at the scene in Coral Bay. I'm saving you time, babe.'

'The scene of what?'

The prisoner shrugged. 'I could've killed you,' he said again, 'but I was paid to miss, just to scare the hell out of you – and if I'm going down, so is the bastard who paid me.'

Suddenly Georgia's insides went to mush as the words he was saying suddenly made sense.

At that moment, she did the best thing she could have done. She stopped talking to the prisoner. Even in Cyprus, interviews conducted in cells are inadmissible in a court of law, so she arranged to talk to him in a proper interview room, recording and videoing the interview and offering him legal representation.

She was assisted by the male detective, who

273

sat quietly by whilst she interviewed coldly and clinically, extracting the information she needed whilst at the same time holding herself together from splitting apart. At the end of the session, the prisoner was returned to his cell and after making her fellow detective swear a vow of silence, she got in her car and headed back to Pafos, driving as though in a tunnel all the way.

Despite the detective's assurances that he would keep quiet, Georgia suspected, rightly as it happened, he would tip off the man she was on a mission to see. The world of the male detective is a very closed, defensive one as she well knew, and so, instead of making her way to Pafos police station as might have been expected, she went to an apartment in the residential part of town first. By then a searing rage was burning through her veins with the heat of a volcano.

She had a key, let herself in silently.

Tekke emerged from the bedroom with a heavy holdall in his right hand, surprised to see Georgia waiting for him in the lounge. He stopped abruptly, fear and resignation in his tired eyes, but also a determination in his orbs.

'Don't try to stop me,' he warned her.

'I won't,' she said. 'I'll just say you weren't here.'

'I don't want to hurt you.'

'The hurt's been done,' she whispered and swallowed. 'Why?' she asked hoarsely.

He shrugged. 'Because I was – am – jealous of you; because I wanted you to see it's not a job

274

for a woman. I wanted to be your saviour, to be there for you; because I wanted you to be my wife and because I love you.'

The words resonated falsely around her mind. 'So you arranged for someone to take pot-shots at me, to scare me in the hope I'd stop being a cop and be your wife? Not a well-thought-out plan, was it?'

'On reflection, no.'

'You're a dinosaur.'

'And you're in the wrong job. So excuse me.'

'Where will you go?'

'To the north, then Turkey. I have relatives there. I'll be untouchable. Please don't stand in my way.'

Georgia emitted a heavy sigh. 'You know I can't let you go, don't you?'

Tekke shrugged. 'Don't try to stop me.'

He shouldered past her, barging her out of the way and made it to the door. He opened it and turned before stepping into the corridor outside. 'You could have been my wife.'

'I don't think so. Part of being married is supporting the dreams and aspirations of each other. You could never have done that.'

He twisted out into the corridor, Georgia a few steps behind him, but as soon as he went to the stairs, three uniformed cops emerged from the shadows and surrounded him. He stopped, dropped his bag and turned slowly towards her. He looked sadly at her for a moment, then launched himself at her, screaming, 'Bitch!'

Tekke never laid a hand on her, because she was ready for the attack. She reacted instantaneously and her bunched, steel-hard fist crashed into the side of his head. He was sent spinning into the arms of one of the uniforms, who tossed him back across to the other two who swiftly handcuffed the detective and forced him down to his knees.

Georgia leaned down and whispered in his ear, 'What a way to end a relationship.'

'Time to talk,' Georgia said. Facing her across the desk was a sour-faced Tekke, defiant and uncooperative. 'I'm not interested in what you did to me,' she stated. 'Someone else will deal with that. What I need is a lead to get me on the trail of a cop-killer, a man who is capable of shooting a man from over half a mile away, and I know there won't be many of those in the world, let alone on Cyprus. You obviously have excellent contacts – so give me a name, someone I can start with who will put me on the right path. What's between us now is purely professional,' she concluded, then added, 'If you do this I might be able to help you.'

'The hunter has become the prey,' he snorted, sat back and wiped his tired face, stretching his sagging skin.

'I want a name. I want to move quickly. I want to make an arrest. I want to capture a cop-killer. I hope you want the same, Tekke – or is your mind now too twisted and despoiled to do the right thing?'

He didn't answer.

It was 2 a.m. when she got the call. She was

awake, hadn't been sleeping, her mind flashing and regurgitating images, encounters and conflicts; Tekke, Henry Christie, the shooting on the plane, being shot at ... a multitude of things all vying for space in her mind. She desperately needed to drink heavily, but knew she could not afford to even let a drop pass her lips. She needed to be right on top of her game because she was under real scrutiny.

Her mobile phone chirped as she sat in front of the TV watching a satellite-beamed British cop show from the eighties. A cup of cold coffee was on the table in front of her.

'DI Papakostas,' she answered. It sounded strange in her mouth, the new rank.

'He wants to talk.'

She was already dressed, even if it was the same set of clothes she'd been wearing forever, it seemed. She arrived at the police station in ten minutes. Five minutes after that she was sitting opposite Tekke in an interview room.

'I'll give you a name.'

Her tummy muscles contracted.

'On one condition.'

'Which is?'

'This was all one big mistake, a fabrication, all lies designed to sully my good name by a scumbag hoodlum with a grudge. Discredit what he says, let me go and I'll move to Larnaca, take up the new job and we'll never meet again. I walk out of here, reputation intact. You say it was just an unfortunate happening.'

She pretended to think about it. 'Why should I do that?'

'Because I deserve a second chance?'

She almost wet herself at that one.

'Because of us,' he added.

She could smell his body odour from where she sat. Could see his rough-looking face, was amazed she had ever fallen for him.

'Only if the name leads to something.'

'You'll have to work at it, but it will,' he promised.

As much as Georgia Papakostas knew she was forging a path through the Cypriot police force which other women might follow, she was realistic enough to be aware that a woman alone, albeit a newly promoted detective inspector, however sassy and tough she might be, was still swimming against a cultural tide, particularly in the criminal underworld, which could easily drown her. As far as crims were concerned she was just a woman and possibly not to be taken as a serious threat. Because of this she did the only sensible thing available to her: she employed some muscle.

She hand-picked two tough, uniformed cops, re-dressed them in plain clothes and headed back to Nicosia the following morning. With these guys in tow, towering behind her in shades and with folded arms and oozing seriously bad attitudes, she barged her way through doors, into betting shops, pubs, bars, clubs, following the name Tekke had given her. She was like a mini-tsunami, surging with power and purpose.

One name led to another, then another and so on. Finally she was given a name – whispered to her with fear and trepidation – in a seafront bar in the resort of Polis. She was also given a location and a heads-up that the man was on the move.

With no time to organize a proper squad, the three of them, armed with Glocks and protected by Kevlar body armour, found themselves back in Nicosia, cautiously climbing the stairs of a notorious tenement block until they reached the fourth floor. They turned quietly along the landing strewn with the discarded paraphernalia of drug use.

As is often the case, the arrest that is expected to be the most problematic turns out to be easy. As Georgia's two companions in crime took up positions on either side of the target apartment door and she faced it, ready to flatfoot it off its hinges, it opened unexpectedly.

A man appeared, maybe thirty-three, a haversack slung over his shoulders, and was as startled as Georgia. But she was first to react. She charged him shoulder-first into the breastbone with a scream of a banshee which also incorporated the fact she was a police officer and that he was under arrest.

He recovered well, contorting away like a dancer in the tight confines of the vestibule, but backed up by the two burly cops, he was soon pinned to the floor. Even if he'd been a martial-arts expert he would have stood no chance.

Georgia straddled him, her crotch across his chest, knees pinning his shoulders down. The other cops spread over the rest of him. Georgia's gun was pointed directly into his face, over his left eye.

'You,' she panted, 'are under arrest for murder.'

She then read him his rights.

A sniper rifle and ammunition for the same, together with maps of Pafos airport and photographs of the location were found in the haversack. Questions poured at him as detective after detective tried to elicit a confession. Nothing came.

The man was positively identified after his fingerprints were forcibly taken and entered on the International Fingerprint Recognition System.

Fourteen hours after his arrest, Georgia entered the interview room and sat down opposite, a sheaf of paper rustling in her hands. She was close to exhaustion, but the prospect of a major breakthrough, assisted by caffeine in the form of coffee and energy drinks, kept her on track.

The man averted his eyes.

'I know you are Bernardo Rosario, twenty-four years of age. Born in Naples. Emigrated alone to the United States of America ten years ago to escape the heat of the Neapolitan cops who were on your heels following the shooting of a judge in Naples. Since then,' she consulted the papers briefly, 'you have worked in various capacities for the Tantini family in New York and Miami. Most recently your talents have been channelled into working as a gofer, delivering what needs to be delivered, where and when it needs to be delivered, to whom it needs deliver-

280

ing. You deliver weapons and other goods. Am I right?'

Rosario shrugged, gave nothing away.

'So I have to make an assumption here – that you have also become a killer.' This remark made his eyes twinkle slightly – a reaction. 'You have been found in possession of a firearm which has been used to murder a Cypriot police officer, together with ammunition for that weapon. The bullets found at the scene and in the body of the dead cop can be proved to have been fired by the weapon in your possession. Your fingerprints are on the weapon, yours alone. So what I have is you, a dead cop and a murder weapon – a complete triangle.'

She gazed unblinkingly at the prisoner. 'Think about it.'

He did. Stewed for two hours. Then she went back to see him.

'I have no doubt in my mind that I can send you to prison for life and in this country, life means life. Think about it.'

More stewing.

Two hours later she was back again. She smiled and said, 'You'll die in prison.' Then she stood up and left him again.

Twenty minutes later he was buzzing desperately to see her.

'I'm all ears.'

He looked as though he'd been hyperventilating, was trying to control his breathing and his

281

mental and physical state.

'But just one more thing before you start,' she cut in before he could speak. 'You have managed to avoid extradition to Italy for the murder of that judge, but I can assure you if by some freak of fate you manage to walk free from a Cypriot court – which you won't – then I'll ensure you get taken back to Italy to face that murder charge.'

Before he could say anything, she left the room again.

He was screaming for her within five minutes, pounding the cell door, jamming the ball of his hand on the call button.

She sat him down, calmed him. His eyes were wild. He was sweating profusely.

'I need protection,' he panted. 'I need my freedom.'

'In exchange for what?' she asked blandly.

'A name.'

'Just a name?'

'By telling you this, I'm bringing a death sentence down on me.'

She regarded him with disbelief, sat back, her eyes running over him.

'I don't know who the sniper was, but it wasn't me,' he said. 'I just delivered and picked up the weapon. Nothing more.'

'In that case you're no good to me. I think I'll prosecute you for murder. I will make it stick.'

'But you know I didn't do it.'

She pouted. 'Justice isn't about the truth, but I

tell you what, if – *if* – you can answer my questions to my satisfaction I might be able to get you on to a witness-protection programme. But do not misunderstand the balance of power here. I call the shots. I say how it goes.' She jabbed a finger into her chest. 'Me. It's not a negotiable thing and at the moment I feel you're not pulling your weight, I pull the plug and we go back to square one.'

He looked at the floor. 'I'm a dead man,' he muttered.

Georgia shrugged. 'Your decision – a full life sentence or a witness-protection programme followed by a new identity, a new life – on the run, obviously, but that's what you are anyway. A fugitive. It's just that other people will be after you rather than cops.'

He raised his eyes. They played over Georgia's face.

'Walter Corrigan,' he said.

SIXTEEN

They were back at the Tram and Tower, Henry Christie, Karl Donaldson and the person who, uninvited, had jumped into the back seat of Henry's Rover in Lord Street, Southport – none other than Georgia Papakostas.

She had brought them up to date with the developments in Cyprus and they'd listened intently with hardly a question or murmur, both men's eyes transfixed on this Eastern Mediterranean beauty. Annoyingly for Henry, her eyes kept wandering to Donaldson and it was plain to see she was taken in by the good-looking bastard. He wanted to interject, 'He's happily married, you know?' but managed to keep his trap shut knowing that Donaldson had never strayed, even when his marriage had hit a rocky outcrop.

After the initial shock of Georgia joining them, they had quickly decided to head back north, then west, across the River Ribble and have a brain-dumping session at Henry's local, where he knew he would have no trouble getting a lock-in if required. Ken, the landlord, was very accommodating, even more so than usual when the trio landed on his doorstep just as he was closing up for the night. He almost tripped over his bearded chin when standing aside for them to enter.

Donaldson rubbed his eyes as she finished her tale, concluding with how she had got to Southport.

Corrigan's villa had remained under surveillance with the trusty Piali doing the honours, and a man believed to be Corrigan returned after a short time and then left with bags packed. Georgia, already alerted, followed him to the airport and discovered he was on a flight to Manchester. Because she had only been given his name by Rosario and had not had the opportunity to unravel his connection to the shooting, there wasn't enough suspicion to arrest him. Having said that, she didn't want to lose him.

Using her muscle as a cop, she blagged a seat on the plane. Her passport and a minimum amount of luggage were rushed to her by a colleague, and she boarded the plane right behind Corrigan, sitting two rows behind him – and didn't have a clue what she was playing at. She was also very much aware that she hadn't even told her bosses what she was doing either. Operating on a whim was not like her, normally being someone who mapped out every move with excruciating detail, but she was finding it exciting.

'I'd managed to arrange car hire at Manchester and more by luck than anything, I managed to follow him to South ... South...?'

'Port,' Henry said.

'And the hire car's still there,' she added.

'Brilliant,' Donaldson cooed, locking eyes with her.

Oh God, Henry thought bitterly, seeing her eyes go all gooey. He's going to fuck this one. I just know it ... buggeration! He knew he had missed his chance and it was as if the time they'd spent in Cyprus hadn't happened.

'OK, guys,' he said. 'What does this leave us with?'

They regarded him, waiting for the answer.

'Hope that was a rhetorical question, Henry,' Donaldson said.

'You mean it's down to me to pull this together? I don't even have a clue what's going on.'

'After you buy the drinks for us, it might come to you.'

'OK – but first things first. Georgia.' He turned to her. 'You need somewhere to stay.'

'Any suggestions?'

'There's one of those Travelodges or Premier Inns just outside Blackpool. I've crashed there a few times. Why don't you fix up a couple of rooms for us there, Henry?' Donaldson put in quickly. 'Use Ken's phone. He won't mind.'

'I thought...' Henry looked at his friend and was about to say, 'you were staying with me and Kate.' He didn't bother finishing his sentence. Now it was certain – Donaldson *was* going to veer off the straight and narrow. 'Nothing,' he said absently. He rose dispiritedly and with a heavy heart set off for the bar where Ken was totting up the night's takings. Feeling truly sick, he made the call to the hotel and booked two rooms, then returned with three drinks clasped between his fingers.

'OK, H, what have we got?' Donaldson folded his fingers behind his head. Georgia waited expectantly, but looking very tired. Henry held his head between his hands and thought for a while, then raised his face.

'We have two high-ranking detectives consorting with a known Mafia mover and shaker. Dave Anger, Paul Shafer and Walter Corrigan. Corrigan is connected to a man called Rosario?' He looked at Georgia for confirmation – yes. 'And Rosario delivers weapons for the Mob, in this case the rifle that killed an innocent cop, but was probably intended for Paulo Scartarelli, now in custody in Lancashire.'

'We actually don't know if they are consorting. Maybe they're scamming Corrigan, on to something big we don't know about,' Donaldson said.

'Maybe, but until I know differently, then they are consorting,' Henry said, probably because that was what he wanted to believe. 'Now, is this connected?' he posed the next question. 'A man I believe could well be responsible for the murder of two hookers in Preston has been shot by the police in Merseyside and it seems that this dead guy, Jonny Motta, has been eliminated from the murder enquiry even though it looks as though he's the prime suspect. Just say that Motta did kill the prostitutes, then another coincidence is that they're believed to have come from Albania, just like the prostitute Scartarelli murdered.'

'Vague, vague,' Donaldson almost tutted.

'You come up with something better,' Henry

said sulkily, a jealous streak a mile wide inside him.

'I haven't got anything better,' Donaldson admitted. 'Except that Scartarelli and Corrigan *are* connected, even if it's only by the use of that villa in Cyprus.'

'It would be interesting to see if we can find a link between Scartarelli and this Motta,' Georgia said. She was taking it all in, moving it around even though she was exhausted. 'If there is, it completes the circle. Corrigan – Motta – Scartarelli – and your officers, Anger and the other one.'

The tame landlord Ken appeared bearing a large plateful of sandwiches, with several varieties of fillings. He placed it on their table.

'On the house. I can see brains ticking.'

'Ken, you are a star.'

'And I'm also off to bed. Help yourself to any bottles or shorts if you want anything more and we'll settle up tomorrow. Leave by the front door, but make sure it's locked behind you.'

Georgia dived into the food, suddenly ravenous. The men ate more sedately, munching thoughtfully.

'You've been hankering to see Scartarelli,' Henry said to Donaldson. 'Why don't we all go and have a word with him?'

Henry crept into bed at 2.35 a.m., sweaty, alcohol-breathed and very tired. He muttered some sort of apology to Kate, who made an unintelligible response, though it was clear she wasn't over the moon at his appearance. Henry tried to

288

sleep, but his mind refused to allow it as it mulled things over.

Problem was, Henry actually enjoyed mulling things over, trying to make some sort of sense of the cards he'd been dealt. He also didn't like jumping to too many conclusions but he liked putting them together and testing them to destruction. That was how breakthroughs were made: sifting, sorting, trying things out. And that was why, thirty minutes after going to bed, he was up again in his dressing gown, sitting in the conservatory with the blinds drawn, pen and pad to hand. He wrote out a list of names, characters and some notes.

Three dead prostitutes

Jonny Motta maybe killed two of them

Paulo Scartarelli killed the third one – over a year ago having been ID'd by hooker on death-bed. So the cops had to do something about it. Not much, though. Just circulated as wanted. Not much detecting going on! Police Authority ordered cops to do something – hence me, Operation Wanted.

Walter Corrigan. Cyprus. Mafia – linked to Scartarelli – he ran there but accidentally located by Georgia!

Corrigan – Scartarelli – does Corrigan want him dead? (Fails, kills a cop) Cops in Cyprus get act together. Find Rosario, Mafia gun supplier who fingers Corrigan as the contractor?

Corrigan leaves island, comes to UK.

Seen i/c Anger/ Shafer – big, old-time buddies What are they up to?

Have Lancs cops really eliminated Motta properly. I know it's the guy I fought – fingerprints in neck. Maybe the fingerprints I took will prove it!

Am I just linking stuff that has no connection? Is everyone guilty? Is anything connected? Prob not.

Is KD screwing GP!!!!

Henry scrubbed a few heavy lines through the last entry and tried not to think about it. He read through the notes and thought, But what's my job here? The answer was to tidy up the shooting of a man by police officers in Liverpool.

Then he had another thought. The original IPCC investigator met his death in suspicious circumstances. A hit-and-run. Should that be investigated again? Did that have any bearing on anything?

He found his way to the drinks cabinet and poured himself a healthy shot of Grants which he swallowed in one, making him bare his teeth in reaction.

'Bed,' he declared.

He was up at seven, shaved, showered and the rest. Over a strong filtered coffee he sent texts to Jerry Tope and Bill Robbins, asking them to meet him at Leyland police station, where Scartarelli was being housed prior to his court appearance. Neither replied.

He had also arranged to pick up Karl Donaldson and Georgia on his way through, even though it stuck in his craw. What would they look like? Flushed and sex-sated. Yuk!

He popped back upstairs to say goodbye to Kate, who was flat out on her back and snoring loudly. Having kissed and closed her mouth gently with the tip of his finger, he went back down and picked up his mobile phone, which was ringing: Karl.

'What?' Henry said grumpily.

'Don't bother to pick us up, we'll make our own way over in my tank.' He meant his Jeep.

'Whatever,' Henry said, thumbing the end-call button, certain he heard a familiar female giggle in the background before the connection was axed. Darkly he drove to Leyland via the M55 and M6, exiting at junction 28. The police station was less than five minutes from the motorway, right next to the Magistrates' Court and opposite a large Tesco superstore. He parked at the back of the sports centre, also opposite the station.

Henry's mood did not lighten when he let himself into the nick and made his way up to the canteen, which was completely devoid of personnel now that the canteen facility had been axed. It had been replaced by self-service machines dispensing pre-packed breakfasts that then needed heating in a microwave, all in the name of cost-cutting. The morning social had been well and truly curtailed here.

He grabbed a frothy coffee from another machine and took a seat by a window overlooking the road out front, waiting for the arrival of his colleagues.

Bill Robbins landed first, followed shortly

291

after by Jerry Tope.

The other two were noticeable by the lateness. Morning sex, Henry thought jealously.

His trustworthy team got a coffee each at his expense and sat by him.

'What's happening?' Bill asked.

Henry explained why they were at Leyland – a subject which got some shocked reactions from the men – then asked Jerry if he had made any progress on the IT front.

'Of course, but nothing so far with the CCTV stuff, I'm afraid. However...' He produced a copy of an email, which he passed to Henry. 'This was sent to Dave Anger from Paul Shafer.'

Henry twisted it around and read it. *'Keep up the good work. If we keep our heads down and don't lose our nerve, this'll smell very wealthy – eventually. OK for S'Port meet?'*

Henry thought it over, then raised his eyes. 'Anything else?'

'Not on that subject.'

'OK – keep on it.'

'There is something else, actually. That expense account, Operation Wanted. I've discovered something interesting and I—'

Henry frowned. 'Not for here and now, Jerry. Will it keep?'

'Mm, OK. Mind if I keep digging on it, though?'

'Do what you want,' Henry nodded.

Donaldson and Georgia strolled into the dining room, both bouncing following their night of passion. At least that was how Henry saw it. They had picked up the ID badges that Henry

292

had arranged for them at the front desk.

'Glad you could make it,' was the most original greeting he could manage.

'Morning, guys,' Donaldson beamed as Georgia rushed to Bill and gave him a big hug. Bill responded in kind and held on for just a moment too long for decency, but she didn't seem to mind. They exchanged a few how-are-you's and then Henry introduced her to Jerry Tope, who was mesmerized.

'Jerry,' Henry cut into his reverie, 'I believe you've got some IT-based things to pull together?'

'Yeah, boss.' Reluctantly he slunk away, tearing his eyes from Georgia only as he went out through the door.

Henry did have to admit she was stunning, dressed in tight jeans, a loose blouse and denim jacket. He scowled at Donaldson, who winked playfully at him, then they all sat at a table whilst Bill scurried about getting more coffees.

'What's the plan, H?' Donaldson asked, stretching and yawning.

Henry gave him a double-take, then took a breath to clear his mind of the horrible image he had of the Yank and the Cypriot 'doing it'. He had never been so utterly jealous of a man having sex with a woman before. Just wasn't like him.

'I'll go down to the custody office and check where we're up to with Scartarelli. He should be about ready to be taken over to court and I reckon the time he spends waiting in a holding cell will give us the opportunity to speak

293

to him.'

'How much time could that be?'

'Depends how many people are up this morning. We'll just have to suck it and see.'

Donaldson nodded. 'OK, bud.'

'If you guys want to wait here, I'll go down and see what's happening.'

Although Leyland police station is the one used by Lancashire Constabulary to house suspected terrorists and other serious offenders, it is still a fairly quiet nick in comparison, say, to Blackpool, where chaos reigns 24/7. It is one of the force's most recently constructed stations, comparatively speaking, and was built with extra security because it was an opportunity not to be missed as no other station in the county had high security. And it was handy geographically, being so close to the motorway network.

Making his way down the flight of stairs to the custody office on the ground floor, Henry bumped into no one, even in the corridor leading up to the cell complex.

He buzzed at the steel door, looked at the security camera, flashed his warrant card and was allowed in.

The custody sergeant was a bruiser called Eccles. He glanced up from his paperwork – literally, he was reading the newspaper – and smiled. He knew Henry from old. They had about the same length of service and their careers had intersected occasionally over the years.

They greeted each other warmly and asked

294

brief questions about families and shared friends.

'So, Henry, what can I do you for? Scartarelli, I'll bet.'

'Yeah. I want to arrange for some people, including myself, to have a chat with him for intelligence-gathering purposes.'

'No probs.'

'Has he had his brekkie yet?'

'Had everything,' Eccles confirmed.

'I'll go and get my colleagues,' Henry said enthusiastically. 'One's from the FBI – whoow! – and another's a Cypriot cop.'

'Only one thing...'

'What would that be, Chris?'

'He's already gone to court.'

Henry's eyes automatically rose to the clock on the wall, which read 8.27. Court didn't start until ten, so Scartarelli's transfer across was early by any standards.

'Yeah, I thought that, too,' Eccles said, reading Henry's mind. 'The escort came early and wanted to take him, so who was I to refuse? I made them take the other remand prisoner, too, even though they weren't interested in him. Another one you were involved with, by the way – Downie?'

'I know him all right.'

'He's been charged with some jobs over here, indecency and deception. Looks like he'll be in for a long stretch, as will the Italian, of course.'

'That's good to hear. Er, who actually came for Scartarelli?'

'A new security company...' Eccles rooted out the custody record and flicked it open. 'Dell

House Security. They've just taken over the Sec-Ser contract, apparently, though I hadn't heard about it. Must be keen to make a good impression, hence the earliness.'

Henry scanned the custody record which showed a company stamp and a scribbled signature on the line indicating that Scartarelli had been handed over.

'I'll just mosey through, if that's OK. I'll fix up the interview with the guards.'

'Whatever.'

'Buzz me through.'

Henry walked across to the steel door which was the entrance to the short underground tunnel leading from the police cells to the holding cells underneath the Magistrates' Court next door. It was a brightly lit tunnel, concrete-lined, less than twenty metres in length. Henry walked briskly along it and came to the next door, which opened into the holding area. This contained a number of cells, interview rooms and an office as well as an electric shuttered door for the prisoner loading bay, big enough for a large, single-decker prison bus to reverse into.

The first strange sensation for Henry came when he was able to get through to this complex through a door which should have been locked and manned by someone controlling it. He could just push the tunnel door open and it swung gently on its well-oiled hinges.

He stepped into the holding area.

All the lights were on ... but there was no one at home.

At the least there should have been a guard in

the office, clearly visible through the big plate-glass window. No one sat there.

Henry crossed to the office and looked in through the window, just to confirm it was empty and that a guard wasn't tying shoelaces or something.

It was empty.

'Hello,' he called.

No sign of any of the prisoner escorts.

He walked over to one of the cell doors and looked through the window. The cell was empty, too. The next cell along was also empty. However, much to his relief, the third cell contained the two prisoners who'd come across from the police cells.

Scartarelli was inside, as was the other remand prisoner, Downie, sitting side by side on the bench.

As Henry's face appeared at the toughened-glass window in the cell door, both prisoners turned their heads to look sourly up at him. Neither gave him a welcome smile. Both still had their wrists shackled by rigid handcuffs.

Downie recognized him first and jerked a middle finger at him. Scartarelli had a tense expression on his face.

Henry gave them a little tinkle of his fingers, turned away and went back to the office. He picked up the phone and dialled through to the custody office next door.

'Chris, it's Henry...'

'Boss,' the custody officer said before Henry could speak, 'can you make your way back ... something odd's just happened.'

297

'Uh – yeah ... shouldn't the escorts still be over here with the prisoners?' Henry asked.

'Yeah, well that's what's odd. The escort's turned up.'

Henry frowned. 'Be there in a sec.'

He hung up and hurried back down the corridor, being buzzed back into the custody office by Eccles. There he immediately saw two uniformed security guards with 'SecSer' emblems on their tunics.

'What's happening?'

'These guys are from SecSer. They've come for the morning remand prisoners. Seems a bit of a cock-up. They say they've never heard of DellHouse Security and that SecSer still have the contract. What do I do now?'

Henry stood stock still for a moment, pondering this, mulching it slowly.

'There's no sign of the escorts in the court holding area,' Henry said, jerking his thumb in the direction.

'Eh? They should be there.' Eccles screwed up his nose.

'Or maybe they just snuck off for a brew?' Henry suggested. 'Or maybe not...' A feeling of dread coursed through him. He got his mobile phone out of his pocket and as he tabbed through it for a number, he crossed to the court-corridor door and said, 'Let me back through, Chris,' as his hand wrapped around the handle.

'What shall we do?' one of the SecSer guards asked.

'Sit tight,' Henry said, yanking the door open on the buzz and entering the corridor with his

298

phone pressed to his ear. 'Bill, it's Henry ... Get down to the cells ... Bill? Fuck!' The signal had disappeared as Henry entered the corridor, but he hoped that the brief, urgent message had got through before the signal let him down. He moved up a gear and trotted down the corridor.

Ahead of him he heard two dull thuds close together, then two more, then one more ... and he knew what had made the sounds.

Gunfire.

His trot became a compelling spurt and he flew through the door into the holding area.

Now his dull-dumb brain had got into gear and his sharp eyes took in everything: the fact that the shutter door to the prison bus bay was now three-quarters open, that a black Range Rover with smoked windows had reversed into the bay; that the door of cell number three was open. But above all that a masked man was backing out through the cell door, holding a semi-automatic pistol of some sort and that a sliver of smoke rose from the muzzle of the gun.

The guy was wearing overalls and trainers and for a fleeting second did not notice Henry as the detective pirouetted through the door. But that didn't matter, because there was a second man, similarly dressed, standing by the rear of the Range Rover who did see Henry and uttered a shouted warning. That man, too, was armed with a pistol and it was aimed at Henry.

Henry caught a scream in his throat as he dived to one side and rolled towards the toilets as two bullets whooshed past him, embedding themselves just above his head in the wall.

The man coming out of the cell pivoted in his direction, and suddenly Henry was very open and unprotected, nothing between him and this gunman except for a few metres of open space. As the guy swivelled, he went into a low crouch and swung his arms around and pointed the sharp end of the isosceles triangle formed by his rigid arms at Henry – meaning Henry was in the sights of the gun.

But Henry still had some momentum, and scrabbling like a demented sprinter, he rolled on to one knee and threw himself at the toilet door, crashing through it into the gents and rolling towards a cubicle just a second before the man fired.

Henry scrambled down to the far end of the lavatory whilst at the same time trying to get his mobile from his jacket pocket. At the far wall, he regained his feet and stepped into the last cubicle, turning and peering out to see if he had been followed and was about to be executed. He was in no doubt that was the fate which had just befallen one, or both, of the prisoners in their cell.

He knew for definite that Scartarelli was now a dead man.

He was more than all thumbs as he tried to redial the last number he'd called. Holding the phone clamped to his ear, Henry waited for the gunman to appear and dispatch him, tremors of fear pulsating through him.

But all he heard was an engine revving, the screech of tyres on the shiny concrete surface of the bus bay.

They'd gone.

Henry stepped out of the cubicle.

Bill answered the phone.

'Bill – two, possibly three gunmen escaping from the holding cells under the courts. Black Range Rover, fogged windows, 54 reg – that's all I know – get it circulated now! Possible deaths down here. Get the helicopter up, too.'

Henry was speaking as he walked out of the toilet, stopping just beyond the door. There was the smell of cordite in the air. A wisp of exhaust smoke rose in the loading bay, the only evidence that a vehicle had just been there, together with the tyre marks on the surface.

Nostrils flaring, heart pounding, he stepped slowly towards the open cell door, knowing he'd come across an assassination squad conducting business. He was right.

Scartarelli was dead. He had taken four of the bullets, by the looks of him. Two to the chest – bang-bang – right over the heart, two in the head as compactly aimed as the other two. Both had entered the front of his skull and removed the back of it, splattering it all over the cell wall behind him. He was slumped on the bench seat, having slithered sideways to his left, leaving a trail of blood down the wall.

The last bullet had been fired into Anthony Downie, just one into the side of his head. He was as dead as Scartarelli.

Recalling the brief conversation Henry had had with Scartarelli on the plane in Cyprus, Henry mumbled, 'Oh yes, mate, it definitely was you they were after.'

301

He wiped the back of his hand across his mouth, inhaled a steadying breath and stepped out of the crime scene as the corridor door opened as Donaldson, Georgia and Bill burst through. Their morning-time sexual haze was now very much wiped off their faces – or so Henry thought with satisfaction.

SEVENTEEN

Henry had to fight the instinct, which had occasionally served him well, to commandeer a cop car and go out in hot pursuit of the Range Rover. He knew he would be more useful and effective staying put at the court and the police station. There was a hot crime scene to protect and preserve and a manhunt to coordinate. On top of that there was a double murder enquiry to get up and running – but first things first.

Trusting Donaldson to protect the murder scene, Henry dashed back to the custody office and phoned the Force Incident Manager in the comms room at HQ. He filled her in succinctly with the current situation and after that left the hunt for the Range Rover down to her to sort. Then he snaffled a PR from Sergeant Eccles in custody, promising to return it. He was on his way back to the crime scene when he heard a local patrol call up.

'Charlie Five – urgent.'

'Go ahead,' the comms operator responded.

'Behind a Black Range Rover, 54 registered, just turned into Worden Park, vehicle now accelerating away from me...'

'Roger that ... Other patrols to acknowledge and make to the area.'

This time, as Henry surged through the door

303

into the holding-cell area, he decided to let his instinct direct him. He ran in shouting, 'Bill – you stay here, guard the scene, do the necessary. Georgia, you stay with him ... Karl,' Henry held up the PR, 'fancy a run out in your Jeep? Suspect vehicle spotted nearby.'

Instantly Donaldson said, 'You got it.' He was a true man of action and didn't need a second invitation.

'Follow me.'

Henry ran out through the shutter door and headed towards the front of the police station where Donaldson had parked up. Donaldson loped easily behind him, pointing his remote locking fob at the car.

'Heading towards Worden Hall,' the officer, call sign Charlie Five, said coolly over the PR, referring to the fact that the vehicle he was following was now in Worden Park and heading in the direction of Worden Hall in the centre of the park.

'I'll bet they have a change of transport lined up in there,' Henry guessed as he slid into the front passenger seat next to Donaldson, who started the massive four-litre engine and pulled out of his parking spot. 'DCI Christie to comms – please reiterate – extreme caution. These men are armed and extremely dangerous.' He turned to Donaldson and pointed at the big Tesco supermarket over the road. 'Right across the car park,' he directed the American, then sat back and added sourly, 'A bit like World War Two ... us Brits do all the hard work, then you lot come along and get the glory.'

'Eh?'

'Georgia Papakostas?'

Donaldson began to laugh.

'Across here and right across the town square,' Henry said, directing Donaldson across the supermarket car park and instead of leaving by the usual route by road, he told him to drive across the flowerbeds, then over a tiny cobbled square to join Worden Lane, which led to the park. Henry knew where he was going. Not because he'd been a cop in these parts, but because many of the driving courses he'd attended had used these roads regularly because of their close proximity to headquarters. The area was often rife with cops on driving courses.

The Jeep scoured deep tracks into lawns and flowerbeds and bounced over the tiny square on to Worden Lane as instructed.

'Straight on,' Henry said, holding on for dear life.

Donaldson rammed his foot on the gas pedal, things becoming much more urgent as Charlie Five screamed, 'Shots fired, shots fired...'

'Faster,' Henry said, seeing the walls of the park approaching.

Charlie Five was a patrol crewed by one cop, Rob Howard, a rather grizzled PC who, though counting his pay days to retirement, was still as keen as mustard and still loved the buzz of coppering and loved seeing villains behind bars.

He was one of only two mobile-response officers on duty in Leyland that morning. If he was honest, it had been a dull early shift and he

305

was anticipating buying a fried breakfast from the Tesco restaurant across the road from the station, his usual early shift treat.

In all honesty, Howard had been tootling, certainly not breaking any pots that morning. Very few jobs had come in and as the circulation about the Range Rover came up and the serious incident at the court, his whole demeanour changed. He had been lazily heading back to Tesco and when the wanted vehicle's details came over the radio he was, in old-fashioned police parlance, heading in an easterly direction along Langdale Road towards Worden Park. He reached the junction with Worden Lane, the road which skims the perimeter of the park, and stopping there just saw the tail end of a vehicle turn into the park gates some two hundred metres to his right. To be honest he wasn't sure if it was a Range Rover, but it was definitely an off-roader of some sort.

He screwed his Astra patrol car to the gates and plunged into the park, seeing that the vehicle at the far end of the car park was definitely a Range Rover – as described in the radio circulation.

His right foot hit the accelerator and his finger hit the transmission button on his PR.

The Range Rover flew out of the car park on to the narrow road snaking through the park and into the small car park behind the Arts and Craft Centre attached to the old hall. PC Howard was only seconds behind it as the 4x4 skidded to a spectacular, muck-chucking halt and two masked men leapt out, brandishing weapons in the PC's direction.

Howard, no coward, knew he was in deep trouble, as he had got too close in his enthusiasm. The two men jogged menacingly towards him, no hurry, and raised their guns at him. Howard slammed the gearbox into reverse, not the easiest gear to find quickly on that particular Astra, and slewed backwards away from them, screaming into his PR as two bullets thudded into the radiator.

'Shots fired, shots fired,' the PC's voice squawked distortedly over the PR, the sound of his engine revving in the background.

Donaldson swerved in through the park gates, urged on by the voice and that of Henry Christie yelling in his ears.

'Go, go, go,' he said dramatically, even though a little voice in his skull told him how stupid that sounded, despite the circumstances.

A woman walking her dog had to leap out of the way, dragging her poor pooch, almost strangling the little beast.

'Straight on,' Henry said.

The Jeep bounced across the tarmac and ahead of them they could see the Astra reversing, but not the gunmen who were hidden by the hedge surrounding the Arts Centre car park.

The Astra reversed wildly back down the road, but then the PC lost it and ran it off the edge of the road into soft grass, the wheels spinning.

'There!' Henry said. He pointed across the wide meadow towards the far end of the car park as the Range Rover emerged on to the grass and

307

sped towards the park exit. Donaldson grimly yanked the steering wheel down and bounced the Jeep off the road on to the grass, going diagonally for the Range Rover, even though it was some two hundred metres ahead of them.

Donaldson's pride and joy was now in its element, but so was the Range Rover, which tore across the open space, bounced back on to the park road and raced towards the park gates.

Henry gave the commentary over the radio: 'Range Rover now on the road leading to the park exit. Three on board, I think, all males. For your information I am following in a green Jeep, a private vehicle...' Henry held tight as Donaldson's 4x4 shot up the banking from the grass and on to the road. Even though he was strapped in, he bounced high and smacked his head on the roof, and was thrown hard against the door. Undeterred, Henry continued into the radio, 'Vehicle heading at speed towards Worden Lane.' His voice was level and controlled over the air.

The Jeep screamed its way through the automatic gear box.

Ahead of them the Range Rover reached the park exit, skidded out on to the main road and went right. Henry relayed this, then turned to Donaldson. 'Won't this bus go any faster?'

The American shot him a warning glance.

'Big car, little dick,' Henry said spitefully.

'Up yours,' Donaldson said as his car passed through the gates and emerged on to the main road – and was broadsided by a large articulated milk lorry coming in the opposite direction.

EIGHTEEN

'That was lucky.'

'Luck is comparative.'

'We got out alive, unscathed – a miracle.'

'Admittedly that *was* lucky.' Henry could still feel the impact, the unbelievably loud crash and crunch, the tearing of metal. He could see the Jeep being spun and lifted across the road into the front garden opposite. The airbags deploying. The thoughts made him go cold. 'The other side of the coin is that – actually, the other *sides* of the coin are – your precious American piece of shit is a write-off and your reckless driving allowed three major villains to escape.'

'You sound pissed at me, but do I detect an undercurrent of hostility, even deeper than the facade?'

'Fancy talkin' for a Yank,' Henry said. 'Maybe your brain got mashed after all.'

'Hey!' Donaldson stopped and spun Henry around. They were at the front of Leyland police station having returned from a four-hour sojourn at the infirmary at Preston for a check-up following the crash. Bill Robbins had collected them and was walking behind them as they bickered their way towards the station. 'You got somethin' to say, say it, pal!'

309

Henry glowered at him and shook his arm free. 'I'm annoyed because villains got away – OK? And once again, no doubt, I've had the proverbial investigative rug pulled away from under me. Duh!'

'OK, fair enough.'

Henry shook his head, annoyed.

'I thought you were pissed at me for more fundamental, personal reasons.'

He shook his head again and walked in through the front revolving doors of the station to find the small foyer crammed full of the media, a hum of anticipation reverberating around the room. A double murder at the Magistrates' Court. Juicy stuff. Great headlines and a story that would probably run for weeks.

Henry stopped, not expecting the sea of humanity, some might say dregs of the earth, but knew immediately that such a serious, violent incident would be a magnet for all sections of the communication trade. There were probably about thirty people crammed in there, but through them all he caught sight of Georgia sitting squashed on a chair in one corner. She did not spot him or Donaldson immediately. Henry eased his way towards her.

'Why are you here?' he asked.

She jumped to her feet, hugged him, then hugged Donaldson longer and said, 'How are you, how are you?'

'To say we came face to face with the business end of a milk truck, we're doing fine – a remarkable story of survival. If either of us had been going any faster...' Henry left the words unsaid.

'As it is, I've got a bruised arm and he's got a thick head. But that doesn't answer my question – what are you doing out here?'

'I was asked to leave by Chief Superintendent Anger.'

Henry left Donaldson and Georgia in the foyer, the American chivalrously saying he would stay and keep her company and that he had some arranging to do re his car and its recovery and replacement anyway.

Henry went through into the guts of the station and up the steps to the second floor, where he knew all the activity would be located in terms of the investigation. He found that the canteen had been transformed into a Major Incident Room as if by magic. It was hardly recognizable as the room he'd had a coffee in earlier.

It was buzzing with activity, many people having been brought in quickly at short notice. Henry recognized some old regulars, those detectives who were brought in for investigation after investigation. Those who knew their roles backwards and could be relied upon time after time to do the business.

He walked through the hastily arranged tables, which were already starting to conform to the model in the MIR operating manual.

Henry loved it. He felt like he was in his element. There was nothing better than being part of a murder squad, no buzz to beat it.

And it was something that had been cruelly taken away from him by the advent of Dave Anger at the helm of FMIT.

Henry knew he would probably have no part in this investigation and it hurt to think so. He'd already been informed that Jack Carradine had been put in charge and was calling the shots. That had been revealed to him whilst in the casualty waiting room.

Henry spoke to a detective sergeant he knew, one of those reliable specialists brought in for his knowledge of evidence-logging.

'Hello, Henry.'

'Where's the SIO?'

The DS pointed in the direction of the corridor. 'CID office ... There's a briefing going on.'

Inside, Henry growled. 'Thanks.'

'Henry – you don't know where Jerry Tope is, do you? I know he was doing a bit of work for you, wasn't he?'

'On his mobile, I assume. Why?'

'We've been trying to contact him for this job, to run an intelligence cell.'

'I'm not sure exactly where he is.'

'OK, ta.'

Henry went to the CID office. He paused outside, his hand on the doorknob, suddenly feeling a little woozy. He wondered if he was suffering from delayed shock from the crash. Maybe he shouldn't even be at work, but back home being tended by Kate.

He knew that if it had been a normal day, not one on which a double murder had occurred, or one which he'd been shot at by a gang of assassins, then he might well have gone home, put his feet up and watched *Diagnosis Murder*, rooting for Dick van Dyke.

However, today wasn't like that.

He'd stumbled across a murder being committed, almost took a bullet himself, chased the offenders and almost come to another sticky end under the wheels of a heavy goods vehicle. So there was no way on God's earth was he going to go home and suck his thumb.

He recovered his composure and opened the door to the CID office.

The office was not particularly large and it didn't take much to fill it, and the twenty-five to thirty detectives, some sitting, most standing, did just that. Henry had to ease his way behind them, then stand on tiptoe to see over their heads to the front of the office where the SIO was addressing them.

DCI Carradine was the centre of attention and it was clear from what he was saying that Henry had missed the briefing almost in its entirety.

'So that is where we stand,' Carradine said, drawing the briefing to a conclusion. 'That will be the focus of the enquiry, because we believe that the second man in the cell was just unfortunate – wrong place, wrong time – and he was killed simply because he was a witness.' Henry guessed that Carradine was talking about Downie. 'These men,' Carradine went on, 'are obviously very dangerous individuals and we are dealing with a highly organized group of people who will stop at nothing to further their aims and stay free.'

Henry caught sight of Dave Anger sitting down at the front of the office next to the standing Carradine. Henry's nostrils flared.

313

Carradine continued, 'Fortunately no police officer was injured this morning, but we do salute the obvious bravery of PC Howard ... Rob, where are you?' Carradine looked around and beckoned Howard out of a knot of uniformed personnel. 'It's guys like this who make Lancashire Constabulary the police service it is, the best in the country.' Carradine beamed at the old rugged cop, who shifted with embarrassment in front of everyone. A little ripple of applause went round the room, with one or two appreciative 'well dones' added. Carradine slapped Howard on the shoulders and the PC moved gratefully away from the limelight. 'You'll get a bravery award for this, I'll personally see to that ... However, guys and gals,' he said turning his attention to the rest of the audience, 'from now on we do not put ourselves in the firing line for this job. Everything is done by the book and in reference to the health and safety of everyone.' Carradine took a breath. Henry wondered if he should put up his hand and say, 'I nearly got shot, too. Will you pat me on the back? Put me forward for a bravery award? Bet you won't, you fucker.' He didn't. In spite of the very real temptation. Carradine continued, 'So, folks, you know your pairings, so go and see the allocator in the dining room, which is now the MIR. He will already have some jobs for you to be doing. Get on with them. The sooner we move, the better chance we have of catching these villains. Any questions before you go?'

Somebody asked, 'Any news on the Range Rover?'

'Nothing yet. Checkpoints are in place, the helicopter's up, GMP and Merseyside have been alerted, and we're about to brief the news media, so it'll be regional soon. I'm sure it'll turn up sooner rather than later. Anything else? No? OK, folks, let's get to it. Back here for debrief at 8 p.m. unless told otherwise.'

The briefing dispersed, detectives filtering out past Henry at the door, one or two nodding at him, others just averting their eyes as though he was a pariah.

Eventually everyone had gone with the exception of Carradine and Anger at the front of the room.

Henry sauntered towards them.

Anger stood up, collecting a sheaf of papers. 'Good brief, Jack,' he was congratulating the DCI, probably for Henry's sake, then he turned to Henry. Carradine stood slightly behind him, smirking.

'Ah, Henry, I wondered when you'd show your face again,' Anger said scathingly. 'Not too badly injured, I hope?'

'I'm OK. Luckily no one was injured.'

'I'm glad to hear that, I really am,' Anger said insincerely.

'Yeah, we're all glad you're OK,' Carradine added, but shook his head.

'Unfortunately I missed the briefing,' Henry said. 'I was otherwise engaged in casualty, as you know. I wonder if you have the time just to run things past me again, bring me up to speed.'

Both men regarded him as if he were stupid.

'Why would we want to do that, Henry?'

315

Anger asked.

Henry's heart began whamming inside his chest. 'Because...' he began.

'Nope,' Anger said sharply. 'You won't be part of this investigation in any capacity whatsoever ... Having said that, don't go anywhere.' He pointed at Henry. 'You stay here in this building because we want to talk to you. Get comfy, get a brew. We have a press briefing, then we'll be busy with other aspects of the job and then we need to have a little sit down and a chat with you.'

'I tell you what,' Carradine chirped up. 'You can make yourself useful if you want to – get into the MIR and help get it set up.' He said that as though he was doing Henry a great big favour. 'That should keep you busy enough until we have the time to see you.'

It could have been much worse. The administration of Major Incident Rooms was something Henry had been involved in as a DC and he had enjoyed the responsibility of getting a few up and running in his time. It was therefore no hardship to assist the office manager to get it all running smoothly, to bring in the HOLMES computer terminals, that is the Home Office Large and Major Enquiry System, and start to get information loaded on to them.

He knew what he was doing, and despite the fact he wanted to be in charge, he swallowed his pride and made himself useful because an enquiry such as this needed to have a well-run back room on which the detectives doing the jobs could rely.

Yes, it could have been much worse, but it could also have been much better.

And the problem was, Henry wasn't sure how to take things forward in relation to what he knew about Dave Anger and everything else he had uncovered in the past few days which was unsettling.

Did Anger's meeting with Corrigan have anything to do with this morning's murders, Corrigan having that connection to Scartarelli?

That was the biggest question burning a very deep scar in his brain.

At one point he made his way down to the enquiry desk to see Donaldson and Georgia, but found they were not there. He tried to contact them by phone, but got nowhere with that. Nor could he find Bill Robbins, who seemed to have done a disappearing trick, too. He guessed Bill was helping Donaldson to sort out the damaged Jeep and that Georgia had gone along with them. He expected to hear from them soon and left messages for each of them on their mobiles, a particularly caustic one on Donaldson's.

The day went quickly by because he made himself busy and soon it was 8 p.m. and time for the debrief. Again, Henry would normally have found this to be an exciting time, another of those important stages in a murder enquiry when all the detectives came together at the end of the day, buzzing with news or the lack of it, reporting back, doing a bit of bonding and hopefully going for a few jars to bring the day to a close afterwards.

317

Henry felt detached from it as he listened to the jacks going through what they had uncovered.

Everything was positive, but there were no firm leads and the Range Rover hadn't turned up.

Carradine listened and then told them what he had been doing that day – arranging the post-mortems, supervising the terrible crime scene, press liaison, intelligence and other such stuff. Anger sat by him, proudly watching his protégé.

At the end of the debrief, Anger rose to his feet, looking solemn.

'Thanks for all your effort today, it is much appreciated. As you've been told, there will be many more detectives and uniformed personnel drafted in from tomorrow and this investigation will really get going.' He bunched his fist to emphasize his words. 'We will look for a 7 a.m. briefing – so everyone get a good night's sleep because tomorrow will be a long day and I imagine that every day after that will be a long slog, so you need to prepare yourselves for that likelihood. This will be a long investigation, make no bones about it, but I know that with people like you, it will be a successful one. So, thanks again and good night. I'll see you all in the morning.'

They dispersed, Henry overhearing a few plans for drinks, although no one asked him along.

Not that he wanted to go. He wanted to speak to Dave Anger and then get home, regroup his team and decide on the way forward.

As the last of the detectives left the office, Henry, Anger and Carradine were the only three staying behind.

Henry swallowed as they looked at him through hooded lids, like vultures looking down from the branches at an animal that wasn't quite yet dead.

Anger smiled. 'Henry, at last. We need to talk.'

They retired to the divisional chief superintendent's office on the floor below, Anger apparently believing he had a right to use it as he had a key for the door.

'Sit.'

Henry sat on a chair on the public side of the office whilst Anger slid around to the other side of the desk and parked himself on the chief super's chair, which hissed as the air escaped from its thick leather.

Carradine came into the office and positioned himself behind the door, remaining standing, arms folded, a blank look on his face.

Henry, therefore, was between the two of them, the rock and the hard place. 'Nice,' he said looking at the office. Henry knew the divisional chief superintendent quite well and the walls were egotistically adorned with lots of pictures of the guy and his many certificates.

Anger and Carradine did not respond, maintaining their silence.

Anger then leaned on the desk with his right elbow and right hand bunched into a fist.

'Let's just have a look at this, shall we?' he said. 'Firstly,' his thumb flicked up, indicating the first item on the agenda, 'you need to tell me why you and your gaggle of ragtag mates were going to speak to Scartarelli. Secondly,' his first finger flicked up, item two, 'you need to explain why a man of your experience jumps in a car and goes on a chase, instead of staying at the scene and getting a strategic grip of a very serious incident. Then,' his middle finger came up out of the fist, agenda item number three. Henry wondered if he would have enough fingers to cover all the items that he wished to cover. 'Number three, why did you even consider using the vehicle of a private individual to conduct such a chase? It was reckless and you have put the Constabulary, once again, in a very unfortunate position. People could have been killed. As ever, you are stupid, foolish and short-sighted.' Anger folded away his fingers back into his fist. 'I'm waiting, Henry.'

'Anything else?' Henry asked.

'Lots of things, actually.'

Henry shifted uncomfortably, now feeling very worried about his situation. He tried to sit back and look as though he was relaxed.

'You really are an arsehole, Henry,' Carradine could not resist saying. 'You poke your fucking nose into everything that doesn't concern you, don't you?'

'I do my job.' He gave his eyebrows a quick flick up and down. 'Know what I mean? Unpleasant as it might be.' He cast his eyes from one man to the other, trying desperately to work out what was happening, to read their minds, then he turned to Anger. 'Dave, maybe I'm the one who should be asking the questions here.'

'Run that one by me,' he said harshly.

'OK.' Henry steeled himself and blurted, 'Do you know a man called Walter Corrigan?' then wished he hadn't revealed this card, but knew now he'd have to go with it.

Anger's immediate response was, 'No, why should I?' and Henry had to admit it was a pretty smooth riposte to a nooky question.

'He's a fixer for various people connected to organized crime, a very bad man.' Henry didn't want to say the Mafia, because it sounded all too corny.

'Means nothing,' Anger said with a twitch of his mouth. 'I get the impression you're just trying to deflect blame away from yourself here, because I don't know what the hell you're leading up to, but I know it's probably bollocks.'

'You do know Paul Shafer, though, don't you? Detective superintendent in Merseyside?'

'I know him, of course I do.'

'Old mates?'

'Look, Henry, I've no idea what you're trying on here, and I think it's time now for *you* to face facts.'

'Did you see Shafer last night?' Henry ploughed on, undeterred.

'No. Why? What are you getting at?'

'Right,' Henry nodded. 'Fine. I'll be off, then.' He rose to leave.

'You'll stay right there. I haven't finished with you yet, pal.'

'I've finished with you – and you,' he added, looking at Carradine. 'Another old mate, if I'm

321

not mistaken.' Carradine flinched.

'OK, as of this moment,' Anger declared, 'you are suspended from duty pending the investigation into your total lack of judgement today in putting the lives of civilians at risk.'

Henry gave a short laugh, side-stepped past Carradine and walked out of the door.

He hurried down the steps and let himself out of the police station, standing at the front of the building as he waited for his heart rate to subside.

The day had gone cold and the night was drawing in. Street lights were on and a spat of rain hit his face.

Everything about him had tightened to breaking point. His muscles were rigid, his fingers tensed into fists, his teeth clenched and he had to force himself to calm down before a blood vessel burst in his head and he had a stroke.

He fished his phone out of his pocket and checked it. It had been on silent for most of the day, and he thought he might have missed some return calls, but none showed, except one from Jerry Tope, who he hadn't even tried to contact.

He returned the call.

'Jerry, it's Henry – where've you been all day?'

'Digging around.'

'I assume you heard what happened here?'

'I did.'

'They were after you for the Intelligence Cell.'

'I gathered, but I have been a bit busy with a few things, not least of which were the prints

322

you got off Motta.'

'Go on.'

'You were right, there were some partial prints taken from that Fiat Panda you gave the dead hooker a lift in – but they'd been well buried, but y'know me, I found 'em.'

'I'll congratulate you when you give me some good news.'

'I got a fingerprint expert to do a comparison between them and the ones you took from Motta's body. They matched.'

The implications of this sank in, but only confirmed what Henry really knew. Jonny Motta was the guy he'd fought and chased in Preston and therefore number-one suspect for the murders, especially if his prints had been found in the Panda. And yet, in Jerry's words, 'they had been well buried'. Henry would have to find out exactly what Tope meant by that, but if it was true, next question was, 'Why?'

'Thanks, Jerry. I'll see you tomorrow.'

Henry ended the call, then dialled home to speak to Kate as he walked across to the car park behind the sports centre opposite the nick, where he'd parked his Rover.

'Hi, babe.'

'Henry, I've been so worried. How are you?'

'Bearing up. I'm OK, just want to get home and get to bed.'

'I'll have some food waiting. How long will you be?'

He walked around the side of the sports centre and across the unlit car park, trying to jerk his keys out of his pocket as he went.

323

'Half-hour, maybe. See you, honey.'

He folded his phone and slid it inside his pocket and walked to the side of the car.

The blow to the head felled him instantly and he was unconscious before he hit the ground.

NINETEEN

Henry rolled and his head crashed against the side of something hard, then he rolled back again, his head smacking something else and it was the combination of these two blows that brought him back to painful consciousness.

He groaned, opened his eyes, but could see nothing. He was in complete darkness. Then he rolled again and bounced, tried to steady himself with his hands but found he could not move them. They were pinned behind him, his wrists cuffed with a pair of old-style police handcuffs, although he did not know this at the time. All he knew was that something metal was cutting into his skin and it hurt like hell.

He was disorientated, could not work out anything and fought for control of his mind.

He bounced again and there was the sensation of movement as he cracked his head against something again.

'Ahh!' he gasped.

His head started to clear and he tried to straighten out his legs, still not certain what was happening to him. The back of his skull was throbbing and, he guessed, bleeding. It felt as though there was an open wound there, gaping wide.

325

He was in so much pain. And he was in a grave.

His legs would only go so far, then they touched something hard.

As his senses returned, he identified the sound of a car engine and then it came to him. This was no grave, this was the boot of a car. He'd been jumped on, smacked to the floor and now here he was, trussed up and living the chicken dream. First the chicken in his childhood, then the prostitute in the back of the Panda, and now him for real. All pushed and folded into a space not big enough to accommodate them.

He retched with fear and panic, but was not sick, although there was a terrible taste in his mouth and he spat. At least his mouth hadn't been taped up.

The car stopped suddenly and Henry rolled forwards, once again catching his head on something that felt like a piece of iron. Then they were on the move again, but it was no smooth journey.

He pulled his wrists apart, testing what he now knew to be handcuffs, linked by a chain. They were not as strong as rigid cuffs, but they were well capable of doing their job without a problem.

'Not good, not good,' he intoned, again that panic rising in him like bile.

The car swerved around a corner and Henry tried to brace himself and roll with the momentum in a controlled way, jamming his feet against the side, but he struggled and hit his head again on that hard thing.

'Hell!'

There was something sticky and wet down his neck. He knew for certain it was his own blood, lots of it. His shoulders were saturated with it.

Then he felt himself going woozy and there was another bump in the road, followed by another swerve around a corner which made him crash his head again and he did see stars, but managed to fight against unconsciousness. He had to stay awake.

Suddenly the car slowed and stopped.

He could hear voices. Then the clatter of a shutter door opening, at least that's what it sounded like. The car stopped again and there was the sound of the door again – closing? Had they arrived at their destination? The car moved slowly forwards, then reversed, then stopped. The engine was turned off.

Voices, footsteps, came closer. Two car doors slammed shut.

Then the boot lid rose, a dim light came into the boot, making Henry blink, even though it wasn't a strong light, and he looked up at the two men standing above him.

'Henry, you're awake,' the first one said.

'At least we won't have to carry you, which is something,' the second one said. 'How's the head.'

'Sore.'

'Good.' The man reached in and with two hands grabbed Henry's lapels, hauling him up and over the lip of the boot, then allowing him to crash to the concrete floor, unable to protect himself. His forehead smashed down with a

327

clunk and he rolled on to his back, moaning. The man booted Henry in the side and said, 'Get up, fucker.'

Henry brought his knees up and rocked himself up into a sitting position and from there unsteadily managed to get to his feet, finding his true height and looking into the hateful eyes of Jack Carradine, DCI.

Carradine smiled cruelly and punched Henry hard in the lower stomach, doubling him over. He followed this with a double-handed smack on the side of his head that dropped Henry to his knees. It was a very good blow and as Henry hung there, as if he was looking over a balcony, he knew a couple of his teeth had been dislodged and he spat out a mouthful of blood and saliva.

Then Carradine pulled him back to his feet.

'That felt good.'

Henry was breathing in short, painful gasps. He would have liked to have given a witty rejoinder coupled with a threat, but knew there would be no profit in it and it would only serve to encourage Carradine to hit him again, if in fact he needed an excuse to do so.

And he didn't need an excuse.

Henry took the next punch to his liver by rolling back against the car, trying to remain upright, but the follow-up one, hard to the lower intestine again, sank him back down to his knees. He was then in a position which Carradine could not resist, as he took the opportunity to put both his hands on the back of Henry's head and then ram it down on to his upcoming knees.

Something cracked in Henry's face and he went sprawling across the floor. The knee jerk had missed his nose, but had connected with his right cheekbone and broken it easily. Henry had had this broken not so very long ago and it had taken a long time to heal, but now it was smashed again and this time he was sure it would not repair. Maybe it didn't need to repair, though, he thought. I won't need it better if I'm dead.

'Get him up,' the second man said to Carradine. The second man was Dave Anger.

Carradine heaved Henry up by the scruff of his neck, causing Henry's head to loll uncontrollably.

On his feet, he staggered a few steps before regaining his balance. His cheek was throbbing madly and he could even now feel it swelling.

He managed to get a quick glance at his surroundings, before Anger pushed him in the back towards a short flight of concrete steps. He was able to climb them assisted by Carradine, who roughly dragged him up and into a short corridor and then through a thick metal-panelled door into what Henry knew was the basement custody office at Preston police station.

They had brought him to a police station. How rich was that, he thought as he was bundled past the unoccupied sergeant's desk, then left down the cell corridor and kicked into a cell, where he went down on both knees. A fucking police station. They were in the old cells at Preston police station, which were unused since the advent of the new operating centre. Henry could not help but smile at their cockiness as he pulled himself round and sat up against the bench. He knew no one ever came down to the cells any more, as they were basically out of bounds to anyone working in the station. And who was working here now, he wondered. At this time of night, just the staff in the divisional comms room and the CCTV room – and that was it. No one would have any reason to come down here anyway.

The cell door reopened and Carradine stood there.

'Get up.'

'What if I don't want to?'

'I'll kick you to death here and now.'

Henry eased himself up from the floor on to the bench bed, then up to his feet. Carradine jerked his head and stood back to allow Henry to walk past.

'Interview room one,' he was ordered.

He shuffled slowly down the corridor, turned left and then went through the open door of the said room.

The table was gone, but there were three plastic chairs in a triangle.

Carradine pushed him down on to one of them, then sat down himself. Henry looped his cuffed hands around the back of the chair, the only way in which he could sit, letting them hang behind him as he leaned forward.

Anger came in and sat on the third chair.

'Henry, you are a right royal pain in the arse.'

'Fine by me. But *you* must be into something so fucking deep...' he started. 'And for how long? You bastards have been at it for years...'

Carradine shot forwards and smashed his open hand across the side of Henry's face, whipping his head around dislodging a tooth. Running his tongue around the inside of his mouth he collected more blood and saliva into a spitball.

'Gob it out on the floor,' Carradine ordered him.

Henry leaned forward and let it drizzle out. He had decided he wanted to leave as much of his DNA around the place as possible. Then he looked up at the two men.

Anger stood back and considered him. 'I know we've never got on, Henry, and I suppose this is going to be the end of things for us, but I'll do you a favour. You tell me what you know, who knows what, and your end will be swift. I won't say it'll be painless, but it'll be swift.'

'You're gonna kill me?'

'You're the man who knows too much.'

'I know fuck all – that's the irony – but I suppose this somehow pulls some of it together. Tell you what, you tell me what you know, and I'll tell you what I know.'

'Doesn't work like that, I'm afraid, and it's all far too complicated to explain to you now.'

'It's gotta be something to do with prostitutes and people-trafficking,' Henry persisted.

'Good stab,' Anger conceded.

'You've got something going with your mates in Merseyside, haven't you?'

Anger shrugged. 'I'm afraid it's not up for discussion, Henry.' He shifted on his chair and fished his mobile phone out of his pocket. It was

331

flashing. He put it to his ear as he stood up and answered it. After a short conversation, he said, 'He's here and wants to see him.' He nodded at Henry. 'I'll let him in.'

'OK.'

Anger left the interview room, so that Carradine and Henry were alone.

'So why didn't you want to put Jonny Motta in the frame for that double murder?' Henry asked him.

Carradine thought for a few seconds. 'He had to be taught a lesson, a lesson about turf, a lesson about respect, a lesson about consideration for others. The only way he'd get that was through a bullet in the head.'

'Or in the chest, as it happens.'

'Or the chest. Same difference.'

'So a police raid was set up, knowing that the end result would be Motta's death?' he asked incredulously. 'You couldn't rely on that to happen, surely?'

He sniggered. 'If you happen to know where Motta was and the lead firearms officer was on your side, you could.'

'Shit,' Henry said. *Even the firearms team was involved in it.* 'So he was murdered in cold blood? Did he even have a gun – or was it planted on him?'

Carradine shrugged as if he didn't care. 'Eventually the IPCC report will say self-defence and this'll all go away.'

'What's going on, Jack? What the hell are you involved in?'

'Long, long-standing stuff, but as Dave said,

you're the one here answering questions, not asking them. You'll just have to work it all out.'

'And then you'll kill me?'

'Prob'ly kill you before you have a chance to work it out, actually.'

'People are expecting me. They'll be wondering where I am.'

'We'll make sure you don't turn up, then. We're good at covering our tracks.'

'I'll bet you are, *I'll just fucking bet you are!*'

The door of the interview room opened and Dave Anger entered, followed by two others – Detective Superintendent Paul Shafer and a man Henry did not recognize, but guessed was Walter Corrigan.

Henry glared up at them, his head rolling, spittle and blood oozing out of his mouth, the cut at the back of his head still dripping blood down his back. His cheekbone was continuing to swell and turning a nasty shade of purple as it did.

'This is him?' Corrigan asked. Anger nodded. 'Do we know what he knows?'

'Not yet – haven't got to work on him properly.'

'Is this a suitable place?'

'It's fine – this floor is sealed from all the floors above it. No one can get access.'

'OK – but get it done quickly.'

Shafer pushed forward between Anger and Corrigan. 'Hello, Henry, not looking too sprite, are you?'

'Go fuck yourself.'

Shafer glanced at Corrigan. 'Want some help with him?'

333

'Please.'

Both men removed their jackets, flexed their fingers and Henry's eyes flipped from one to the other and he started struggling against the handcuffs.

'You have half an hour,' Anger said, 'so make it good.' Both men rolled up their shirtsleeves, violence building up in them. 'I'll be up in comms when you've finished, if you'd like a look at how Lancashire Constabulary operates, Walter.'

'Sure thing.'

It was as if Anger, cool and confident, was showing a town councillor around the police station. They left Carradine and Shafer ready to perform.

Henry's whole body was sagging on the chair, his face a mass of throbbing pain, blood dripping from his mouth. He spat on the floor again – more DNA – and looked up through his one good eye at the two men standing over him. He knew of a few people who'd been killed – not just tragically died – in police cells and their deaths had resulted in media frenzies. He had never expected that his own end would come in a cell and that, because of the way these men would cover it up, no one would ever know where, when or how he had died. The last place anyone would look would be an unused police cell. And not only that, it would be more than likely that Anger and Carradine would be the investigating officers – if his body ever turned up, that is. He doubted it would.

'I don't want you to willingly tell us anything,'

Carradine said. 'I want to kick it out of you.'

'I'm not going to tell you anything, other than you're well and truly fucked ... so go ahead, do what you have to do.'

Carradine stepped forward, swung back his right hand. Henry braced himself but knew he would be sent flying off the chair, nothing he could do but go with it, curl up into a ball and hope he went into unconsciousness quickly.

The blow came, hard and powerful, and Henry did tip off the chair and roll up to the wall, bringing his knees up. Carradine came in after him and tried to stomp on his head, but Henry jerked away, seeing the foot descending on him, but he could not get away from the next flatfoot stomp which caught him squarely on the temple, sending shockwaves through his cranium. He realized he was probably going to be kicked to death – and he knew how bad that could be after having investigated a couple of murders committed that way. It was nasty and brutal.

But then something happened he did not immediately comprehend.

It was as though a Tasmanian devil had entered the interview room, a whirling blur of fists and feet, and Carradine suddenly fell to his knees and then to his stomach, whilst behind him Shafer too was splayed on the floor, a burly figure kneeling on his spine.

Karl Donaldson had burst in, followed by Georgia Papakostas and Bill Robbins.

Donaldson had instantly seen what was happening and had floored Shafer before the man had even turned to see who was behind him –

335

one chopping blow to the neck, another power fist-drive at the back of the skull and he had dropped like a sack of spuds. Bill had jumped on him then, as Donaldson turned his attention to Carradine. The DCI had spun round, and that was a problem for him, because the punch delivered by Donaldson into the side of his head felled him to his knees and broke his jaw at the same time. The second punch dropped him into fairyland.

Hardly breathing at all, Donaldson swooped down to the beaten Henry Christie and lifted him into a sitting position. Henry swooned a little, but still managed to insult Donaldson. 'Fuckin' last-minute Yanks again.'

'Yeah, pal, we always save the world.'

Georgia was behind Donaldson. She knelt down next to Henry and touched his face. He winced away.

'Can you get these things off me?' He jiggled his hands tied behind his back. 'One of them must have a key.'

A few seconds later he was on his feet, his hands free, rubbing his wrists, which were red-raw. He staggered slightly and Georgia grabbed him to stop him falling.

'Thanks,' he said.

Donaldson rose from the task of putting the handcuffs on Carradine and looked at Henry.

'You OK, pal?' He was rubbing his knuckles.

'As could be expected ... Look, Anger and, I think, Corrigan are in the building. Anger's showing him the comms room, would you fucking believe?'

'Hey, when you think you're untouchable you're at your most vulnerable,' Donaldson said.

'I want Anger,' Henry said, brushing past Donaldson, stepping over the still unconscious Carradine and then over the prostrate form of Shafer with Bill Robbins still sitting on him. 'You think you two could keep these two bastards down for a few minutes?' It was a rhetorical question, aimed at Bill and Georgia. 'Karl, c'mon, let me show *you* the comms room. You can have Corrigan.'

Henry limped quickly away, his head still reeling, his body hurting, but a gritty determination seething within him as he made his way out of the deserted custody office to the stairs, which he took two at a time, Donaldson close behind him.

'We went looking for Corrigan when we knew we wouldn't be allowed back into the cop shop,' Donaldson explained as they went upwards. 'Picked him up in Southport and, to cut a long story short, we followed him here with Shafer – a three-car tail, my hire car, Georgia's hire car and Bill's pool car. We were brilliant.'

'You could have got here a mite sooner,' Henry whined painfully as they reached the third floor, on which the comms room was situated. He led Donaldson through the double doors at the top of the stairwell, turned left and pushed open the door of the comms room.

The room was set out rather like the bridge of the Starship *Enterprise* but on a smaller scale and not as shiny. There were four operators sitting at their consoles, two receiving the incom-

337

ing calls and two radio dispatchers, with the comms sergeant sitting at a separate desk, a pair of earphones on as she monitored everything the operators were doing.

And at the far end of the room, Dave Anger and Walter Corrigan were standing and chatting, Anger showing his honoured guest something on a notice board.

Henry stood at the door.

He must have been a terrifying figure to behold, his face smashed and billowing out with the swelling, blood down his shirtfront as well as down his back.

One of the female comms operators looked sideways at him and screamed, 'Oh my God!' making Anger turn.

Henry's figure must then have become even more fearsome, as, with a howl of rage, he leapt over one of the radio consoles, slithered across it leaving a trail of his blood and went for Anger, who, taking in what was happening, shoved Corrigan away from him and ran for the door at the far end of the room which led to the stairs on the opposite side of the building.

Another operator screamed. The sergeant pulled her earphones off and rose to her feet, only to be knocked back down by Henry as he used her to help propel himself after the retreating Anger.

'He's yours,' Henry shouted to Donaldson, and pointed to Corrigan, who had been pushed into a corner of the room.

Anger had disappeared down the steps, but Henry was not far behind him, throwing himself recklessly down, not taking any note of the pain in his body, being so focused on capturing Anger.

They raced down three flights. Henry gained on him all the time, until they reached the footwell in the basement, where Anger barged into the double doors, expecting them to be open, but they were locked and he was trapped as Henry reached the top of the flight of steps and stopped, knowing he had his man.

Anger's back was to the doors.

Henry came down the steps one at a time, a terrifying expression on his battered face.

'Just you and me, now, Dave,' he said quietly on reaching the last but one step.

Anger did not reply, but launched himself into Henry. They both fell backwards on to the concrete steps, Anger raining punches into Henry's stomach and ribs as they rolled and fought. Henry's arms wrapped around Anger, trying to halt the onslaught, holding him tight. But it was like fighting a demon and they rolled off the stairs on to the landing, crashing against the locked doors.

Anger broke away and scrambled to his feet and as Henry tried to do the same kicked out desperately, his foot connecting with Henry's side, hurling him over. Henry scrambled to the corner of the landing as Anger came at him – then he turned in the confined space and dived at Anger's midriff, using all the strength he had in him to topple the chief superintendent over.

Even as he fell backwards, though, he caught Henry a stunning blow on the face which sent

339

him reeling away and before Henry could recover, Anger was on him again, punching hard and repeatedly, and Henry felt his legs go to jelly and he knew he was going down.

But he also knew that this was not the way it was going to be. Drawing on something from the depths of his whole being, he roared like a bear and broke through the pounding of Anger's fists. His forearms forced Anger's arms away from him, opening the man up, and with the millisecond he had to take advantage his hands came out wide and with as much power as he could muster, he clapped his hands hard. Only thing being was that Anger's head was between them and the slightly cupped palms smashed down on Anger's ears. The force of the blow sent a ripple of agony through his ears. The effect was to burst one eardrum.

Anger screamed and reeled away, but Henry paid no heed and went for him. He went for him with a frenzied attack. By hauling strength from deep within he beat Anger down to his knees and then to the floor. He did this until every ounce of power dissipated out of him and he sank to his knees, then on to all fours, next to Anger, who lay there moaning, beaten and defeated, drifting in and out of consciousness, his glasses lying discarded by his side.

As a final symbolic act, Henry got to his feet, stood on them and crushed them.

TWENTY

Once, long ago, this same terrible thing had happened to Henry Christie – he had woken up in a hospital to find Robert Fanshaw-Bayley sitting on a chair next to the bed, looking anxiously at him as though he cared. Back then FB had been a detective chief superintendent and Henry had just survived the attentions of a hit man called Tiger Mayfair, but only just. He'd been in hospital to recover from his injuries and waking up to see FB had almost been a setback to speedy recovery.

'We can't keep meeting like this,' FB said, this time. He too apparently remembered the previous occasion well.

Henry, who had spent a day and a night at the Royal Preston Infirmary purely for observation, and pumped up with nice pain-relieving drugs, eased himself into a sitting position. He had nodded off but didn't know how long he'd been asleep. Could have been five minutes, could have been five hours.

'Time is it?'

'Three.'

He squinted with his good eye. 'Am I right in thinking Kate's coming to collect me at five?'

'Yeah – apparently the doctor thinks you'll be

341

all right.'

'Nice doctor.'

'How are you feeling?'

'Fine, fine.'

'You gave Dave Anger a hell of a pasting.'

'Good.'

'He's still in hospital – down the corridor, here.' FB jerked a thumb. 'Being looked after by two uniformed cops.'

Henry was stiff and sore, despite the pain relief. His face was a bloated mess, his head had one deep cut in it, now stitched, and was a mass of swellings the size of eggs, but nothing, other than his cheekbone, was broken. Again.

'He's making a complaint of assault against you.'

'His prerogative, he can do what he wants. I'll counter-sue,' Henry mumbled as he spoke through thick lips, because that was the best he could do.

'I don't think his claim will be going anywhere under the circumstances,' FB reassured him. There was a pregnant pause, then FB said, 'You think you're up to being told what's happening in the big wide world?'

'Pass me that water, will you?' FB reached for a glass of water on Henry's bedside cabinet, which he handed to the patient who took a sip through cracked lips. 'Ugh – it's warm, and there's no whiskey in it.' He took some more, then said, 'Fire away.'

FB gathered his thoughts. 'As you can imagine, they're not a very talkative bunch, but we've got some good detectives drafted in from

GMP doing the business on them and, bit by bit, a picture is forming of what it's all about. We haven't been able to talk to Anger yet, because he's been in hospital since you threw him down a staircase and jumped on him.'

'Take it one step at a time. I don't yet have a fully functioning brain.' Henry held up a finger to prevent FB from making a smart retort.

'It can probably be traced back a number of years,' FB began. 'And all this shit stems from a protection racket that Dave Anger and his Merseyside mates were running, allowing criminals to operate brothels and street prostitutes, which was a very lucrative addition to a cop's salary.' Henry shook his head sadly. He hated bent cops. 'The racket was run mainly in Liverpool, but a bit of trading was done up here in Lancashire. Scartarelli was involved in it, but he apparently had a bit of a temper where the women were concerned and unfortunately this led to him killing one who'd been plying her body in Blackburn. Don't know why he did it, but he did, possible she might've wanted out. Unfortunately for him, the girl named him before she croaked. *Fortunately* for him, the murder investigation was headed by Dave Anger and Jack Carradine, both still involved in the protection racket in Liverpool, even though they were Lancashire officers. Extra pocket money.'

FB looked distressed and Henry could guess why: he had been responsible for bringing Anger into Lancashire from Merseyside to head up the FMIT team. It must have hurt to know he had selected and employed a very corrupt officer.

'They were able to manipulate the enquiry and although they had a named suspect in Scartarelli, they didn't pursue him as vigorously as they might have done, mainly because they knew him and he was running the racket they were involved in protecting.' He paused. 'With me so far?' Henry nodded. 'They let him get away, basically, but for anyone looking at the investigation from the outside it would have seemed as though they were doing the best they could.'

'So more recently, where did Jonny Motta fit into this?'

'He was trying to muscle in on the business, not knowing that the cops were involved in protecting it.'

'Why kill the prostitutes in Preston, though?'

FB sighed. 'Probably something we'll never get to the bottom of. Why do blokes kill prostitutes anyway? We think he was trying to get them to work for him, coercing them by violence, and it went too far, unfortunately for them.'

'And for him, too,' Henry said. 'Because how was he to know that the protection racket included some members of the police firearms team?'

'You know that bit?' FB sounded surprised.

'It's something I covered in discussion with Jack Carradine before he started kicking the shit out of me.' Henry leaned back, feeling groggy. 'Head's pounding like a jackhammer.' He snorted. 'I suppose I must consider myself lucky. I mean, Dave Anger could well have had me killed for sleeping with his wife, couldn't he?

344

Even though she wasn't his wife when I slept with her,' he added as a rider.

'Lucky break there, Henry,' FB agreed.

Henry rolled his neck, massaging it with both hands. His brow furrowed. 'Where does Corrigan fit into all this and why was Scartarelli killed?'

FB shrugged. 'Corrigan is the man behind it all, according to your chum in the FBI.' He said 'chum' quite dismissively, because he didn't really like Karl Donaldson very much. 'He's the guy who arranges for the prostitutes to come across from Eastern Europe, Albania and the like, sorts out their passage and where they're going when they get here and who gets them. Basically, Scartarelli worked for him. But the train of thought is that Scartarelli has been trying to oust Corrigan, even to the point of using his villa in Cyprus without his permission. That's why Corrigan wanted him killed – we think. No one's saying very much, though. That villa, by the way, is actually owned by a legit holding company in the States linked to the Tantini crime family, who I think you've heard of.'

'How'd you find that out?'

'Sent Jerry Tope searching online. He's a bit of a whiz at it.'

Henry smiled. 'He'll get himself into trouble one of these days.' He leaned forward and squirmed himself into a better sitting position. 'Plump up my pillows, will you?' he asked and FB, a grimace on his face at becoming a nurse, pulled Henry's pillows up as requested. Henry enjoyed the attention. It wasn't often FB did something for him.

The two men didn't speak for a while. Henry had had his brain knocked about a bit and his thoughts were jumping all over the place, not much logic to them, his brow constantly knitting together as he thought through something, wondered whether to ask a question, then didn't bother because it was too much like hard work. However, eventually he spoke.

'Can I ask you something?' he said to FB at last.

'Of course.'

'How are Anthony Downie and Jane Kinsella connected to all this?'

'Not sure what you mean – Downie was just in the wrong place at the wrong time and got a bullet in the brain for it. The best witness is a dead witness. No great loss. Who's Jane Kinsella?'

'Operation Wanted?' Henry reminded him.

'Ah, *that* Jane Kinsella.' FB shook his head. 'No connection at all, I don't think.'

'Can I ask you something else?' Before FB could say yes or no, Henry said, 'When you gave me those jobs to do, catching those wanted persons, did you have any inkling whatsoever about all this? Did you know about what Anger and Carradine were up to?' Henry craned his neck to look into FB's eyes. They told their own story. 'I'll take that as a yes.' His mouth pursed, he closed his eyes and rested his sore head back. Eyes still closed, he said, 'You fucking knew or suspected something was going on, didn't you?'

'OK, I did, as did the Chief Constable of

346

Merseyside. Shafer and others have been suspected for a long time of being involved in various criminal activities. So what better man to get involved in it than you? We'd been looking for a way to get into it for quite a while now and when I got that rocket from the Police Authority, it just seemed to slot into place. I knew that when you started delving, something could well happen. Always does with you. The other two wanteds were just so you'd think I wasn't pushing you in a particular direction.'

'So I wouldn't suspect anything. You complete and utter bastard,' Henry said.

'And then when Motta was killed ... gold dust,' FB said brightly. 'I have got a real sweetener for you, though.'

'What would that be?' Henry said bitterly.

'After the shit has settled on this, I'm going to put a superintendent in charge of FMIT rather than a chief super.' He paused dramatically. 'It's yours if you want it – unless you want to retire instead, that is?'

'You think that offering me promotion will be a sweetener?' Henry asked incredulously ... but even as he spoke, his mind started to work out the big difference between a superintendent's pension and a chief inspector's pension. He said, 'You could be right.'

The surprise was that when Dave Anger was released from the hospital into police custody proper, he wanted to talk, and talk he did. He had formed the impression that Carradine, Shafer and Corrigan had been confessing all, an impres-

347

sion that wasn't corrected by the detectives tasked to interview him.

In the end, with the half-stories from Shafer and Carradine, nothing from Corrigan, and more than enough from Anger, it all started to come together.

With regards to the shooting of Jonny Motta, the detectives learned that the IPCC investigator, McKnight, had been a bit too good and had stumbled upon several bank accounts owned by the police officer who pulled the trigger. They showed regular amounts dripping in and accumulating. Investigating further, he discovered more accounts belonging to firearms officers that did not seem quite right. He never knew for certain whether these finds were or were not connected to the shooting, but he knew they had to be investigated.

When Shafer got wind of this, he arranged for a fatal accident to occur to McKnight, who was under the impression he was going to meet a secret witness with information about the shooting. Shafer had then brazenly spoken to and sympathized with McKnight's grieving widow and been handed all her husband's work-related documents, including a notebook detailing all his finds.

And, finally, Anger named the people responsible for killing Scartarelli in the court cells: three firearms officers from Merseyside, also implicated in the protection rackets and who had taken part in the raid on Motta's flat.

Lancashire officers, who also arrested the firearms PC who had shot Motta and claimed he

348

was acting in self-defence, arrested them in dawn raids – and when those four were in custody, everything crumbled.

'Yeah, that's where we're up to,' Henry Christie said. It was four weeks later and he was on the phone in his new office in the FMIT building across the sports field from the headquarters main building. Sat opposite him, feet up on the other side of the desk, was Karl Donaldson. Henry was on the phone to DI Georgia Papakostas of the Cyprus Police. He was giving her the regular update of the progress of the investigation, even though he was not actively involved in it himself, merely a witness. 'Yeah, I know,' he said, 'still no name for the sniper. Sorry about that, but we'll keep digging if you will. It would be tragic not to get someone arrested for killing a cop, even if it was by accident. Good luck with it. Yeah, I'm doing fine, thanks ... OK...' The conversation was drawing to a close. Donaldson dropped his feet and mee-mawed for Henry to give him the phone. Henry snarled at him. 'Someone here who wants to speak to you...' He gave him the phone.

'Hey, babe, how y'all doing?' he said, thickening his accent. 'Me, fine, I'm fine ... what about you? When do I get to see you again?'

At that, Henry stood up, annoyed. He gave Donaldson a middle finger and stalked out of the office into the corridor and looked up and down at what was to become his new kingdom – FMIT. He hadn't yet been promoted, as FB promised, but had been allowed to move into the

349

office on the middle floor of the block pending this. He had taken great delight in getting the labourers to gut what was once Dave Anger's domain. Now it was his and would be for as long as possible.

Donaldson appeared at the office door and regarded his British friend with a half-smile.

'You think we really did it, pal?'

Henry returned the inspection, looking his American friend up and down, considering the question. He shrugged. 'She's a very beautiful woman.'

'Not as beautiful as my wife,' Donaldson said.

'But you let me think, for all these weeks...'

'I was enjoying myself.'

Henry's desk phone rang and he moved Donaldson out of the doorway to get in and answer it. He listened then said, 'Be there in a few minutes ... see you.' He turned to Donaldson. 'Fancy watching a real cop in action?'

'Is there one around here?'

'If you were much smaller, thinner, lighter, wore thick glasses, had false teeth and one leg, I'd smack you very hard and then run ... Come with me, I have things to do.'

Henry, Jerry Tope and Donaldson strolled into the accounts department on the middle floor of headquarters where Madeline Rooney sat at her desk. She was sporting a wonderful tan from her recent holiday in Florida and it was set very nicely against the new expensive and very low-cut dress she wore.

'You two guys stay here,' Henry told his

350

companions, then crossed the office to Madeline's desk, taking a seat at the end of it. She hadn't seen him approach, being quite engrossed in her nails that looked as though they had been recently manicured.

'Henry, darling,' she said brightly. She lowered her eyes and tilted towards him, displaying a wonderful view of her chest, which Henry remembered well, despite the intervening years.

'Hi.' He smiled.

'What can I do you for? Remember I'm a happily married woman now, but there could be *one* exception to the rule.' The breasts wobbled enticingly.

Henry gave a sigh. 'I'm not sure how to say this, Madeline, but I suppose I'll get straight to the point, if that's OK?'

'Yeah, whatever.'

'Did you have a good holiday?'

'Oh, wonderful, absolutely wonderful. Great villa, Disney, the Gulf Coast, the Keys ... you name it, we went, me and John – and the kids,' she added with a hesitant afterthought. 'Why, do you fancy going? I've got loads of brochures and things.'

He shook his head. 'No,' he said patiently, leaning forwards himself, but keeping his eyes to hers. 'It must have cost a fortune ... how did you finance your trip?'

'What sort of question is that? We saved for it.'

'You mean like the way you saved for your new car? And the way John saved for his? And everything else you've bought in the last couple of months.'

'What are you saying?'

'I've seen your bank accounts, love.'

Her mouth shut tight and she swallowed. He went on, 'Lots of deposits in there that match lots of withdrawals from Lancashire Constabulary accounts, including Operation Wanted.' He raised his eyebrows. 'You knew you'd get caught in the end, didn't you?'

She turned her attention to the computer on her desk and her hand covered the mouse. 'I suppose I'd better turn this off. I presume we'll be going from here.'

'Yeah,' Henry said quietly. 'Once we've got John, too. Shall I caution and arrest you here, or would you like me to do it in the corridor?'

'Corridor, please.'